Going Deep

USA TODAY BESTSELLING AUTHOR
NIKKI ASH

He's serious. Committed.
Unstoppable.

Alice: How long is forever?
White Rabbit: Sometimes one second.
-Lewis Carroll

Prologue

GISELLE

"I KNOW YOU'RE CHEATING ON ME! ADMIT IT!" Mom chucks a vase across the room at Dad, who doesn't duck quick enough, and it hits his shoulder before it crashes onto the tiled floor, breaking into a million pieces.

"I hate you!" she shouts with tears streaming down her cheeks.

She turns around, her possessed eyes searching for another item to throw. My dad uses that moment as an opportunity to wrap his strong arms around her tiny, fragile body from the back. She kicks and screams, trying to get out of his hold, but he's stronger. "Let go of me! I'm going to kill you! You're such a piece of shit liar!"

Ignoring the hateful words she's spewing, he pulls her down onto the couch as I pop the lid to one of her prescription bottles and shake out two pills.

While he's holding her down, I pry her mouth open and push the pills down her throat. She tries to gag, her manic gaze hitting me with so much hate, it sends chills racing up my spine.

She continues to kick and thrash around while Dad holds her tight, waiting for the pills to make their way through her system and temporarily calm the beast inside her.

She was doing so well the past few months, I thought for sure they got her meds right this time. She was so happy and cheerful. It was as if she was on cloud nine. Until she wasn't. And now, once again, it seems we're back to where we started.

Once Mom's lids begin to droop, Dad lessens his hold on her, and my sister makes her presence known.

"Is Mom okay?" she asks quietly, afraid if she speaks too loudly, she might poke the beast, which in our many years of experience is never a good thing.

"She's okay, Addy." I cut across the room and pull my scared sister into a tight hug.

When she was little and Mom would lash out, she would hide in her bedroom until one of us would come and get her.

Now that Adrianna is older, she no longer hides. She's too worried about our mom hurting herself or one of us. But because of how violent mom can get, Dad and I make her hang back while we get her under control.

"Dad, I think she needs to see a psychiatrist again," I say to my father. "Her pills aren't working. We can't keep drugging her like this."

My eyes dart to my mother who is lying lifeless on the couch, still in my father's arms. My heart breaks every time we have to sedate her, but we don't have any choice.

It's either that or she will end up hurting one of us, and then when she wakes up and realizes what she did, she will sink even further into depression. It's a shitty no-win situation.

Dad silently shakes his head in frustration as he lifts my mom and carries her to their bedroom. Once he comes back out, he grabs his briefcase and cell phone and heads toward the front door without saying a word.

This is what he always does when she gets like this. Hides away at his office. Sometimes he'll be gone for days at a time, but it's pointless to call him out on it.

He's the only breadwinner in this family, which means we need him. He pays the bills and attempts to take care of our mom. And I love him, even if many days I also hate him.

When he comes home and smells of another woman's perfume, I want to smack him senseless, yet at the same time, I can understand why he does what he does.

He's married to a woman who is so far gone most days, he spends more time taking care of her than actually being with her.

Their kisses have turned to tears, and their love that once upon a time shined through during even the darkest of days has been covered by a dark, black cloud that has been stagnant directly over our life for too many years.

"Dad," I call out, refusing to let him run this time. We can't keep doing this. "She needs help."

"What do you want from me, Giselle?" he snaps. "Our insurance barely covers the appointments, let alone the medications. The doctor has tried every drug imaginable, and nothing fucking works. I'm doing the best I can." And without waiting for my response, he's out the door.

"I found this," Adrianna says softly once the door has slammed shut. I turn around to see what she's talking about, and in her hands is my acceptance letter to NYU Paris I received in the mail last month. The deadline to accept is coming up.

"How many times have I asked you not to go through my stuff?" I swipe the paper out of her hands.

She frowns, and I immediately feel bad.

"I was looking for your eyeliner. I'm sorry. Now, tell me you're going." Her voice is demanding, and her hand goes to her hip. I have to bite down on my bottom lip to stifle my laugh at my little sister's attitude. "Giselle, tell me you're going," she repeats.

"Addy..."

"No, don't you dare 'Addy' me. I don't want to hear some bullshit excuse about you needing to stay here for Mom. She's been like this for as long as we can remember, and it's never going to get better. This is your out." She snatches the paper back from me, waving it in the air. "Run, Giselle, and don't look back."

"One, you're thirteen, don't say bullshit." She rolls her eyes and tilts her head to the side, waiting for me to continue. "And two, I can't leave you—" Before I can finish my sentence, Adrianna cuts me off.

"One, you're not my mother, and mine is too depressed and out of it to give a shit what language I use."

She purses her lips together in defiance, daring me to argue. I know her words aren't meant to be hurtful. We've grown up taking care of one another.

But with me being five years older, I've always tried to be the mother she's never really had. However, as she gets older, she often says she prefers for me to act like her sister and not her mom, which is understandable. But that doesn't stop me from trying.

"And two," she continues, "this is your dream, to study interior design in Paris, and there's no way you're not following it, just to stay here in this hellhole for me. I'll be fine. You're going to do whatever you're supposed to do to let them know you'll be there, and then you're going to get on that damn plane after graduation and get out of here."

Tears prick my eyes as I stare at my beautiful, grownup sister. Sure, she's only thirteen, but because of the life we've had to endure, she's been forced to grow up twice as fast as other kids her age.

I can't imagine being across the pond from her for a week, let alone for years, and with us having no money, who knows when I'll be able to come back and visit. But for her, I will find a way.

If I have to work full-time while going to school, I will. I'll do whatever I have to do to make sure she's okay.

"I'm going to miss you," I tell her.

She snakes her arms around my waist and rests her head on my shoulder. "And I'm going to miss you, but in five years I'll be out of here as well, and I can tell you one thing. I'm not staying here for mom. I love her with everything in me, but I can't live like this forever."

"Promise me that if you need me, you'll call. I don't care what I'm doing, I'll come home," I murmur.

"I promise. Now, can I borrow twenty bucks? I'm meeting some friends at the movies." She backs out of our hug and bats her lashes innocently.

I sigh dramatically then giggle. "Sure, how about I drop you off on my way to Christian's house?"

Adrianna rolls her eyes. "I don't need my big sister to hold my hand on the subway."

"I know you don't *need* me to, but I would feel better if I did. I'm heading that way anyway."

Adrianna huffs in annoyance. "Fine, but only because I know you'll withhold the money until I agree. Let's go."

After checking on our sleeping mom, we head out to the Rye Metro station. After making sure Adrianna makes it safely to the IMAX theater in Rochelle—and only once I see her and her friends go inside—I head back to the station, jump on the 6 and take it to Lafayette. I get off then take the F to the Lower East Side.

The entire trip is a good seventy minutes, and I'm lucky enough to get an actual seat, so I use the time to pull up the online application to NYU Paris.

Without giving myself time to second-guess my decision, I click accept. Even with the help of financial aid, I'm not sure how I'm going to be able to afford it. But my sister is right, this is my dream, and I will always regret it if I don't follow it.

When East Broadway lights up, I stand and make my way to the doors, so I can exit. I climb the steps and glance around for Christian. He said he would meet me here. I spot him across the street and wave.

I know he sees me when his face breaks out into a huge grin. With black curly hair, onyx eyes, and dozens of tattoos running up and down his arms, he is the epitome of a bad boy.

He's also my best friend and boyfriend. I run across the crosswalk and throw myself into his awaiting arms. He lifts me up, twirls me around in a circle, and kisses me passionately.

"*Mi Amor*," he murmurs against my lips.

It's been almost a month since I've seen him, and I've missed him like crazy. Because he's a year older, he graduated a year before me and attends NYU's School of the Arts. His dream is for his band, Down Coyote, to one day get signed. We've been dating for close to two years now and I hate that in order for both of us to follow our dreams, it will mean living four thousand miles away from each other.

"What do you want to do today?" he asks excitedly, and my heart fractures.

"I was thinking we could go back to your dorm. I need to talk to you."

His steps falter, and he eyes me skeptically before he says, "You've decided to go." It's not a question, he knows I've already made the decision. He knows me that well.

"I have," I say. "It's just that—"

"You don't have to explain, Giselle, I get it. It's a once in a lifetime opportunity and a chance for you to break away from your mom for a little while. You deserve this. But what does that mean for us?"

"It means we enjoy the next couple of months together, and once it's time for me to go, we say goodbye."

I've always been a realist, and I'm not about to hold either of us to being in a long-distance relationship.

While Christian was my first kiss, my first love and the first guy I had sex with, it's not fair to expect him to remain faithful to me while I'm overseas for school for the next four years, if not longer.

"Okay," he agrees, "but promise me one thing."

"What?"

"When you return to New York, I'm the first person you look up after you see your sister." He pulls me into a hug and gives me a soft kiss on my lips.

"I promise."

"I know this isn't the end for us, Giselle," he says. "This is just a minor detour. One day you'll return, educated and cultured, ready to take the design world by storm."

A grin splits across my face at the thought. "

I'll be a famous musician, making millions and living in a penthouse apartment on the Upper East Side." He waggles his eyebrows. "We'll be a power couple, baby."

He kisses me again, and I nod in agreement. Is it possible? Everything he's saying about our future...Can we really have it all? I guess only time will tell.

Chapter One

GISELLE
SEVEN YEARS LATER

"Fuck yes. You like it when I ram my cock into you, don't you? Scream my name when you come all over my fucking cock."

I refrain from rolling my eyes as Paul 'rams' his cock into me. And I'm using air quotes to emphasize the word *rams*, because let's be real here, when the guy is only working with a four—maybe five—inch dick, he isn't ramming anything into anyone.

But he thinks he is, so I guess it's the thought that counts. Not that it matters. He's Paul Cohen, a multi-billionaire real estate tycoon who owns a good portion of the Upper East Side.

I wouldn't care if he had a one-inch dick and wanted me to call out his mother's name as long as he keeps wanting to fuck me.

"Oh, Paul," I call out dramatically.

He looks down and grins at me as several beads of sweat fall from his face and land on my chest.

And because we're fucking missionary, and he can see every face I make, I have to force myself not to cringe.

But internally, I'm screaming, "Ewww! Fucking gross!"

How someone is able to work up that kind of sweat in only—my eyes dart to the clock and see it's 9:08 p.m.—seven minutes is beyond me. But if his nasty sweat and breathless grunting is any indication, we're going to call this a wrap in under ten minutes. Not a record time, but pretty damn close.

Wanting to speed this along, I squeeze my vaginal walls together in an attempt to grip his dick—not that it does much good. His groans get louder, his thrusts turn frantic.

"I'm coming," he grunts out, and my eyes go to the clock again. 9:10 p.m. Damn, I'm good. Just under ten minutes, like I predicted.

"Oh yes, Paul," I call out, putting all the years of my doing Kegel exercises to use as I force my muscles to clench around him and fake my orgasm.

He stills on top of me, pulls out, and climbs off the bed, going to the bathroom to dispose of the condom.

I wait until he comes out, then, grabbing my clothes off the floor, head inside to quickly clean up. I'll shower once I'm home, but I hate the lingering smell of latex.

After washing my face—because eww, sweat!—and hands, I make my way back out to the bedroom. Paul is in only his boxers, and is lying on the bed, scrolling through his phone.

"Have you called Henry?" I ask, referring to his driver who always brings me home.

"Any chance I can talk you into spending the night?" He looks up from his phone and shoots me a playful grin.

He may have a small dick, but he's not hard on the eyes. Between his mop of blond curls, his striking emerald eyes, and the adorable dimple that peeks out of his left cheek when he grins, he's extremely good-looking in that boy next door sort of way.

And if I were any other woman, that grin would have me climbing back into his bed. But I'm not, and his grin does nothing for me.

"Sorry, it's already after nine. I really need to get going. I have work in the morning."

He nods, knowing there's nothing he can say that will convince me to stay. I've been there and done that, and it will never happen again. Sleeping together leads to feelings, and feelings lead to your heart being shattered into a million pieces.

"See you Wednesday night?" he asks, getting out of bed to walk me to the door.

"See you then."

After grabbing my clutch from the table in the foyer, I turn the knob to open the door, when Paul's arm snakes around my waist, and he pulls me in for a kiss.

"Goodnight," he whispers against my lips.

"Goodnight."

It's a thirty-minute drive from the Upper East Side—where Paul lives—to Brooklyn Heights—where I live. I use the time to check my text messages and emails. I see one marked as urgent from my boss, so I click it open first.

Giselle,

Please advise. Mr. Caprice has forwarded his wife's requests, and she would like to discuss them with you tomorrow. Please confirm a time. He has listed times that will work for her.

Thank you,

Lydia Strickland

CEO

Fresh Designs, Inc.

I scroll through the requests and grin when I see everything Elizabeth Caprice is requesting are all the suggestions I made when we did a walkthrough of her home a couple weeks ago.

With a degree and master's in interior design, my dream was to land a position with the largest interior design company on the East Coast, and I actually achieved it.

I've only been working under Lydia for just over a year now, and while the pay is downright embarrassing since it's an internship, I'm confident if I keep going the way I am, I'll land myself a permanent position, with decent pay, soon enough.

Most internships here last between one year and eighteen months. I just need to hold on a little bit longer.

After checking my schedule for tomorrow, I email Mr. Caprice back to confirm a time. When I feel the car come to a stop, I look up and see we're here.

"Thank you, Henry," I say before jumping out of the backseat like I always do before he can get out to open the car door for me. The poor guy must be in his eighties, and there's no reason why I can't open my own door.

"Goodnight, Miss Winters," he calls out as I shut the door.

It's a good ten-minute walk to the building I live in, so I pull up my sister's name on my contact list and call her to see how she's doing. She's a sophomore at the University of Boston and lives in a sorority house, so there's a good chance she'll still be awake.

"Giselle!" she shouts into the phone when she answers, making me pull it away from my ear. A few seconds later, the noise is gone. "Sorry about that. It's the Spring Social. The entire campus is like one giant party. How are you?"

I smile on the inside at how happy my sister sounds. She deserves to be carefree and enjoy her four years of college.

I was worried when, during her senior year of high school, she came out that she's gay. Not because I care which sex she prefers, but because I was nervous others might not be as accepting, and she would feel like an outcast at her school.

I worried for nothing, though, because she's excelling both socially and academically, and even has her first serious girlfriend.

"I'm good," I tell her. "How was your first week back to school?" Adrianna has just begun her spring semester.

"So good! I got into the lab I was telling you about. It will mean taking fifteen credits instead of twelve, so I'll have to work twice as hard, but I'm so excited."

"The microphysics lab you told me about?" I confirm.

"Yes! It's extremely rare for a sophomore to be approved to take the class, but Professor Gent said with my grades and the fact that I was the top scorer in her chemistry class, she feels I will be successful."

"That's amazing, Addy. I'm so proud of you."

My words come out slow, so she can't hear the emotion laced in them. I swallow down the lump in my throat and swipe a falling tear, reminding myself this is why I'm doing what I'm doing. For Addy. And for mom.

"Thanks, Sis."

"How's Stacey?"

Stacey is Adrianna's girlfriend. They met in one of their science classes and hit it off right away. They've both picked the same major, which I imagine gives them a lot to talk about.

"She's great. Busy with school and softball."

"I look forward to meeting her."

"Yeah, maybe over spring break."

"Sounds good."

Adrianna's quiet for a moment, and when she does speak, her voice is soft and hesitant. "Umm...listen." I hear the nervousness in her tone, and I'm instantly worried. "The registrar's office sent a final notice. If I don't have the remaining balance paid by Monday, I'm going to have to withdraw from my classes. I know I was just going crazy over the lab, but I can take less classes if you need me to. I don't want—"

"Stop it! I'm sorry. I've just been so busy at work, it slipped my mind. I'm walking inside my building right now, and as soon as I get to my room, I will pull it up and pay the bill."

"Are you sure?" she asks, and my heart tightens in my chest. It wasn't supposed to be like this. Damn my father!

I inhale deeply then exhale to collect myself. The last thing Adrianna needs is to hear me crying. "I am one hundred percent sure."

"Okay, thank you."

"You're welcome. Hey, I'm about to get on the elevator, and I don't want to lose you. Have fun at your party tonight, and we'll talk soon."

"Okay! Love you."

"Love you too."

We hang up, and before I get into the elevator, I type out a quick text to my *other* boss and hit send.

ME

I need more hours.

BIANCA

Noted.

I take the elevator up to the third and top floor of the brownstone I share with my best friend, Olivia Harper. And by share, I mean she owns it, and I pay pennies to live here with her.

I met Olivia our freshman year of college in Paris. I was assigned a flat mate, and after only one week of living with her, I was almost positive I was going to kill her in her sleep.

While most students spent their first week of school trying to figure out which classes they wanted to keep or drop, she spent the week sleeping her way through the entire lacrosse team...in the middle of the night...while I was trying to sleep.

As fate would have it, Olivia and I were in the same Art History class. She mentioned being lonely in her two-bedroom flat, so I offered to move in.

We lived together during all four years of college and two years of getting our master's degrees. During which time, our friendship went from flat mates, to best friends, to sisters.

She is the yin to my yang. Which is why when she said she needed to move back to New York last year, I packed up my stuff and followed her home.

I'm quiet as I open the door, unsure of who's here and not wanting to wake anyone up if they're sleeping. But when I walk inside, I see Olivia is sitting on the couch watching television with her sweet baby boy in her arms.

He's drinking a cup of juice, but when he hears the door creak open, his head pops up, and he grants me the most adorable toothy grin.

"Hey, how was your night?" she asks, pausing whatever she's watching to give me her full attention.

"Good." My answer is too vague for her liking, and she frowns.

"Were you on a date or working late?"

Knowing she won't stop until I give her the information she wants, I sit down next to her and put my arms out for Reed.

He drops his cup and climbs into my lap. I give him an extra tight hug, inhaling his baby scent, and he giggles.

"Hey there, my little love muffin. Did you miss me?" I coo. Reed plants a big, wet kiss on my cheek, and my heart soars. "I missed you too."

He scoots out of my lap and slides down the couch and onto the ground, toddling over to where some of his toys are. I watch him for a second before I realize Olivia is still waiting for me to answer her question.

"I was on a date."

"With who?"

"Just some guy."

"What's his name?" she presses.

"Paul." I give her a look that says I don't want to discuss him, but she ignores it.

"That's a nice name. Is it serious?"

"Not really. Where's Nick?" I ask in an attempt to change the subject. Olivia grins at the mention of her baby daddy-slash-fiancé, momentarily forgetting about my date.

"Jacksonville. They've made it to the playoffs. We're flying out Saturday for the game."

Nick Shaw is the starting quarterback of the New York Brewers. While he has his own place in the Lower East Side, he's more often than not wherever Olivia and Reed are.

"That's awesome!"

"They might be Super bowl champs for the second year in a row." Olivia beams. "How's work going? Anything new on the big account you've been working on?" she asks.

"Actually, yes!" I get excited thinking about the email I read earlier. "The client loved all of my suggestions, and we're meeting tomorrow morning to discuss moving forward."

"That's fabulous! One day you will be the most sought-after interior designer on the East Coast, and I'll get to say I'm your best friend."

She grins, and my heart swells at the way my best friend always sees the best in me. She has no doubt in her mind that one day I will achieve my goals and dreams. If only I was as optimistic as she is.

"Now, let's talk about your birthday." She claps her hands together in excitement.

I groan. "Livi, c'mon! Can't we just pretend I'm not getting any older and forget my birthday altogether?"

"Nope and nope! I know you're crazy busy these days between work and making up for all the years you haven't dated..." She gives me the stink-eye, telling me she isn't happy with my lack of details. "So, I'm calling dibs on you next Friday night. Birthday dinner followed by a night out. Corrine and my dad are watching Reed."

When I open my mouth to argue, she shoots me a rare glare that has me cringing slightly. She's not going to accept any excuse I try to give her, so I don't bother. I'll just need to let Bianca know I can't work next Friday, which sucks since I literally just asked her for more hours—and more importantly, I need them.

"Okay, Friday." I nod with a smile, and Olivia squeals in excitement.

"Yay! We're going to have so much fun!" Her phone goes off, and when she checks to see who it is, her smile widens. "Reed, Daddy is calling. Come say hi." She hits accept and Nick's face appears on the screen.

"Hey buddy," he says as Reed crawls over to the couch to see his dad on the other end of the line.

Figuring Olivia will be busy on the phone for a good while, and wanting to give her some privacy, I sneak away into my room.

After taking a long hot shower and getting dressed into my comfy pajamas, I open my laptop and pull up my bank account information. Then I open another window and log into Adrianna's school site.

It's going to be tight, but if Bianca can give me some additional hours, I think I can swing it without going into the negatives. Not that I have a choice, since the alternative is my sister not taking all the classes she's signed up for—and that's definitely not an option.

I click on her semester bill and type in my credit card information then hit submit. I refresh my bank site and the balance drops from five figures to four. I type another text to Bianca with an apology that I can't work next Friday night then remind her I can work any other day.

Closing my laptop, I turn my light off and crawl into bed. Then I remember I never called my mom tonight.

Damn it.

I look over at the clock and see it's too late now. I'll just get up a few minutes earlier tomorrow and call her before I get ready for work.

Chapter Two

KILLIAN

"WING T 69 BOTTLENECK RIGHT!" NICK YELLS, announcing the next play we're going to run through.

During any given practice, we'll go through dozens of different plays. With our team making it to the playoffs for the second year in a row, all eyes are on us—many wanting us to succeed, but a lot wanting us to fail.

When you become the Champions after not even making it to the playoffs in over a decade, it's a given everyone will be ridiculing every move your team makes, questioning if you can do it again, or if it was just a one-time deal.

I've been with the New York Brewers since I was drafted my senior year in college, and after finally earning a ring, I can tell you, one isn't enough. Especially when my best friend Nick has four of those damn things—three from the team he previously played for, and one from last year when we won during our first season of playing together since college.

The Super Bowl was almost a year ago, and I'm still high on the win and craving another one. It's what keeps me motivated every game as we get closer to the Super Bowl once again.

We won our first playoff game against Jacksonville last weekend. That's one game down. Only three more standing in the way of us getting that ring.

We break into formation and then the ball is hiked. Everyone scrambles to their position on the field. Nick steps into position and throws the ball right into my awaiting arms, which of course I catch, and run down the field for a touchdown.

Coach Harper blows the whistle, and everyone congregates around him. "Good practice, everyone. You have the next two days off to rest. Practice Saturday and we play Pittsburgh Sunday. Don't get into any trouble. I don't need to remind you that we're only three games away from being Super Bowl champions."

Everyone cheers at his words then head into the locker room to shower and change.

Coach Harper pats Nick on the shoulder. "See you Friday, Son."

Nick nods and smiles. "Yes, sir."

Coach Harper is the father of Nick's fiancée, Olivia, and the grandfather to their son, Reed. You would think it would be awkward for Nick to be playing on the same team his future father-in-law coaches, but the truth is, Stephen

Harper is more of a father to Nick than his own father is. He never gives him special treatment, but it's clear they have a good relationship.

When Nick was picked up last year, Coach spent every day helping him work out and get back into shape after his injury.

Once I'm packed up and ready to go, I turn my cell phone back on and see a missed call from my publicist. I give her a call back. "Amber, how's it going?"

"Good, thanks for returning my call. I just wanted to remind you tomorrow night is the party with Bugatti to announce your endorsement deal with them. Several major investors will be there."

I grin at the thought of signing a deal with Bugatti. My first big purchase I made after I signed with New York was a Bugatti Veyron, my dream car.

I've owned several others since then, but the Veyron will always be my favorite. So, when my agent, Mike Miller, was approached about me signing an endorsement deal with them, it was a fucking given.

It's common for football players to endorse various items and companies such as insurance agencies, clothing lines, and different health food companies.

But being named MVP of the Super Bowl last year has opened endorsement gates I never imagined possible— including getting a special edition made of my favorite car.

Amber continues. "I'll email you the details again, just in case you lost them." The woman knows me way too well.

I suck at remembering anything other than when to catch a ball. "Will you need a date?" she asks.

"Yeah, thanks."

We hang up, and as I'm grabbing my gym bag, I spot Nick walking over to me, his own bag slung over his shoulder. "Ready to go?" I ask.

"Hell yes."

We head out of the stadium and toward my car. Because we live in the same building, we often ride together. Driving in New York sucks, which is why we only live about ten minutes from the stadium.

"So, listen," Nick says, "there's a little get together Friday night for Giselle's birthday. We're going to dinner and then out afterward. Olivia knows we have curfew, so we won't be out too late. I know you and Giselle aren't exactly friendly, but it would mean a lot to Olivia if you'd go. Giselle doesn't have many friends."

"How is that my fault? Maybe if she wasn't so unpleasant to be around, more people would like her. Then you wouldn't need me to increase your number of guests."

I know I sound like a dick, but I'm not lying. I have no clue how Olivia and Giselle are even friends, let alone best friends.

While Olivia is sweet and soft-spoken and just an all-around nice person, Giselle is the complete opposite in every way: blunt, loud, and not at all nice.

"She's not really that bad. You just have to get to know her. She's like a Pitbull. She looks vicious, but once you pat

her head, she'll roll over, wag her tail, and lick you to death."
Nick shrugs.

"You realize you just compared her to a dog, right?"
When Nick's brows furrow in confusion, I shake with
laughter. "A bitch?"

His eyes widen. "That's not what I meant!"

"Well, if the shoe fits...or should we say paw?" I laugh
harder at my own joke. "So, who else is going?"

"Her sister might come down, and Celeste will be there."

I start laughing all over again at the mention of Celeste.
"What?" Nick asks.

"I just can't get over the fact that your current fiancée is
friends with your ex-fiancée."

Nick glares, and it only has me cackling harder as I press
the ignition and head out of the parking lot.

"Bro, shut the fuck up. Celeste was barely my fiancée."

He's right, but I still have to give him shit about it. I
met Nick and Celeste our freshman year of college. Nick and
I shared a dorm, and Celeste was his childhood friend who
was a few years younger but always hung out with us.

She was and still is a gold-digger. She might be hot as
fuck, and a huge model who owns a few successful businesses,
but that doesn't change the fact that her entire goal in life
is to make money and marry a guy who will give her more
money.

I will never understand how in the world Nick has not
only remained friends with her over the years, but almost
married her last year.

"Whatever you say. Have you guys found a home yet?"

Nick groans, and I laugh some more. I shouldn't get such a kick out of this man's life, but I can't help it.

Nick and Olivia are the only two people I know who are engaged to be married, can afford to purchase a new home—hell, fifteen new homes if they want to—but instead live separately.

"I think Olivia is putting off moving because of Giselle. Since they've met, Olivia has always found ways to take care of Giselle without making it look like she is, and if she moves out, Giselle will be more or less homeless."

"What do you mean?" I ask, turning onto our street.

Olivia owns a beautiful brownstone in the heart of Brooklyn Heights, and there's no way she would kick Giselle out. Those two women are closer to being sisters than best friends.

"If Olivia moves out, Giselle will never stay living there knowing her friend is only continuing to pay the mortgage for her, and there's no way she can afford to take over those payments."

That's for sure. You would never know it, but Olivia's mother, who died when she was younger, left Olivia a huge inheritance. The woman could probably afford to purchase the entire building she lives in.

Giselle, on the other hand, comes from the same background as me: middle-class working family who lives paycheck to paycheck.

"I could be wrong, but I don't think it's normal to be married and live in separate homes," I joke.

"Which is probably why we still haven't gotten married. I love how selfless Olivia is, and that she wants to put her best friend first. And I get it. Giselle moved back to New York just for Olivia. But fuck, I just want to marry her and live under one damn roof. I feel like a kid in a divorced home, bouncing back and forth between our places."

"Well then, Giselle is just going to have to do what everyone else does and stand on her own two capable feet."

I pull into our parking garage and turn the car off. When we get to the elevator, Nick presses the button for my floor then the one directly above for his.

"I'm sure you guys will figure it out," I tell him. "It'll suck once you do move, though. How will you come down to play Madden with me?"

Nick laughs. "Don't worry, honey, I'll always find time for you." He winks.

The elevator door opens on my floor. "I have that endorsement party for Bugatti tomorrow night, so I won't see you until Friday. Text me when and where to meet you guys and I'll be there."

Nick nods. "Thanks, man, and congrats on your deal."

I thank him then step off the elevator, the door closing behind me.

"TABITHA, YOU LOOK BEAUTIFUL." I STEP OUT OF the limousine and give my date a kiss on her cheek.

She's dressed in a black floor-length gown, and her blond locks are up in a bun of some sort. Amber came through, as always.

"Thank you, Mr. Blake," she gushes as I help her inside before walking around to the other side, so she doesn't have to slide over in her dress.

"Please, call me Killian. Tonight, we're going to a party to announce and sign my endorsement deal with Bugatti. They're planning to run the ads during the playoffs and Super Bowl. There'll be some pretty big investors there."

"Understood," she says with a smile.

We make small talk on the way to the Four Seasons where the party is being held. Tabitha is polite and professional, and I can already tell tonight will be a good night.

Once we arrive, we're escorted back. I'm met with several people who introduce themselves, including the head of the design team who is in charge of making the special edition.

"This beautiful car will only be available to fifteen people," Travis boasts, clearly proud of what his team has created.

"I'm just honored I'll be one of those fifteen people." I shake his hand.

"That's so exciting," Tabitha whispers enthusiastically.

I begin to tell her it's a dream come true when I spot someone I know out of the corner of my eye and wonder why in the world she's here at my party.

"Excuse me for a second. I see someone I know."

I make my way over to the bar where she's sitting on a cushioned stool, and when I get close enough, I notice she's sipping on what looks like some type of scotch.

Of course, she is.

While most women would choose a fruity drink of some sort, Giselle chooses the hard stuff. Her brown hair is pin straight down her back, and her blood-red dress fits every curve of her damn body perfectly. When I approach the bar, the bartender asks what I would like.

"Jameson whiskey sour, please." I lean one elbow against the bar top and face her. "What are you doing here?"

She takes a slow sip of her drink before she gives me any of her attention. "I'm assuming the same thing you're doing here. Celebrating the endorsement deal for a..." Her voice trails off as she realizes just who the endorsement deal is for. "*You?*" She shoots me a side-eye, her nose scrunching up as she takes another sip of her drink.

"Yes, me, and I'm almost positive an interior design *intern* isn't needed for any part of this deal, so I'll ask again, what are you doing here? Did you crash the party in an attempt to find some rich guy to latch onto?"

She cackles, throwing her head back like what I just said was the funniest thing she's ever heard.

Then, she stands, and because I'm standing directly next to her barstool, the front of her body rubs up against mine, and her perky tits, which are overflowing out of the top of her dress, press against my chest.

I force myself to keep my eyes on hers as she leans into me and whispers, "I'm here with the man you made the deal with, silly. The man, who in about sixty minutes, will be nestled between my thighs, fucking me senseless. And if I wanted him to, would give me ten of these stupid ugly cars."

Giselle smirks snidely as she edges out from between the stool and me, remembering to take her drink with her.

"There you are, lovely." Roman Ette, the man responsible for this deal taking place, comes over and rests his hand on Giselle's back, giving her a chaste kiss to her cheek. "I should've known you ran off to the bar."

He smiles at her, and Giselle giggles. *What the fuck!* She actually giggles. Who the hell is this woman, and if she's dating him, why is she crying broke?

"You know me too well, Roman. I was actually on my way back to find you. I was only gone but a minute." She giggles some more. "Were you missing me already?"

"Always." He shoots her a wink then turns his attention back to me. "Mr. Blake, I heard the guest of honor arrived." He extends his hand and I shake it. "Are you excited to see your special edition?"

"I am, sir. This is truly a dream come true."

I spot Tabitha making her way over, but for some reason, everything I found to be beautiful about her suddenly seems so plain. I refuse to acknowledge my thoughts have anything to do with the woman still standing in front of me, currently eye-fucking a man more than twice her age.

Tabitha stops at my side, and I make introductions. "Tabitha, this is Roman Ette."

"Nice to meet you, sir." She smiles politely.

"And this is his date." I make it a point not to mention Giselle's name, refusing to give her any importance, just to piss her off.

So, I'm shocked when Tabitha says, "Nice to meet you, Giselle."

My eyes dart over to Tabitha first, who doesn't seem to notice her slip-up—maybe she knows her?—but then my gaze goes to Giselle. Her glacier-blue eyes which normally appear cold, go wide with what looks like worry, and I know right away something is up.

"Do you two know each other?" I ask.

"We do." Giselle quickly speaks first. "We went to school together."

"Oh, really? Where did you go to school, Tabitha?" Her eyes are now as wide as Giselle's.

"We went to NYU—" Giselle begins to say, but I cut her off.

"I asked Tabitha."

"We went to NYU," Tabitha says.

"Really?" Roman says, joining the conversation. "I thought you went to school in Paris?" His question is aimed at Giselle.

"I did. NYU Paris," she says, her perfect smile never faltering.

But as I rake my eyes down her body, I notice she's wringing her hands together—something I'd seen her do a few months back when she was worried about her mom. It's her telltale sign she's nervous. Why would Giselle be nervous? Unless she has something to hide.

"Yes, NYU Paris," Tabitha agrees, but unlike Giselle, she isn't as good at faking it. Her voice wavering with each word she speaks.

Roman smiles, none the wiser, but something feels off. My gaze meets Giselle's, and for the first time since I ran into her, she isn't glaring at me.

Instead, it's almost as if she's pleading with me to drop it. Her eyes are no longer icy—they're vulnerable, exposed. I've seen this look from her before. I remember it well because it's not often Giselle allows herself to appear weak.

My thoughts go back several months to the night we spent in the Hamptons with our friends. We had been partying at AM Southampton until Olivia got too drunk and Nick felt it was time to head home.

As we were all climbing the stairs, Olivia, in all her drunken glory, decided to assign each woman to a princess. Celeste was labeled Belle, and Giselle was Rapunzel, but that wasn't the part that got my attention. What did was what Olivia said afterward:

"And one day you're going to meet a prince you will trust with all of your secrets, and he's going to save you just like Flynn Ryder saved Rapunzel."

Giselle's eyes went wide, much like they are now, as she silently pleaded with her best friend to shut up.

But her eyes weren't angry—they were scared. She's always been a damn contradiction: strong, yet she relies on her best friend to support her. Hard working, yet she dates rich men who want nothing more than a trophy wife on their arm.

Maybe I was focusing on the wrong part of what Olivia said. On the part about her needing to be saved, when what I should've been paying attention to, was the part about her having secrets. Is it possible there's more to Giselle than what meets the eye?

The rest of the night goes smoothly, and I force myself to push any more thoughts of Giselle out of my head. It doesn't matter what she's hiding. None of it is my business. Giselle isn't my business. And the last thing I need in my life is a lying, sneaking, secret-keeping woman. I've dealt with those type of women more times than I can count, and I've learned my lesson the hard way. I'll be damned if I put my hand on the hot stove after getting burned.

Once the night comes to an end, Tabitha and I say our goodbyes. When we're a few minutes away from her apartment, I can't help myself. I told myself I didn't care what Giselle is hiding, but I can't get her off my mind.

"What did you major in at NYU?" I ask.

Tabitha flinches. "I... um... I didn't make it that far." She shrugs. "I dropped out." Her eyes dart everywhere in the limo but at me.

I open my mouth to ask her another question when she squeaks out, "Oh, we're here." She scoops up her clutch then quickly swings the door open. "I hope you had a good night." She smiles awkwardly then slides out, shutting the door behind her and scurrying up the sidewalk like her ass is on fire.

Oh yeah, something is definitely up.

Once I'm back home, I shower and change into some lounge pants. I try to get Giselle off my mind, but it's not happening. I lie in bed and turn on the television, willing myself to drop whatever I'm thinking. But the more I try not to think about her, the more I do.

A memory surfaces from our night in the Hamptons— after Celeste, Nick, and Olivia disappeared into their rooms, and I thought Giselle had done the same thing.

"Hey! Do you mind?" Giselle snaps at me.

"Sorry, I didn't realize anyone was in the bathroom." I should've knocked, but when I grabbed the knob and it opened, I assumed it was empty. Now that I know it is indeed occupied, I should close the door, but instead my eyes are frozen on Giselle's sexy body.

She's wearing a powder blue lace bra that matches her eyes, her nipples hard and pebbling through the thin material.

My eyes drag down her body, over her toned stomach and land on her tiny matching lace panties. Without thinking, I lick my lips as I imagine what her cunt would taste like. It's been a long time since I—

"See something you like?" She smirks and takes a step forward. "Too bad I don't fuck athletes."

Her hand lands on my chest. She pats it condescendingly, effectively snapping me out of my trance as she saunters past me, out of the bathroom, and leaves me standing there with a raging hard-on.

I think what confuses me the most about Giselle is while everyone is privy to that version of her—the beautiful woman who hides behind her ice-queen persona—I've seen another side of her. A side I'm not even sure Olivia has ever seen.

The next morning, Giselle gets a phone call from her sister that her dad left her mom. She has no way of getting there, so I offer to take her.

After a completely silent two-hour drive to Rye, we pull up to her house. Giselle quickly unbuckles her seatbelt, throws open the car door, and runs up the short sidewalk to her parents' house.

It reminds me a lot of the home I grew up in before I could afford to buy my parents a nicer place. A single-story home on zero lot land with paint probably twenty years old peeling off the walls.

There's a beat-up looking Ford Focus in the driveway that must be at least thirty years old.

I step out of my vehicle and my eyes land on some teenagers who are currently standing on the street engaging in what looks to be a drug deal.

One of them gives me a curt nod, and I hit the alarm on my car, knowing damn well it won't really do any good in a neighborhood like this.

I walk into the house to find Giselle and her sister talking. Their words come to a halt when her sister sees me.

"Who's this?" she asks, and Giselle introduces us. "This is Killian, a friend of Nick and Olivia's. He brought me here."

"Thank you." She wraps her arms around Giselle in a hug. "I'm so sorry. She won't come out, and I have to get back to school. I didn't know—"

Giselle pulls back. "It's okay," she says, cutting her off. "Go, and don't worry about a thing. Just focus on your classes. I will make sure mom is okay. I promise."

She gives her sister another hug, then pushes her out the door. Once it's closed, her back hits the wood and she lets out a deep sigh. Her eyes close, and for just a small moment, she appears softer. She doesn't look anything like the closed-off ice-cold woman I've come to know the last couple months. That is until she opens her eyes back up and speaks.

"You can wait outside. I don't need you here."

Her blue eyes are once again hard, and she glares at me like I'm the enemy. Without waiting for me to speak, she blows past me down the hall.

I'm about to go back outside when I notice she's trying to pry the door open with a screwdriver.

"What are you doing?"

"What does it look like?" she snaps. "Having a fucking tea party? I'm trying to open the door! My mom locked herself in there."

I walk down the hall and take the screwdriver out of her hand. "That's not going to work."

"Well, I need to get in there. Can you break it down, please?"

"You sure?" I ask. "The doorjamb will probably splinter."

"Yes. My mom...she could be..." She doesn't finish her sentence with words, but instead with her terrified eyes.

I tell her to stand back, then I kick the door, and just as I predicted, it opens but the frame splinters, and pieces of wood fall to the ground.

"Thank you."

She rushes into the room while I stay in the doorway. Her mom is on her bed, sobbing, and Giselle climbs on to the bed and pulls her head into her lap.

"He's gone," her mom cries. "He left me."

"It's okay, Mom," Giselle says in the same melodic tone parents use when trying to soothe their upset babies.

Wanting to give them their space, I back out of the doorway and walk back down the hall to wait in the living room.

I haven't even sat down on the sofa when I hear screaming and shouting coming from the bedroom.

"It's all your fault! I hate you!" The voice isn't Giselle's, so it must be her mother. I start to walk back toward the bedroom.

"Mom, please calm down."

I stop in my tracks, unsure of what I should do.

I hear something crash, and then Giselle says, "Mom, stop, that hurts."

My feet move of their own accord into the bedroom, where I see Giselle's mother dragging Giselle by her hair to the center of the room.

"Mom, you're hurting me!" she yells, but her mom doesn't stop.

"Everyone left me! You, your sister, now your father!"

When her mom turns her back toward me, pulling Giselle into a standing position, I come up behind her and cage her arms in my own.

I'm not sure if I'm doing the right thing, but I can't just stand here and watch her hurt her daughter.

Giselle's mom appears to be shocked at first, her head tilting back to look at me, but then she starts to fight back.

For a tiny little thing, she sure is strong. She thrashes about and tries to kick me in the groin, all while screaming for me to let her go.

Giselle runs out of the room, and a few seconds later, returns.

She stabs her mom with a needle into her neck, and a few minutes later, her mom's body feels like dead weight in my arms.

"You, umm...you didn't kill her, did you?" I ask nervously.

"No, it's a sedative. We try not to use it unless it's necessary. I knew there was no way I would be able to get her to swallow her pills. Thank you for holding her down. Usually her nurse is here, but she has the weekends off when my dad is home. You can lay her down."

Carefully, I lift her and set her on the bed. She's definitely out.

Giselle walks over to the dresser and opens the drawer. "Damn it!"

"What's wrong?"

"My dad really did leave. All of his clothes are gone."

She slides open the closet door and there's a huge empty spot.

"What's wrong with your mom?" I ask.

"She suffers from depression, and we can't seem to find meds that work." She pulls out her phone and dials someone. "Donna, it's Giselle. Listen, my dad left. All of his stuff is gone. Until I can figure everything out, can you stay with her?" She goes quiet, listening to the person on the other end. Then she says, *"Yes, of course you will be paid accordingly."* She listens some more and then murmurs, *"Okay, thank you,"* before ending the call.

"If you're afraid of your mom being alone, we could bring her with us," I offer.

"She hates to leave her house, and since I live with Olivia, that's not an option. I'm not about to bring my shit to her doorstep. I'll figure it out. I'm sorry you had to see that."

She smiles softly, but it's a sad smile, and my heart hurts for her. But then her eyes meet mine, and it's as if she's just remembered she isn't supposed to be nice to me.

"You can wait outside in the car. Once Donna gets here, we can go," she says, clearly dismissing me, her mask rising back over her face to hide her emotions.

The ride home was once again silent. When we arrived at her place, she quickly thanked me and got out, and since then she's never once mentioned her mom again.

I have no idea what happened—if her dad returned, or even how her mom is doing. I haven't asked, and she hasn't spoken of it. I shouldn't even care. It's not my business. *She's* not my business.

So then why are you thinking about her?

Chapter Three

GISELLE

I'm sitting at the table in my favorite Japanese restaurant with Celeste, Killian, Nick, and Olivia. Adrianna didn't make it down because she had an important cram session she needed to attend for an upcoming test, and I insisted she stay there to prepare.

Nick and Killian are discussing their win against Jacksonville and what they need to do to beat Pittsburgh.

Olivia is showing Celeste pictures of Reed since she's been out of the country the last few months. She launched her new clothing line worldwide last year, and she's been traveling all over to promote it.

We're all here to celebrate my twenty-sixth birthday, and the only thing I want to do is go home and get some sleep.

I'm beyond exhausted from all the hours I've worked this week. But because I know tonight means a lot to Olivia, and I've been pushing her away recently, I keep a smile on my face as I listen to everyone around me converse.

"You ended up staying longer than planned. Did you meet anyone special while you were away?" Olivia asks Celeste, waggling her eyebrows playfully.

Celeste laughs. "Funny. Actually, I am dating someone. His name is Chad Vacanti."

"Good for you," Olivia says. "Is it serious?"

"As serious as two people can be who have busy careers." Celeste shrugs.

"So, in other words, he's a workaholic like you," Olivia volleys back playfully.

"No, he's *dedicated* to his job and works hard like me. He's a VP for the investment banking firm he works at. He had to fly over to the UK for some business, so we met up while I was there. It was nice."

Killian chuckles, and everyone looks his way.

"What?" Celeste glares.

"Nothing." Killian smirks.

"Just say it," Celeste insists.

"It's nothing, really. I'm just glad you finally found your millionaire." He pops a piece of sushi into his mouth and chews, then adds, "I take it you found him on Wall Street? Tell me, Celeste, does he know he's dating a gold-digger?"

"Screw you!" Celeste hisses. "For your information, my company's fourth quarter earnings grossed over six-point-five million dollars in profit, asshole."

Everyone at the table stills in shock. Holy shit! Celeste really is doing well for herself. Go her!

"Damn, Celeste!" Nick pats her on her shoulder. "That's awesome."

"Congratulations," Olivia adds.

"Seriously!" I say, "That's awesome."

"Thank you." She smiles proudly.

"Then why the hell are you still searching for your happily-ever-millionaire?" Killian questions.

"Killian," Olivia chides.

"What? It's just a question," he says.

God, he's such a judgmental ass!

"I'm not looking for a millionaire." Celeste takes a deep breath and her eyes dart all over the place, like she's suddenly uncomfortable. "There's nothing wrong with wanting a man who's stable and has his life together, who can afford to pay his bills." She huffs. "Never mind, you wouldn't understand." She lifts her glass of Sake to her mouth and downs it.

"So, what you're saying is, if you met a guy who, let's say, works full-time, pays his bills on time, but only makes five figures a year, you would date him?" Killian challenges.

Celeste shoots daggers his way, and Killian laughs. Before she can answer, Nick jumps in. "Kill, stop, man."

Killian shrugs and downs his beer.

I don't know what his deal is tonight, but I do not want to be on the receiving end of his inquisition.

My goal is to lay low and pray he doesn't call me out on seeing me last night. I'm already regretting the fact that

I goaded him by telling him I was going to fuck Roman and that his car was stupid and ugly.

It's really not either one. On the contrary, it's one of the most beautiful cars I've ever seen, and it has all the bells and whistles.

Olivia, feeling the need to change the subject, turns her attention on me. *Great...* "How's Paul?"

"Who?" I ask before I can catch myself, forgetting I gave her a name the other night.

"Paul, the guy you went on a date with last week."

I notice Killian sit up higher in his seat, his eyes widening marginally as he stares at me, like he's just as interested to know my answer as Olivia is. *Damn it!*

Ignoring Killian's stare, I focus my attention on Olivia when I answer. "I'm actually not seeing him anymore. It didn't work out."

Olivia frowns. "I'm sorry."

"How's Roman?" Killian asks.

My eyes dart over to him, and the asshole is fucking smirking.

"Who?" Olivia asks, confused.

I glare at Killian, silently warning him to shut up. He's doing this to mess with me, but he doesn't understand this isn't a fucking game. He's not only messing with my life, but he's messing with my friendship with Olivia.

Instead of heeding my warning, his smirk turns into a full-blown grin as he says, "The guy I saw Giselle at the party with last night."

And he just had to fucking go there...

46

"You went on a date last night?" Olivia asks. "When I asked you where you were, you said you were working."

I drag my gaze from Killian to look at Olivia. The hurt in her features is evident, and I feel like the world's shittiest friend.

I consider how to word my answer before I speak, because up until this moment, I've technically never lied to Olivia, and I have no clue how to twist this so I'm not lying now.

But before I can answer her, my name is called, and when I look over my shoulder, my heart drops at who is calling it. *Christian.*

Seriously, can this day get any worse?

He approaches the table, and I feel everyone's eyes on us.

"Hey, I thought it was you." Christian grins nervously.

Asshole should be nervous. The last time I saw him, he was balls-deep in a groupie in his hotel room, only days after he told me he loved me.

We had gotten into a fight regarding a text I saw on his phone. I left upset and sat on the bench outside of his hotel room, trying to figure out how to handle what I saw.

Not even an hour later, I made the decision to go up and talk to him about it. I think I was hoping he would convince me what I saw was a big misunderstanding. Only, when I got up to his room, he had already found another woman and was fucking her on the couch. That was a year ago, and I haven't seen or spoken to him since.

"It's me," I say dryly, not bothering to smile back.

He doesn't deserve anything from me, let alone a fake emotion. He lost the right to get anything from me the day he chose to throw our friendship and relationship out the window for some random groupie's pussy.

Christian glances around the table before his eyes come back to me. "It's your birthday." It's not a question—he's just remembered.

"Yep...Happy Birthday to me," I say.

Nobody says anything for a good thirty seconds, until Killian chooses to speak up, breaking the silence. "Wait a second. Aren't you Christian Ortega, the lead singer for Down Coyote?"

"That would be me." He nods with a small but genuine smile.

Christian lives for the moments when people recognize him. His dreams came true. His band was signed, and they rose to the top. It's too bad the industry destroyed him.

With the fame came the parties, and with the parties came the drugs. With him being high as often as he is—or at least was during that short time I was around him again—I don't even know how he enjoys his success.

The morning after I found him fucking the groupie, he called me as if nothing happened. He blamed the drugs, promised he would stop getting high. He swore he didn't even remember having sex with her.

He called several times, begging me to forgive him, but I told him it was too late. The damage was done. I can forgive a lot of things, but I can't forgive cheating.

The fact is we never would've worked out anyway. Seven years apart changed us both. We're no longer the naïve young teenagers we once were, and there's no going back.

Sometimes when I think about the way Christian behaved, I wonder if that's what happens to my mom. I know the drugs Christian was on aren't the same as my mom's, but I wonder if maybe she doesn't remember what she does or if it's possible she's reacting a certain way because she's on so many different drugs. If we just took her off of everything, maybe she would see things more clearly. I can't be sure, though, and I'm too scared to find out.

"We're just finishing up dinner and are about to head out for some drinks," Killian says, snapping me out of my thoughts. "You should join us. Any *friend* of Giselle's is welcome. Or wait, are you her boyfriend?" Killian smirks devilishly.

Christian's hand grips the back of his neck nervously, unsure of what to say.

Thankfully, Olivia jumps in. "You need to walk away right now, asshole. I know about you cheating on my best friend. Go back to your groupies and stay away from her."

Her voice is barely loud enough for the entire table to hear, and while her intent is to sound big and bad, she just sounds adorable, but I still love her even more for defending me.

"I think it's best if you go," Celeste adds. "It's clear you're not wanted here." Celeste has heard all about Christian and what he did to me on several girls' nights out.

"Look, I'm sorry. Would it be possible for us to talk?" Christian asks, and this time Nick jumps in.

"You heard the ladies. You're not wanted here."

"This is between Giselle and me," Christian snaps.

"No, it's really not," Killian says, shocking the crap out of me. He and Nick stand, and Christian backs up. "I didn't realize when I extended my offer, you were a cheating piece of shit. So, not only am I rescinding my offer for you to join us, but I suggest you walk out of this restaurant and lose Giselle's number. If she wants to call you, she'll do so. But until then, get fucking lost."

Christian's hands go up in surrender, and he looks at me like he wants to say something, but luckily, he thinks better of it and walks away.

"I'm so sorry, Giselle." Olivia gets up and comes around to my side of the table to give me a hug. "I love you."

"I love you too," I whisper. "Thank you, guys." Tears brim my lids as I look around at everyone who just stood up for me, including Killian. I might not have a lot of friends, but the few I do have are pretty freaking great. And while Killian isn't my friend, it means a lot that despite how much he doesn't like me, he still stood up for me.

"Growing up I never really had any friends," I admit out loud. "My family kind of has some issues." My eyes dart to Killian who has seen them firsthand. "Christian was not only my best friend but my boyfriend. I never imagined one of the people closest to me would betray me like he did. Anyway, you guys sticking up for me like that means the world to me."

"You would've done it for us," Olivia points out.

"After that, I think we all need to get drunk," Celeste says with a laugh. "That guy was about to ruin my buzz."

"Actually, we have something else planned." Olivia grins. "It's a surprise, though."

"What happened to partying? Getting drunk?" Celeste pouts.

"We will, I promise! After we go to our next stop. But first, we need to sing Happy Birthday." She nods behind her and the waiter comes over with a candle-lit birthday cake. Everyone sings Happy Birthday, then Olivia cuts the cake.

Once we're done eating it, we pile into the limo Olivia rented for the night.

Killian is sitting next to me, and I'm shocked when he leans in close to speak to me. "I'm sorry about what I did in there. Inviting that asshole out with us."

I just don't have it in me to call him out on his shit. So, instead, I say, "It's not your fault. You didn't know."

"True, but we both know I was only inviting him to piss you off." Killian smiles apologetically, and I laugh at his honesty. "So, I'm sorry," he adds.

"It's okay," I tell him.

"We're here!" Olivia announces, and everyone steps out of the limo onto the sidewalk in front of...

"A tattoo shop?" I ask excitedly.

"Yep! I made us appointments!" Olivia clasps her hands together and jumps up and down.

"Hell yes!" I yell, joining her.

"You, umm...you didn't make an appointment for me, did you?" Celeste asks nervously.

"Well, I told him we had a group coming and I wasn't sure who all would want one. He said a couple people would be here," Olivia tells her.

"Oh my god, Livi! This is so exciting!" I exclaim.

"A dream of yours?" Killian asks.

"Of ours." I smile at Olivia. "We both said we wanted one, but we were too scared to actually get them. So we agreed that once we graduated with our masters, we would get tattoos to celebrate. Olivia graduated before me, and by the time I graduated six months later, she was knocked up."

"Must you word it like that," Olivia says through her laughter. "Let's go!"

Linking our arms together, Olivia and I walk into Forbidden Ink, followed by Killian, Nick, and Celeste.

From the outside, it looks like nothing more than a small hole-in-the-wall shop with blacked out windows.

But once we open the door, it's as if we're stepping into a New York City alleyway, and I'm not talking about one behind Fifth Avenue. More like the ones from where I'm from.

The walls are painted to look like graffitied CBS block, but the artwork is far better than anything you would see in the real alleyways. They are eye-catching and beautiful.

The floors are concrete, identical to the sidewalks outside, but cleaner. There are a couple of black leather couches in the front area, and on a black wooden coffee table are stacks of books.

In the right corner is a pool table, and to the left is the front counter. A narrow hallway goes down the middle.

"How can I help you?" the woman sitting behind the counter asks with a smile.

She's pretty, with her silky black locks tied into low pigtails, perfect porcelain skin, and big onyx eyes. Her arms look like beautiful canvases of colorful artwork.

"We have an appointment with Jaxson," Olivia says.

"All of you?" the woman questions, her gaze following over each of us. Then it stops on someone, and her smile widens. My eyes follow her line of vision to...Killian.

"Kill!" She jumps off her stool and runs out from behind the counter, straight into his arms. And if I thought she was just pretty from behind the counter, I was wrong.

She's wearing a flowy yellow top and tiny cut-off jean shorts that on most would look trashy, but on her look seriously hot. She's sexy and adorable, and with her arms wrapped around Killian, I kind of hate her, which doesn't make any sense.

Maybe I drank more than I thought at dinner...

"Quinn, how are you?" Killian asks once they're done hugging.

"Same shit, different day. You here for another tattoo?" She waggles her eyebrows flirtatiously, and it's confirmed, I hate her.

Why? I have no fucking clue, I just do.

Seriously, how much did I have to drink?

"Well, since I'm here, maybe." Killian laughs, and his hazel eyes light up. "But we're actually here for those two." He nods toward Olivia and me. "Olivia, Giselle, this is

Quinn, Jax and Jase's little sister. It's Giselle's birthday, so they're looking to get tattoos."

"How about you?" a deep male voice rumbles.

I turn in place to see a gentleman leaning against the doorframe with his muscular tattooed arms crossed over his chest. He's wearing a fitted plain black T-shirt and ripped jeans, and he's staring at Celeste, who looks completely out of place in her expensive designer dress and high heels.

"Excuse me?" she asks, her nose scrunching up in clear disgust.

The guy lifts off the wall and steps toward her until he's directly in front of her.

"The other two women are here to get a tattoo. How about you? Are you going to finally let me mark this flawless skin of yours?" His finger runs up her arm, and she visibly shivers.

Finally? Who is this guy?

"Don't touch me," she hisses, moving out of his reach.

"Is there a problem?" I ask, not completely comfortable with this guy touching Celeste.

Unlinking my arm out of Olivia's, I step between the two of them, and the guy grins mischievously, not taking his eyes off Celeste.

"Umm...maybe we should go somewhere else?" Olivia suggests.

"I agree. Let's go," I say.

"Wait," Nick says, pulling Olivia in the front of him and wrapping his arms around her waist. "Jase, I would like for you to finally meet my baby mama and fiancée, Olivia." He gives her a small kiss on her cheek.

"Nice to meet you," Jase says. "I've heard a lot about you."

When Olivia looks back at him confused, Nick says, "Jase and I played ball together in high school and college. He was two years ahead of Kill and me."

"We had some great times," Jase says, bumping fists with Nick.

"Did you go to school with them?" I ask Celeste.

It would explain why this guy Jase was acting the way he was toward her. Although, I'm pretty sure she's a few years younger than Nick.

"No." She shakes her head. "I went to public school," she adds softly.

"You met him at the party I took you to, right?" Nick asks. "I forgot about that. Do you two...*know* each other?" His eyes volley between Celeste and Jase.

"Yes, you did," Celeste says dryly, "but I don't know him."

Quinn sneers. "Oh, that's rich! What's wrong? Is my brother not worthy of your memories? Did you block out everything that happened before you ran your stuck-up ass to New York? What are you even doing slumming it in East Village? It's a far ride from the Upper East Side."

"You know what—" Celeste steps directly in Quinn's face "—I don't need to take this shit from you. I didn't know you guys worked here, and if I had, trust me, I never would've come."

"Well, now you know. And FYI, my brothers don't just work here...they own the place. Don't let the door hit you on the way out," Quinn says before turning her back on Celeste.

"All right, everyone, just calm down." A guy who looks similar to Jase steps into view. "Everybody is welcome here. Which one of you is Olivia?"

"Me," Olivia says, raising her hand.

"Nice to meet you. I'm Jaxson Crawford, but everyone calls me Jax. I spoke to you on the phone. I'm this asshole's older brother." He smacks his palm against Jase's chest. "And this spitfire is our little sister." He pulls Quinn into a playful headlock.

"Celeste, it's good to see you again," Jax says, giving Celeste a sincere smile. "Although, with those billboards of you all over New York, I feel like I see you every day." He winks playfully, and Celeste's scowl breaks into a small grin.

"Great, if we're all done with this reunion, how about we figure out who's getting inked?" Jase says, sounding annoyed.

"I want the nice guy," I say, pointing to Jax. "It's my birthday. Livi, you can take the cranky one."

Everyone laughs, and Jase cracks a small smile.

"I might be the crankier one, but I'm still the better artist. Ain't that right, Dimples?" His gaze lands on Celeste, who scowls.

"Bullshit!" Jax laughs. "I'm older, wiser, and a better artist."

"Nah." Jase chuckles lightheartedly. "Just older." Then he looks back at Celeste and his eyes turn smoldering. There's clearly a story there.

"I really need to get going," Celeste announces. Her heels clack against the cement floor as she walks over to me. "Happy Birthday." She gives me a hug.

"Wait! We're supposed to go clubbing after this." Olivia pouts. "Don't go."

"I have an early morning meeting." Celeste moves to Olivia and gives her an air kiss on each of her cheeks since Nick still has his arms wrapped around her waist. "We'll do lunch this week."

Then she makes her way back over to Jax and gives him a quick hug. "It was nice to see you again." She doesn't wait for him to respond before she's out the door.

"I'm going to make sure she gets into a cab safely," Nick says, letting go of Olivia and rushing after Celeste.

When I look over to Jase, his eyes are trained on the door Celeste just exited through.

"All right, so who wants what?" Jax asks.

"I want a quote across my upper back, right below my neck," I say.

"And I want Nick's number tattooed above my ass," Olivia adds seriously.

"What?" I shriek. "No way! Your name isn't Haley, and you don't live in *Tree Hill*!"

Olivia turns around to face me with a huge grin splayed across her lips.

"Oh, thank God, you're joking." I sigh in relief. "Don't do that to me again!"

Olivia laughs. "C'mon, I totally had you there."

"Honestly, as much as you love that show, it wouldn't surprise me if you were serious."

"Kill, you getting anything?" Quinn asks.

"Nah, I think we'll keep it about the ladies tonight, but I do need to schedule a time to have some more of my sleeve done."

Nick walks back through the door. "All right, she's off." He smiles, but it almost looks sad. Olivia must notice because she goes over to him and asks if everything is okay.

"Yeah, I think so. Celeste wouldn't say much. She seemed upset she didn't know Jase worked here, but like I told her, I didn't even know they knew each other like that. Although, based on the way she hugged Jax—" his gaze lands hard on Jax "—it seems she knows the entire family more than she led on."

Quinn snorts. "Oh, we definitely know Celeste."

"Quinn, cool it," Jax chides.

Nick glances over to Jase. "Did something happen between you and Celeste the night of the party?"

You can hear it in his tone, he's not being nosy. He's in big brother-slash-best friend mode.

"Nothing worth mentioning," Jase says coolly.

Nick gives him a long glance then nods, choosing to let it go. He turns his attention back to Olivia. "So, what are you thinking of getting? I remember you once mentioned putting my number above your ass." He waggles his eyebrows.

"Not happening," I tell him. "No friend of mine is getting a tramp stamp. Pick something else."

"That's what I'm talking about!" Quinn raises her hand for a high five. "If only I could say that to every other female who walks in here, asking for a unicorn above her ass."

"Hey, those unicorns helped pay your way through art school," Jax says.

"I still say a unicorn dies every time one is tattooed above a woman's ass." Quinn laughs.

"I'll go first," I offer. "I know exactly what I'm getting."

"Sounds good," Jase says, "You can come back with me."

"You better not take your crankiness out on me." I pin him with a glare.

Jax laughs. "Jase has been cranky his entire life. Well, except for when he was—"

"Enough," Jase says, cutting him off.

His voice is deadly serious, but it only makes Jax grin.

"I want to watch!" Olivia says.

"You might change your mind once you hear that needle." Killian laughs.

"I gave birth to this guy's baby without any meds." Olivia points to Nick. "I'm sure I can handle a tattoo."

Everyone cracks up laughing, and Jase walks me to the third room on the right. "Write down the quote you want." He hands me a pen and paper. "Any particular font you were thinking of?"

"Well, it's from *Alice's Adventures in Wonderland*, so something fun, but not too childish. Surprise me."

"Okay." He grins wide. "I think I know the perfect one."

I hand him back the paper, and he reads the quote out loud. *"I can't go back to yesterday because I was a different person then."*

"Giselle, that's beautiful," Olivia says. "I remember when we read the book in our English class. You doodled that quote in your notebook for like a month."

"Everyone can stay, but you're going to have to take your shirt and bra off for the location you want," Jase says. "Go ahead and get undressed and shout once you're ready for me to come back in."

Everyone exits but Olivia, who looks upset. "What's wrong?" I ask her.

"Your quote is perfect and beautiful, and it made me realize I'm not sure what I want yet."

"We can wait," I tell her.

"No, I want you to get yours, and once I'm ready to get mine, will you come back with me?"

"Of course!" I give her a hug. "Thank you for making my birthday special."

I take my shirt and bra off and hand them to Olivia. Then I lay down on the leather chair face down. "Ready!" I call out.

"Okay, let's do this."

Chapter Four

KILLIAN

We're sitting in the VIP lounge in Provocative, an exclusive nightclub in the Lower West Side. With Celeste gone, it's just the four of us.

Olivia is gushing over Giselle's new tattoo, and Nick, as usual, is gushing over Olivia simply being herself.

I must admit I was shocked by the tattoo Giselle chose. Most women go for the cute and popular. Like Quinn said, the unicorns.

Giselle's tattoo was deep. Although, it shouldn't surprise me. Giselle's actions seem to be throwing me off at every turn. I was stunned earlier tonight when I witnessed her get emotional over her ex-boyfriend showing up.

I honestly didn't think she was capable of feeling anything other than what she feels for Olivia and Reed.

Even when I took her to her mom's house, the entire time she was cold and withdrawn—dealing with the situation, but not appearing to be emotionally affected.

I'm beginning to think there are several different parts to Giselle, and maybe not all of them are so bad.

I think back to Nick's description of her. Maybe she is like a Pitbull. One who is judged unfairly based on her looks but isn't really as vicious as she appears. I know I've definitely judged her.

"It sucks Celeste isn't here, but since we have you both together, there's something Nick and I would like to talk to you guys about," Olivia says. "Actually, two things." She grins excitedly.

"Okay, shoot," I say, taking a sip of my water.

"As you know, Nick and I are planning to get married, and we've finally picked a date! We've decided to get married in June of this year!"

"Oh, Livi! That's only a few months away!" Giselle says.

"Yes!" Olivia agrees. "Also, Reed will be walking better, and football season will be well over so we can go on a honeymoon." She stops talking to give Nick a quick kiss before she continues. "We want a small, intimate wedding, and I would love it if you would be my maid-of-honor."

She hasn't even finished her sentence and Giselle is already leaping across the table and into Olivia's arms. "Yes! Yes! Yes!"

"And I'd like for you to be my best man," Nick adds. "But if you jump into my lap, I'm going to beat your ass."

"Awe, c'mere, good-looking." I shoot him a wink and stand. Nick shakes his head but stands to give me a hug. "Congratulations. I'm happy for you."

"Thanks, man."

"What's the second thing?" Giselle asks once we're seated again.

"We'd love it if the two of you would be Reed's godparents," Olivia says. "We can't imagine anyone else loving and caring for him the way you two do."

"Agreed," Nick says.

"Oh, Livi, you're killing me tonight!" Giselle hugs her friend once more, and when she sits back down, there are tears shining in her eyes. "I would be honored, even if it means sharing my godson with this guy." She nudges me with her elbow.

"I'd be honored," I tell both Olivia and Nick.

"Yay! Thank you!" Olivia squeals. "Oh! I love this song! Let's dance!" She pulls Nick out of his chair, and the two of them hit the dance floor, leaving Giselle and me at the table alone as Justin Bieber sings about not giving up on love.

"You didn't want to invite Roman out tonight?" I ask Giselle, and she glares. "What? I just figured you would invite the guy you're dating out to help celebrate your birthday." I shrug. I wasn't trying to piss her off. I really was just curious.

"Roman isn't exactly the going out to a club and getting a tattoo kind of guy," Giselle replies dryly, then takes a long sip of her Jack and Coke.

Speaking of tattoos..."Does the tattoo you got have a story behind it?"

She eyes me warily, finishes off her drink, and then sighs. "It's from a book I read."

"Which book?" I ask, curious.

"*Alice's Adventures in Wonderland.*"

"The children's book?" I give her a confused look, trying to recall which book that is. I think it's the one with the little girl who falls down a rabbit hole.

"Yes," she sasses. "You would be surprised how deep the story is."

"Really?" I laugh.

I've never read the book, but I've seen the movie once with my niece, and it's hard to imagine how deep the book could possibly be with talking animals.

"Every life and love lesson can be found in that story." She shrugs. "You should read it sometime."

The song changes and Giselle laughs humorlessly, shaking her head.

"Don't like this song?" I ask her.

"Are we playing twenty questions?" she snaps. I hold my palms up and she sighs again. "The song is just so fitting."

I listen to the words for a few seconds. I don't know who sings it, but it's a woman and she's singing about taking a guy home one last time even though another woman is in his heart. My eyes flit to Giselle who's frowning. She reaches over the table and grabs a shot of Johnnie Walker, downing it in one gulp then slamming it on the table.

"Have you ever cheated, Killian?" she asks. When I don't answer right away, she adds, "What? You can ask questions, but you can't answer them?" She reaches for another shot and downs it as fast as the last one.

"No," I say, answering her question, "I've never cheated."

She raises her eyebrows like she doesn't believe me, but after a few seconds, she shrugs and says, "I guess that makes sense. Rumor has it you don't do girlfriends. You can't cheat if you don't commit, right?" She reaches for the last shot, but I grab it first and shoot it back.

She glares daggers my way. "Real nice. I need to get going anyway." She stands and her body sways slightly from all the alcohol she's had to drink, so I stand as well, putting my arm out to help her.

"I don't need your help," she hisses. "I don't need anyone."

"Yeah, maybe not, but you've had quite a bit to drink. Why don't I let Olivia and Nick know we're leaving, and I'll take you home?"

She eyes me skeptically but shocks me when she nods. "Okay, but only because I don't want them to have to leave because of me."

After I let Nick and Olivia know I'm going to get Giselle home, we head outside. Since we all rode in the limo tonight, I told Nick and Olivia they could take it home and I would call for a car service to take us home.

I could call for a separate one for Giselle, but with the amount of alcohol she's consumed, I'd feel better making sure she gets inside safely myself.

The car pulls up and I open the door for Giselle. She slides in, and I go around to the other side to get in. I give the driver Giselle's address.

The ride to her place is silent aside from the music playing on the radio. Giselle stares out the window, and I find myself staring at her reflection in the same window.

A song comes on that catches my attention. It's upbeat... different...and the words hit me hard. I ask the driver to turn it up and he does. The guy is singing about being broken and lonely, but he isn't sad about it. He's reveling in the fact the girl he's with is just as broken and lonely.

My gaze stays trained on Giselle. I can't be sure, but I'm almost positive a tear rolls down her cheek. It's hard to tell.

I glance down at her hand, and without thinking, reach for it. Her head swings my way, her glassy eyes meeting mine before she looks down at my hand covering hers.

Intertwining our fingers, I pull her into my side. She stiffens but doesn't fight me as I wrap my arm around her shoulders and gently guide her head to my shoulder.

"Do you ever feel broken and lonely, Killian?" she asks softly.

"Every damn day," I admit.

She looks up to meet my gaze and nods once.

"Me too," she whispers.

The car arrives at her place, and Giselle thanks me for helping her get home safely.

When I offer to walk her up, she tells me she can handle it, then she leans over and gives me a chaste kiss on my cheek.

As I watch her walk into her building, I can't help but wonder just how many layers of Giselle there are hidden deep down under the surface.

And then I shock the hell out of myself when my next thought is that I'm pretty sure I want to see every one of those hidden layers.

"UNCLE KILLIAN, YOU'RE HERE!" MY ADORABLE niece, Julia, flies down the steps and jumps into my awaiting arms. "I have a new princess movie. Can we watch it, please?" she begs.

"Not right now, kiddo," Dylan says before I can answer her. "Uncle Killian and I have business to discuss." My brother, Dylan, who is also my attorney, is all about business.

Julia pouts, and I pick her up and throw her into the air. "My goodness, I think you've gained ten pounds since the last time I was here."

"Not true." She giggles. "Do it again!"

I throw her into the air one more time before I set her down.

"I think you're taller too." I tilt my head to the side. "How old are you now? Fifteen?"

She giggles some more. "No! I'm four, silly!"

"I could've sworn you were fifteen. Huh."

"Killian, congratulations on the win!" My brother's wife, Christina, gives me a kiss on my cheek.

"Thank you," I tell her. "Two down, two to go."

"You guys got this. Your brother cleared his schedule, so we'll be there cheering you on at the next game."

"Sounds good. How's little man doing?" I rub the top of her pregnant belly.

"He's content in there. The real question is, how am I doing? I'm ready for him to come out." She laughs.

"Only a couple more months, right?"

"Nine weeks, four days," she corrects me with another laugh. "Are you staying for dinner?"

"Of course. Julia and I have a new princess movie to watch, don't we?" I shoot a wink to my niece, who grins.

"Yes!" she squeals.

"Okay, go handle business with your brother. Dinner will be ready in about an hour." Her voice raises a beat louder to let my brother know that's all the time he has to hold me hostage.

"How's Nick doing?" Dylan asks, pouring us both a drink.

"He's good. He and Olivia picked a wedding date and asked me to be the best man. They're getting married in June."

"Good for them. We should all barbecue soon."

"For sure."

He hands me my drink. "All right, let's get down to business."

We spend the next hour going over several contracts, endorsement deals, my bills, and a few new investments I asked him to look into for me.

He commends me on making smart choices with several investments that have made me a substantial profit.

Going into my career, I knew many professional athletes end up broke and filing for bankruptcy. I wanted to make sure I'm never in that situation. If my career were to end tomorrow, I need to know I'll be okay.

"Boys, dinner is ready," Christina yells from somewhere in the house.

"You heard the woman." I stand. "Dinner is ready."

"I think you use my wife for food," Dylan accuses lightheartedly.

"Hell yes, I do," I admit as we head to the dining room. "You know I can't cook, and your wife can."

"Maybe it's time you got a wife of your own," Dylan says with a laugh. He sits down at the table next to his wife, and I sit next to Julia, who is already munching on her chicken nuggets.

"Your date to the party the other night was pretty," Christina says.

"Who?" I ask, placing a piece of lasagna onto my plate and grabbing a roll.

"Well, I guess that answers the question I was about to ask..." Christina rolls her eyes. "If there's a chance she's someone serious." She makes my brother a plate of food and hands it to him before she makes herself one.

"I went to a birthday thing for Olivia's best friend, Giselle, the other night. I wasn't sure if maybe the paparazzi got pictures." I cut up my food then take a bite.

"I was referring to the woman you had on your arm at your endorsement party for that car." She's talking about Tabitha.

"Being as she was rented for the night, I don't think it's anything serious." I shoot Christina a wink, and her eyes go wide.

"You paid for a hooker," she whisper-yells. "Killian!"

"She's not a hooker." I laugh nervously, immediately regretting I said anything. "She's an escort."

"What's an escort?" Julia asks, reminding us of her presence.

"Nobody, sweetie," Dylan says. "Are you all done eating your nuggets?"

"Yes! Can I get the movie ready for me and Uncle Killian?"

"Sure, go ahead," my brother says. Being as they never let Julia leave the table before everyone is done eating, I know I'm about to get shit from him.

Sure enough, as soon as Julia has skipped out of the room, he glares my way. "Bro, you can't seriously think it's okay to hire an escort. Do you know how bad this would look if it gets out?"

"One, Amber handles it for me. It's done through my personal account and it's all handled properly. It's not like I picked her up on the street corner. The women have to sign NDAs and everything. You'd be surprised how many celebrities use escorts for different events."

"How did it come to this, Kill? How did you become the guy who rents women instead of trying to meet one the right way?" My brother gives me a concerned look. "I'm not judging you," he adds. "I'm just trying to understand. If I recall, you dated a few girls in high school, right? And several in college? What happened that scared you from settling down?"

I know he's not going to let this go until I give him something, but at the same time, I've never spoken about what happened in college. Just thinking about it has me feeling all types of shit I don't want to deal with.

"I'm not the same person I was back then." My words make me think of Giselle's quote and it has me wondering if maybe she is the way she is because of something that's happened in her past.

"I'm a professional athlete, Dylan. Every woman I meet, I wonder if she's with me for my money or because I'm in the NFL. I've met women who've straight up told me they just want to fuck me."

I lower my voice to make sure Julia can't hear me. "The truth is I don't know how to meet a nice woman that I'm one hundred percent sure doesn't have a hidden agenda."

I shrug and take a bite of my food. Once I swallow and take a sip of my water, I add, "I guess I just sort of gave up."

"Well, you aren't going to find a nice woman with no agenda through an escort service." Dylan quirks a brow up. "I get it, I do. I work with dozens of guys in the same situation as you.

"I write up their prenups, and then soon after, I help file their divorce papers." He frowns. "But you can't give up, Kill. You're thirty-one years old and you've never even had a serious girlfriend that I know of."

"I agree, Killian," Christina says. "What about letting me set you up with a friend of mine?" Christina, at one time, was an international supermodel who retired when she got pregnant, wanting to be home with her family. "I think the key is to find someone who is in a similar situation as yours, with her own money, but is also a good person."

I laugh. "Good luck with that."

"Is that a yes?" Christina beams with hope.

"Sure, why not?" I take another bite of my food.

"Yes! You boys do the dishes. I need to start scrolling through my friends list."

Chapter Five

GISELLE

"I'll take the BLT Club sandwich with sweet potato fries and a side of fruit. Thank you." Olivia smiles at the server, who writes everything down before he looks at me.

"And for you, ma'am?"

"Just a house salad, please. Ranch on the side."

The waiter nods and thanks us, then leaves to another table.

"That's it?" Olivia's brows furrow. "You're not on a diet, are you? You look amazing." She hands Reed, who is sitting in his highchair, a toy to play with.

"I'm not that hungry."

The truth is I know I'll be going on a date tonight, which means I won't have to pay for whatever we eat while we're out, so I'd rather wait until then to eat.

Every dollar counts right now, and since I'm not about to let my best friend pay for my meal, I need to be careful.

"How's the charity event coming?" I ask, changing the subject.

Olivia and Nick have decided to take Nick's current charity organization, Touchdown for Reading, and expand it to Touchdown for Reading and the Arts, since Olivia's passion is art. She even works part-time at a children's museum as their Art Education Coordinator.

"So good!" she gushes. "Almost everyone who was invited has RSVP'd, and those who said they can't make it, have made generous donations that will go a long way with all of our plans. You're coming, right?"

"Yeah." I nod as I try to think of a way to get out of it. "Just send me an invite to my email and I'll add it to my calendar."

"Why did you frown?" Olivia asks, handing Reed his sippy cup and some Goldfish.

Only my best friend can be taking care of her one-year-old son and notice my hidden emotions. She's like Superwoman.

"I didn't," I deny.

"Yes, you did," she pushes.

"Look Livi," I say carefully. "You know I support everything you do, but the entire purpose of this charity event is to get donations, right?"

"Right, and to announce the expansion."

"Tell me someone who couldn't make it."

"Umm, Nathan Fillion. He's a huge New York Brewers fan."

"The guy from *Castle*?" I'm almost positive my jaw hits the table. This is even worse than I thought.

"Yeah, he actually has a non-profit organization which provides books to children who can't afford them."

"And how much did he donate because he can't make it?"

"Fifty thousand," she says nonchalantly, like fifty thousand dollars is no big deal.

She grabs a bib from Reed's diaper bag and places it around his neck.

"Livi, how much does everyone have to pay per plate?"

"Ten thousand." She pops open the top of Reed's baby food then freezes, looking up at me. "Wait a second. Is that why you're upset? You think I'm going to expect you to pay that? You're my best friend, Giselle!" She frowns in confusion. "I know you don't have that kind of money."

"Well, someone is paying it."

Olivia's mouth opens then closes as she carefully considers how she's going to word whatever she's about to say, but I don't give her a chance to speak first.

"Either you're paying for my spot, or you're giving me a plate for free, which is it?"

"I paid for your plate." I open my mouth to argue, but she holds up her hand. "It's for a good cause, and really, if I'm honest, I did it with selfish intentions. I need my best friend there. Nick will be busy with everyone, and I was hoping you would be there to keep me company."

Her eyes are pleading, and I let out a defeated sigh. It's not like I'm going to say no to anything she asks of me, even if it's a reminder of how one-sided our friendship is.

"Okay, I'll be there."

I force a smile on my face, mentally reminding myself to seriously look into putting my mom's house up for sale. It was one thing to live with Olivia in college. I was able to somewhat pay my way with the loans I took out. And when we moved here, she thought she would be raising Reed alone, so I justified living with her so I could help out.

But now that Nick is in the picture and they're going to get married and start a life together soon, I need to get myself together. It's not fair to our friendship to continue to take advantage of my best friend's generosity.

"Thank you." Olivia grins as she feeds Reed a bite of sweet peas.

The waiter comes over and sets our food down in front of us. We eat our lunch, and when we're done, we go our separate ways. Me, back to Fresh Designs for a new client consultation, and Olivia, to drop Reed off with her stepmom, Corrine, so she can watch Reed for a few hours while Olivia goes to the Children's Museum.

"Mom? Dedra?" I call out when I walk into my mom's house and don't see anyone in the living room.

"In here, Giselle," Dedra, my mom's nurse, calls out from down the hall.

I throw my purse onto the counter and check the time on my cell phone before stuffing it into my back pocket.

It's already a quarter after four and I have a date I need to be ready for by seven. I should've been here hours ago, but the consultation with Lydia and the new client ran way over the scheduled time. He's a wealthy commercial developer, which means he's very opinionated.

Normally that personality trait would be great because opinionated people tend to know exactly what they want. However, this man isn't one of those people.

He's hired Fresh Designs to decorate his new eight thousand square foot sky rise that he's had completely renovated. And while he had tons of opinions throughout our meeting, he couldn't make up his mind on a single thing.

Then, of course, the subway I take to my mom's house had mechanical issues and everyone was forced to take a detour route, which meant an additional forty-five minutes on the subway.

"Hey, sorry I'm late," I tell her as I walk into my mom's room. She's lying in bed in a fetal position with tears flowing down her face. "How's she doing?" I ask Dedra, who frowns at my question.

"Why don't we talk in the other room?" she suggests.

I come around to the side of the bed and give my mom a kiss on her forehead.

"Giselle, you're here," she cries. "I've missed you so much." My mom snakes her arms around my neck and pulls me into a hug. "Please don't leave me," she begs, creating a fissure in my heart.

"I'm just going right outside to talk to Dedra. I'll be right back. I promise." I press my lips to her forehead once more before removing her arms from around me and stepping into the hallway.

"These meds seem to keep her anger subsided, but now she's sunken into a deep depression." Dedra sighs. "I'm afraid to leave her here alone, Giselle."

"Okay."

I try to do the math in my head of what it will cost to hire another nurse for the hours Dedra won't be here.

I've been getting more hours but paying Adrianna's tuition severely depleted my funds. And I still need to pay her sorority dues and meal ticket, which will set me back a good amount.

"I have a friend of mine who's a retired nurse like me," Dedra says. "She can use the extra money to supplement her social security. I can speak to her about spending a few days a week here."

"That would be great. Thank you." I give Dedra a hug. "I've actually been thinking about putting the house up for sale. If I can make enough on it, I can use the money to get my own place in the city, so she can live with me."

Of course, that will mean having to find my father so he can sign off on the sale.

"I know this is a lot, dear. You're already working too many hours. Just take it one day at a time. You are a wonderful daughter." Dedra smiles warmly. "And a wonderful sister."

"Sometimes it doesn't feel that way." Tears leak from my eyes. "Sometimes it feels like I'm really sucking at life," I admit aloud, suddenly feeling like everything that's piled on my shoulders is just too much to handle and it's all about to come crashing down around me.

"This is a lot to deal with. You are only human."

"Thank you. I'm going to spend some time with my mom before I need to head back."

I head back inside my mom's room and spend the next hour with her. She's momentarily stopped crying while we watch some of her favorite shows she's recorded.

When 5:30 hits, I have to go. I'm already going to be cutting it way too close as it is. I give my mom and Dedra a hug with a promise to visit soon.

When my mom cries, begging me to stay, I consider it, but then remember I have a date tonight I can't miss.

On my way out, I grab the bills on the counter I need to pay since my dad stopped paying them the day he walked out on my mom and lock the door behind me.

The subway is thankfully on schedule, and I make it home with twenty minutes to get ready. Throwing my hair up so I don't get it wet, I shower quickly, extremely thankful I recently got everything waxed.

I get dressed into a cute ivory cold-shoulder lace dress and throw on a pair of brown leather pumps. After switching out my everyday purse for a matching clutch, I head out of my room.

"Hey!" Olivia says, "I didn't realize you were home!" Her eyes skate over my outfit. "Going out?"

"Umm...yeah, I have a date." I smile hesitantly, praying she doesn't give me the third degree about where I'm going and who I'm going with. I'm already running late as it is.

"Okay, well, have a good night," she says, shocking the crap out of me.

"You, too."

After walking three blocks to the corner, I find the limo waiting for me. The driver opens the door for me, and sitting inside is my date, Andrew Parker.

It's our first date, but I've done my research. One of Manhattan's top financial moguls and on Forbes's list of top thirty under thirty wealthiest men.

He's staring at his phone, but once I scoot in next to him, he lifts his eyes and grins, politely putting his phone away.

"You look beautiful," he says smoothly, leaning over and giving my cheek a chaste kiss. "Thank you for joining me this evening."

"You're very welcome," I say while checking him out.

With a shaved head, dark brown eyes, and a strong jawline, he almost looks like a bad boy instead of a billionaire. That is until you get to his expensive suit, which probably cost more than my parents' house, and the TAG Heuer watch he's sporting, which is more than likely the price of a vehicle I can't afford.

I look closely and notice a bit of a tattoo peeking out from under his dress shirt. *More like reformed bad boy.*

We arrive at the movie premiere at AMC Lincoln Square. Andrew explains that one of the umbrella companies he owns has invested some money into the film, which is why we're here.

We walk the red carpet and make our way into the theatre. Andrew is stopped a few times along the way, but it's when he's stopped by one person in particular my heart just about jumps out of my chest.

This seriously can't be happening.

"Andrew! How are you doing?" Killian says, shaking my date's hand.

"I'm doing well. It's good to see you. Making time to see a movie in the middle of the playoffs?" Andrew jokes.

"I figured it was the perfect way to impress my date." Killian looks over at the beautiful woman on his arm. "This is Rochelle."

"Nice to meet you." Andrew nods and places his fingers against the swell of my back. "This is Giselle, my date. We were just heading inside. Why don't you two join us?"

"Oh, I'm sure—" I begin to protest, but Killian speaks over me.

"We would love to."

The next three hours are spent with Killian shooting daggers my way while I ignore them and pretend he doesn't exist.

I couldn't even tell you what the hell the movie was about, and I'm thankful when Andrew tells me he has an early meeting tomorrow, so he unfortunately has to call it a night directly after the premiere party.

Chapter Six

KILLIAN

"THANK YOU, THANK YOU, THANK YOU!" OLIVIA hugs me for the third time. "I would normally ask Giselle to babysit, but she's been kind of busy lately, and Corrine and my dad are having a date night."

"So, pretty much I'm your only option," I say dryly, making Nick chuckle.

"What? No!" Olivia shakes her head.

"Liv, he's joking," Nick says. "I'm going to set out some snacks and a drink for when Reed wakes up, and then we'll go." He gives her a kiss on her forehead before he heads into the kitchen.

"We'll only be gone a couple hours. We have to meet with the party planner to finalize all the details for the charity event. She called and said she needed to reschedule last minute."

"No problem. I would've just been hanging out at home anyway."

"I saw you're bringing a date." Olivia grins. "Is it the woman you were spotted with at the movie premiere?"

"No, she was nice, but we didn't really have much in common," I say, cursing my sister-in-law for setting me up with a woman who's recently divorced and still in the 'I hate all men because my ex-husband cheated on me' stage of mourning.

"Oh, that's too bad. Giselle seems to have the same problem. The woman dates more than anyone I know, which is the complete opposite of how she used to be, yet she seems to find flaws in every guy she's with." Olivia shrugs.

"How did she used to be?" I ask in an even voice, hoping I sound nonchalant.

"For the entire six years we lived together in Paris, she maybe went on a handful of dates. The only thing I can think of is that she was pining for Christian the entire time.

But then we moved back here, they got together, and he turned out to be a cheating asshole." She scrunches up her nose in disgust. "Maybe she's just done pining. I don't know." She shakes her head. "Giselle doesn't really talk to me anymore." The corners of her lips turn down into a frown. She's obviously worried about Giselle.

"All right," Nick says as he walks out of the kitchen. "Snacks are on the counter. Juice is in the fridge. Here's his monitor so you can hear him." He hands me a walkie-talkie looking thing. "I appreciate you coming over to Liv's place last minute. Waking Reed up early from a nap is the equivalent of poking a bear in hibernation."

What's up with this guy and comparing everyone to animals?

"You've poked a bear?" I ask with a laugh.

"No, but I can imagine what it's like. Scary as fuck and has you running the other way in fear for your life."

"Bro, he's only a year old." I laugh harder.

"It doesn't matter." Nick shakes his head then glances over to Olivia. "Brown-Eyes, tell him."

Olivia nods in agreement. "Yep, scary."

When I give them a doubtful look, unable to imagine Reed as anything other than adorable, Olivia adds, "Trust me, you don't want to find out."

"No worries," I tell them. "I'm just going to watch some TV while he sleeps. Take your time. We'll be here. It's all good."

Olivia and Nick head out, and I throw myself onto the couch, flipping through the channels. Practice today was brutal and I'm exhausted, but it was a damn good practice.

I'm confident that if we play the way we practiced today, we'll have a good shot at beating New England this weekend. And if we do, we're in the Super Bowl.

I stretch my legs and flinch at how sore I am. I don't know how Nick does it. He comes home from a grueling practice and jumps right into family-mode.

I feel my eyes begin to droop, so I stand and head into the kitchen to make myself a cup of coffee. The last thing I need is to fall asleep while babysitting. Olivia would come home and murder me in my sleep. Reed waking up early would be the least of my concerns.

The coffee is brewing, when I hear the door open, and a few seconds later, Giselle is standing in front of me.

"What are you doing here?" She has her hands on her hips.

"Babysitting."

Her brows furrow in confusion. "Where's Olivia?"

"She had a last-minute meeting with the event planner for the charity event."

She scoffs. "So, she asked you instead of me?"

"Apparently you're too busy working your way down the most recent Forbes list of the wealthiest bachelors, so Olivia called me."

Giselle purses her lips together and shoots me a glare. "You know what, fuck you," she hisses. "You don't know shit about me."

"I've seen enough to know you're a gold-digger." I shrug.

"Wow! You just love to throw that label around. First Celeste, now me."

"If the shoe fits...What are you doing exactly? Trying to figure out who your best option is, so you're prepared once your best friend finally puts herself before you and moves in with her fiancé?"

Grabbing my cup of coffee, I pour some milk into it and stir, then head back into the living room to sit down.

Giselle, of course, follows behind, her heels click-clacking against the hardwood floor.

"What the hell is that supposed to mean?" she asks. "Nick and Olivia are taking things slow."

"Oh, c'mon, you can't be that dense." I take a sip of my coffee. "Nick has been begging her for damn near a year to move in with him. You think either of them want to bounce their son back and forth between homes? You think Olivia, the queen of fairytales, wants to wait months to marry her fucking prince?"

Giselle frowns. "She never said anything."

"Of course, she hasn't. She doesn't want to leave her best friend homeless."

"I didn't know," she murmurs.

"Well now you do."

Her phone's alarm goes off, and she pulls it from her purse. "Shit, I need to go."

"Another date?" I shake my head. "You should hang out with Celeste more. You two have a lot in common." I laugh. "Although—" I snap my fingers "—she's at least finally standing on her own two feet instead of leeching off her best friend."

Giselle flinches. "I gotta go," she whispers. "As always, it was great seeing you." She turns her back on me and heads down the hallway.

I take another sip of my coffee, *almost* feeling bad for what I said. But the truth is, everything I said is fact. It probably wasn't my place to point it all out, but how could she not have known that's why Olivia is still refusing to buy a home with Nick.

About thirty minutes later, Giselle comes out, dressed in a tight black dress and black fuck-me heels. Her hair, which was down in waves, is now pin straight, and her makeup is a bit darker. And in her arms is Reed, who is smiling and babbling like crazy at her.

"He was sitting up in his crib, so I grabbed him." She hands him over to me. "I changed his diaper."

"I didn't hear anything," I say, holding up the monitor.

"That's because you never turned it on." Giselle grabs the monitor and clicks it on, then hands it back to me. "Goodbye, my little love muffin. Be very bad for Uncle Killian." She glares at me then gives him a kiss on his cheek.

"Have fun on your date." I smirk. Giselle rolls her eyes, grabs her purse, and heads for the door. "Oh, wait, I forgot to ask you…" She stops in her place but doesn't turn around. "What number is this guy on Forbes's list?"

She swings the door open, flicks me off, then slams it closed.

Guess she didn't like my question.

Chapter Seven

GISELLE

"IF THEY CAN GET THIS TOUCHDOWN, THEY WILL be in the Super Bowl," Olivia tells me for the hundredth time in the last two hours.

I don't call her out on it, though. She's just nervous. She paces across the room in the friends and family suite we're currently in.

Reed toddles over to her and pulls on her jersey. She lifts him up so he can see the field and talks to him as if he knows what's going on.

Everybody else is more or less quiet, watching down below as the New York Brewers huddle.

The team breaks and gets into formation. The score is tied with less than a minute left on the clock.

When I walk up next to her, Reed leans over and I take him in my arms. Olivia's eyes never leave the field as she watches Nick call the play.

The players scramble, and Nick looks for an opening.

Killian runs to the left and is open, but as Nick cocks his arm back to throw the ball, he's tackled.

The ball falls to the ground and New England gets it.

There are collective sighs and several people in the suite curse. New England has the ball now, and if they score, New York won't be going to the Super Bowl. The players are walking off the field, and that's when I notice Nick is still down.

"Oh no," Olivia gasps.

We watch as Killian kneels next to Nick. We can't hear what's being said, and a second later, the medic runs out with the coaches.

"Oh god, please no." Olivia's eyes meet mine. "He's grabbing his arm." Tears pool in her eyes.

Reed reaches for his mom, but I hold him close. She's shaking, on the verge of freaking out.

"I need to get down there," she tells me. Then she turns toward her stepmom, Corrine. "He's hurt."

"Let's just give him a minute," Dylan tells her.

Everyone watches in silence, until the gurney is brought out, and that's when we know it's game over.

"Go," I tell Olivia. "I have Reed."

"Thank you." She gives her son a kiss. "Mommy will be right back. I love you." Then she takes off out of the suite, along with Dylan, his wife, and Corrine.

A few minutes later it's announced that Nick Shaw will not be back in the game. New England has the ball. They score and New York is out of the playoffs.

NICK HAS BEEN IN WITH THE DOCTORS FOR THE last hour. Corrine took Reed back to her place since it's well after his bedtime and he was getting cranky. Olivia is sitting quietly in her seat, her eyes glued to the door, waiting for a doctor to come out so she can go back and see her fiancé.

She's trying so hard to remain calm, but I know my best friend, and she's freaking the hell out on the inside. When she first met Nick, he was recovering from a shoulder injury and wasn't sure if he would ever play again—let alone come back to win a Super Bowl.

"Any news?" Killian asks, walking over and sitting next to Olivia. His hair is still damp from the shower and he's wearing a New York Brewers hoodie and sweatpants. He must've come straight from the stadium. A few other players sit down as well but keep their distance. Everyone wants to know how Nick is doing.

"No, the doctors are in with him," Olivia says, her voice strained from holding in her emotions. "They called my dad and Declan back about twenty minutes ago." Declan Thomas is the owner of the Brewers. When the owner is involved, it can't be good.

Killian wraps his arm around Olivia and her head lulls to the side, landing on his shoulder. "It's going to be okay," he murmurs.

His eyes come up and meet mine, and I shift in my seat, remembering what it felt like to be comforted by a man.

When Christian and I were together, he would hold me for hours while I cried over my mom. He would tell me everything would be okay. He was wrong, though. Nothing is okay.

Killian gives me a small, sad smile, and I find myself smiling back.

"Olivia Harper," someone calls out, and we all stand. It's a woman dressed in scrubs. Maybe a nurse. "Nick is asking for you. You can follow me."

Olivia nods silently then turns to Killian. "As soon as I can, I'll text you or come and get you."

She follows the nurse back, and for the next hour, everyone waits in silence. It's late and the waiting room is quiet. The door finally opens again, and Olivia and her dad walk out. Her eyes are puffy from crying, but she forces a watery smile.

Killian and I both stand at the same time and meet her halfway across the waiting room. "You can go see him," she tells Killian, who doesn't waste a second before heading back.

"How is he?" I ask.

"He's going to make an announcement. He's retiring. It's his same arm and he would need surgery again. He doesn't want to go down that road for a second time. He wants to go back to school to study Literature. It's a dream he's had since he was little." Tears fall down her cheeks. "He wants to write a novel." She sniffles.

"Why are you crying?" I ask as I pull her into my arms for a hug.

"I don't know," she sobs. "I'm just being emotional."

She cries harder through her laughter, and I join in until we're both laughing so hard, tears are streaming down both of our cheeks—neither of us having the slightest clue as to why we're laughing or crying.

"I'm going to stay here with him," she finally says once she's composed herself.

"Okay, love you." I give her another hug. "If you need anything, please let me know."

I exit the hospital and grab a cab home. After showering the day off, I climb into bed and snuggle into my blankets, my thoughts going to Killian and the way he held Olivia.

It was nothing more than a friend comforting a friend. But it allowed me to see a different side of him. He might be an asshole to me and Celeste, but it's obvious there's a softer, sweeter side to him he only allows certain people to witness.

Chapter Eight

GISELLE

"I'm sorry, Giselle. I've tried to find another nurse for tonight but haven't had any luck," Dedra says through the phone. "It's Paula's night off and she's not answering her phone."

Paula is the night nurse I've had to hire so my mom is taken care of around the clock. It meant adding more to my endlessly growing pile of bills, but it was necessary.

Hopefully the house will sell quickly, and then I can use that money to pay off some debt and get my own place for my mom and me.

I put the house up for sale a few weeks ago—after Killian pointed out what I already knew—that it's time I stop depending on Olivia and handle my shit—and we've already had quite a few people interested. No offers yet, but it only takes one.

At first, when I told my mom the house was being put up for sale, she called me a selfish bitch and kicked me out, but a few days later, I was shocked when she called and told me she's excited to be moving out.

She's actually been in a great mood lately. Gardening in her backyard and talking about not needing my father and being ready to move forward. I think the meds she's on are finally working.

Of course, I've said that before and then they stopped. The problem now is that when I tried to schedule for her to see the psychiatrist to get a refill, I found out my father's insurance had been canceled. And when I called his job to speak to him about it, I was told he no longer works there.

So now, getting my mom new health insurance has been added to my list of things I need to purchase once I have the money.

I spoke to one insurance agent, but with my mom's medical history, I was quoted ten thousand for the year. It's going to have to happen soon, though, because she can't get off her meds, especially since right now they seem to be working.

"It's not your fault," I tell Dedra. "Of course, you need to be there for the birth of your grandchild."

My phone beeps with an incoming call. It's my sister. I unlock the door and throw my purse down on the counter. "I just got home. I'm packing a bag, and I will be over there soon. Go ahead and go. Congratulations, Grandma!"

"Thank you, sweetie."

We say goodbye, and I throw my phone onto the counter, frustrated that I need to be in so many places at once and I can't do it all.

Just as the phone hits the granite, it starts to ring again, the sound sending me over the edge I didn't know I was standing so close to.

"Fuck! Stop ringing!" I yell out loud, begging my phone to silence. When it doesn't stop, my hand swipes at the offending device and it flies through the air, hitting the wood floor.

It goes quiet for a second but then starts up again.

I walk around and pick it up, seriously contemplating shoving it into the garbage disposal, when Olivia makes her presence known.

"What did that phone ever do to you?" she jokes, but I can hear it in her voice, she's concerned.

"I can't make it to the charity event tonight. I'm sorry." The phone starts to ring again. This time it's Bianca. I send it to voicemail and silence my ringer.

"Is this about the cost of the plate? Because—"

"No!" I snap. "I need to go see my mom. She needs to have someone there with her at all times and Dedra's daughter is having a baby. And the other nurse isn't answering her phone.

"They can't find another nurse last minute, and even if they could, it would cost a damn fortune! She just lives so far! I can't be everywhere at once!

"Once I sell her house and move her into an apartment with me it will make things a lot easier."

My mouth finally stops moving as I pause to take a deep breath. My mind plays back everything I just said, and I quickly realize—too late, of course—I just word vomited all over Olivia.

She stares at me for a second, clearly shocked I just told her more about my life in those fifteen seconds than I have in the last year.

"You put your parents' house up for sale? You never mentioned that." Olivia shifts Reed on her hip, but he squirms, wanting down, so she sets him on the floor. He crawls over to his toys and starts to play.

"It's no big deal." I wave her off.

"Umm, yeah, it is. You grew up in that home."

"It is what it is." I nod toward my room. "I need to go pack a bag to take to my mom's. I'm really sorry I can't make it tonight." I start to head to my room when Olivia calls my name.

"You know I'm here for you, right?"

"Of course," I say, turning around and plastering a fake smile on my face.

"Just because I'm with Nick doesn't mean you're not still my best friend."

My thoughts go back to what Killian said about her putting me before Nick, and the words are out before I can take them back.

"Actually, Livi, that's exactly what it means," I say honestly. "And that's how it should be. Things have changed.

You had a baby, and you're engaged to be married. I'm no longer your problem to deal with."

"Why would you say that? You've never been a problem. You're my best friend."

"Why haven't you moved in with Nick yet?"

"I told you we're taking things slow."

"No, you're not. You're only living here because I told you I wouldn't live here without you if you moved, and you know I can't afford to live in the city on what my internship pays me." My voice elevates with frustration and Olivia flinches.

"I don't mind keeping the place for you."

"I mind!" I yell a beat too loudly, then lower my voice so I don't upset Reed. "I mind you paying for a place for me to live when you won't even be here. It's not your job to take care of me."

"I love you." She sniffles. "I don't know what I've done wrong, but I can't fix it if you don't tell me." Tears fall down her cheeks, and I hate myself for being the cause of her crying.

"You didn't do anything wrong." I step toward her as the front door opens and in walks Nick.

He takes one look at Olivia and glares my way. "What the hell is going on?"

"Nothing," Olivia says, placing her hand on Nick's chest to calm him down.

"It doesn't look like nothing. It looks like you're crying," Nick says to Olivia, then he looks at me. "What's going on?"

"I was just telling Olivia that I've put my mom's house up for sale, so if all goes well, I'll be moved out soon."

The last thing I want is for my best friend's future husband to think I'm leeching off her. For Killian to make those comments, words must've been spoken between him and Nick.

"Unnecessarily," Olivia says through her sobs.

Nick wraps his one good arm around her waist in a comforting and protective manner, and my heart squeezes as I wish, not for the first time, I had someone to hold me like that.

"We both know if I wasn't living here, you guys would already be married and living together."

I look at Nick to deny it, and he frowns but doesn't say a word.

"I asked you to move back here and Nick understands that." Olivia steps out of Nick's hold. "I know something is up with you, but you won't let me in. I haven't once asked you to move out or even indicated I want you to. So can you please tell me why you're pushing me away?"

"I'm not pushing you away. I'm just so sick of our friendship being one-sided."

"One-sided? You don't think I've been a good friend?"

Of course, she would jump to that conclusion!

"No! One-sided meaning me! What have I done in this friendship? You've paid my way for the last seven years. You take me out for my birthdays and buy me expensive gifts for the holidays. You even have to pay for my ticket to your charity event because I can't afford it.

"Meanwhile, what have I ever done for you?" I throw my hands in the air in defeat and blink back my tears, willing them not to come. "Nothing! I've done nothing! And to top it off, I'm the reason why you haven't gotten your happily-ever-after!"

"Are you serious?" Olivia questions. "You were the one who pushed me not to run when I got scared. You're the reason I got my happily-ever-after. And as far as our friendship goes, when I was lonely and lost in Paris, *you* befriended me.

"*You* let me cry on your shoulder for months over my mother's death," she says. "And then, when I was dumped by my cheating ex, it was *you* who ran away with me to New York." She swipes at her falling tears. "When I found out I was pregnant and thought nothing would ever be okay again, you held me in your arms on the floor of the bathroom and promised me it would be."

As Olivia recalls everything she's been through, the tears I was holding back finally fall.

"And even though you hate New York, when I said I wanted to move home, you packed up your stuff without saying a word." Olivia steps forward until she's directly in front of me. "No amount of money could ever pay for the friendship you've given me. Having you in my life is worth a thousand times more than anywhere I pay for us to live, or whatever gift I buy, or the ticket I purchase for you for a stupid dinner. It's just money."

A humorless laugh escapes me. "It's *just* money to someone like you. It's *everything* to someone like me who doesn't have any."

"Is that what this is about?" Olivia asks. "Do you need money? Did something happen? I can help you. Just let me in."

My eyes widen at her words, shocked that after everything I just said, her answer is to offer me money. Having no clue how to even respond to what she said, I turn to walk away.

"I'm sorry!" Olivia grabs my hand. "I didn't mean it like that. I just—I don't know how to fix this! Tell me how to fix this, please. I just want my best friend back."

"You can't, and even if you could, I wouldn't let you." I let out an exhausted sigh. "Look, I'm sorry I've been so distant lately. I'm working a lot and taking care of my mom and sister. It's not you. I'm not moving out because I'm mad at you. Like I said before, it's something I need to do for my mom. I appreciate everything you've done for me, but it's time I stand on my own two feet."

"Wait a second," Nick cuts in. "Did Killian say something to you?" I shake my head, and Nick gives me a hard stare, silently telling me not to lie. "Damn it, he did, didn't he?"

"It doesn't matter if he did or didn't," I tell him, because it doesn't. Everything Killian said was the truth. "Look, you guys have an event to get ready for, and I need to get to my mom's." I give Olivia a hug. "I love you, Livi."

She hugs me back. "This conversation isn't over," she murmurs into my ear.

I nod once then retreat to my bedroom to get packed. My phone vibrates for the millionth time. When I glance at the screen, it shows it's Bianca calling again.

"Hello." I nestle the phone between my ear and shoulder while I grab a change of clothes and stuff them into my overnight bag.

"I've called you a dozen times."

"I'm sorry. My mom's nurse—"

"Giselle," Bianca snaps, "I'm too busy to listen to your latest sob story. That's what you have friends for. I was calling because I'm going to need you to come in tonight."

I stop in my place. "I can't tonight." I squeeze my eyes shut as I wait for Bianca to yell at me.

"Then you're fired," she says in a calm voice which tells me she's serious.

"Bianca..."

"You can go afterward. I only need you for a few hours."

"Okay." I let out a frustrated sigh. "What time?"

"A driver will be there to pick you up at your usual spot in thirty minutes. It's black tie. I've sent you all the info you will need. Also, if it helps, because of it being last minute, you will be paid double." She hangs up without a goodbye.

I finish packing and get dressed. The place is quiet, which means Olivia and Nick must've already left for the charity function. They're bringing Reed with them, and once he's tired, Olivia's stepsister, Shelby, is going to take him home. I hate that I can't be there for her tonight, especially since she spent all that money on my plate just so I could go.

After I step out of the elevator and head down the street, I call my mom to check on her, but she doesn't pick up. I leave her a voicemail to let her know I'll be by in a few hours to see her. When I see the limo parked and waiting for me, I tell her I love her and will see her soon.

I approach the vehicle and notice the driver is someone I've never seen before. And then it hits me that in my rush, I didn't check the info, so I have no clue who I'm going on a date with.

"Good evening, ma'am."

The driver bows slightly and smiles, and I smile back before lifting my cocktail dress up slightly and sliding into the backseat. The door closes behind me, and I look to my right to see my date for the evening.

Dark brown hair—thick and lustrous with blazing hazel eyes. His skin is flawless, and his face is strong and defined with prominent cheek-bones.

My gaze goes to his soft, sharp lips, which are turned down in a scowl. He's wearing an expensive suit that molds his body like it was made just for him, and it probably was.

His tie is emerald green and gold. It brings out the tiny flecks of green in his eyes. It's also the colors of the New York Brewers, which makes perfect sense, since the man wearing the tie is the receiver for that very same team.

My eyes glide back up and meet his, and his scowl deepens. "What the hell are you doing in my limo?"

"Apparently, I'm your date."

Chapter Nine

KILLIAN

WHAT IS SHE DOING HERE?

In a shimmery silver dress and matching heels, why is Giselle Winters sitting next to me inside my limo?

When Bianca, the owner of A Touch of Class, called my assistant an hour ago and said there was an issue with the escort who was supposed to be my date, she assured her that she would have someone else for me.

My assistant notified me that we would need to pick her up in Brooklyn Heights instead of in SoHo, so I told her to forward the info to my driver.

I was going through my emails on my phone when the limo driver parked, so I had no clue we were stopped only about four blocks from where Giselle and Olivia live.

And I never imagined, when the door opened, who would be stepping into my limo.

"What the hell are you doing in my limo?" I ask way too harshly. But I can't help it. The woman has been on my mind way too often lately, and being forced to spend an entire evening with her won't help.

"Apparently, I'm your date," she slings back with a glare. "Who would've thought Killian Blake would resort to paying for a woman?"

"Who would've thought Giselle Winters would resort to whoring herself out?" Giselle's face falls, and I regret my words. "I'm sorry," I say. "That was uncalled for."

"It's the truth." She shrugs, opening the door. "I'm a whore, just like Tabitha...you know, the woman you paid to accompany you to your event not long ago. But I bet you didn't call her a whore."

Oh, shit! Now it makes sense—how Tabitha knew Giselle. They both work for the same escort service.

"I'll call Bianca and see if she can find you someone else...Someone who is less of a *whore*. I didn't know you were my client." She steps outside and closes the door behind her.

Flinging my door open, I go around to her side. She's dialing a number, but I snatch the phone out of her hand before she can make the call.

"Look, I'm sorry for what I said. The woman I was going to take didn't work out. Then the date I hired had to cancel. I'm pretty sure you're my only option."

"Great." She closes her eyes for a long beat before she opens them back up. Her blue eyes don't look cold like they usually do. Today, they look deep like the bottom of the ocean, and if I'm not mistaken, they look sad, burnt out as if the light in them faded.

"If you want to call your boss, maybe she can find someone else," I say as I hand her back her phone.

The last thing I want is to be stuck on a date with Giselle, who would rather be anywhere but with me.

"She told me if I didn't go, I would be fired." She frowns. "I can't afford to be fired."

"All right, then why don't we just go and make the best of it?"

Giselle looks up at me and nods, resigned. "Okay."

We get back in the limo, and I let the driver know we're ready to go. The drive to the event is awkwardly silent, neither of us daring to break the tension in the air.

When we arrive, Giselle's head whips around to me. "Oh my god! This is the Prince George Ballroom." She jabs her finger toward the building.

"Yeah," I confirm, confused.

"This is *the* Prince George Ballroom," she repeats, and this time I chuckle.

"I'm aware."

"Oh my god—"

"You're not about to tell me for a third time where we are, are you?"

"This is where the charity event is. Olivia and Nick's event." Oh, now I see where she's going with this.

"Olivia doesn't know you're an escort, does she?"

"Of course, she doesn't know!" Giselle shouts. "It's not exactly something I'm proud of."

"What I don't understand is if you're escorting on top of working at that design place, why are you always so broke?"

I don't know how much she gets paid, but I know what I pay the company she works for, and it's a small fortune.

Giselle glares daggers my way. "You don't know shit, Killian. Don't you dare make assumptions or pretend to know anything about me or my life."

I raise my hands in surrender, not wanting to piss her off right before we go out in public. "I'm not. It was just a question."

"Whatever, let's just do this." Giselle grabs the handle, but the driver opens the door before she can, and she almost falls out of the vehicle. I circle her waist to catch her, and she shakes me off with a quick "Thanks."

The moment we step out of the limo, the press goes crazy.

At first, I'm worried about how Giselle is going to act in front of everyone. But as we walk the carpet slowly, allowing the press to take pictures, the entire time Giselle has on the perfect game face. She links her arm around mine and smiles for the cameras. When different magazines ask me questions, she stands slightly back while I answer them.

"Can I ask you about your date tonight?" one of the reporters asks. "I don't believe we've seen her with you before."

I feel Giselle's body stiffen next to me, while she waits for me to answer.

"She's actually the best friend of Olivia Harper, the woman who made this entire evening possible." I smile, and we move forward.

"Thank you," Giselle murmurs once we make our way inside.

"Outing you would only make me look bad," I say. "If anyone else asks, I'll give them the same answer I did out there."

We head through the grand ballroom and over to the table with numbers. The woman asks for my name and then hands me two place cards so we can find our seats.

The entire place is decorated in gold, silver, and cream. The outer walls have tables lined with silent auctions for the guests to check out. All of the winnings will go toward Touchdown for Reading and the Arts.

We find our table and set our place cards down. Nobody is sitting at the moment, so I suggest we head over to the auctions.

Giselle follows me through the room while I place bids on a few auctions. When different people stop me to talk, Giselle is sweet and charming—the same way I've seen her act when she's with her other dates.

And then it hits me. All those men I've seen her with. They weren't dates. They were clients.

"Killian, I'm so glad you could make it." Olivia pulls me out of my thoughts and in for a hug. "And who's your date?" She tilts her head to the side, and that's when I notice Giselle is hiding behind me. Laughing under my breath, I move to the side.

"Olivia, I would like for you to meet my date. Giselle Winters, this is Olivia Harper." Giselle raises her head and smiles nervously.

"Oh, my goodness!" Olivia claps excitedly. "I didn't know you two were coming together. I thought you couldn't make it." Olivia wraps her friend up in a hug.

Giselle's eyes bounce from Olivia to me, clearly unsure of what to say, so I answer her instead. "She's doing me a favor. My date couldn't make it."

Nick eyes me accusingly, silently calling bullshit, and I shake my head once, telling him to drop it.

"We're glad you both could make it," Nick says. "Killian, I want to show you something. Join me?" It comes out like a question, but it's anything but.

"I think it would be rude to leave our dates—" I begin to say, but Nick cuts me off.

"It will only be a minute." He gives Olivia a kiss on her cheek with a promise to be right back.

"Where's Reed?" I ask as we walk back over to the auction tables.

"He passed out an hour after we arrived, so Shelby took him back to Olivia's place." We stop in the corner, and Nick turns to face me, hitting me with a hard stare. "Did you say something to Giselle about her moving out?"

"No..." I start to say, but then I remember when I was babysitting and Giselle came home, we had words. "Yeah."

"Dammit, Kill. Giselle told Olivia tonight she's moving out."

"And that's a bad thing, why?"

"Because she's put her mom's house up for sale, and even if it does sell, she can't afford a place in the city."

"Trust me, Giselle is making more money than you think. Besides, it's not like she's your concern."

"It doesn't matter if she's a fucking millionaire. She and Olivia got into it because of whatever you said to her, and now Olivia is upset. I get you don't like Celeste and Giselle, and I'm pretty sure it's a mixture of you looking out for me and you refusing to deal with whatever you've been running from since college.

"But no more treating them like shit for me. I accept both of those women the way they are. Just like I don't know what's going on with you under the surface because you refuse to talk about it, the same can be said for them."

Damn it, he's right. I've been projecting my issues onto Giselle and Celeste, when the truth is, I'm not fucking perfect, and I definitely have no right to judge other people.

"I'm not sure why Giselle agreed to be your date, but maybe you can use it as an opportunity," Nick says.

"An opportunity for what?" I ask in confusion.

"To actually get to know the woman you're on a date with. Who knows? Maybe Giselle will shock you. It's not often you bring a date you didn't have to pay to join you." Nick smirks.

If only he knew the truth...

"I went on a date recently. Fuck you very much," I say in my defense.

"That model Christina set you up with? That doesn't count. We both know she was too busy modeling for the paparazzi to actually pay any attention to you. You would've been better off with one of your paid escorts."

He's got me there. Christina might be down to earth, but her friend definitely wasn't. She barely said two words to me the entire time, more concerned with who was taking our photograph or interviewing us. It was obvious she was using me to get back into the spotlight. And the few words she did speak to me were about how much men suck.

"Don't you think it's time to deal with whatever has been eating you up inside? Maybe you could give someone a chance. Let someone in. Not every woman is a gold-digger." I want to explain to him that it's more than them being gold-diggers... it's about protecting myself. But if I say that, he'll want me to explain, and I'm not prepared to go there.

"Maybe not, but most women aren't anything like Olivia," I point out.

"How would you know if you refuse to give anyone a chance?" Nick pats me on the shoulder. "I'm going to dance with my fiancée. Be nice to Giselle." He gives me a pointed look.

"Yes, sir!"

I follow him back over to where the women are standing and talking. Nick leads Olivia onto the dance floor, and Giselle is left standing there alone.

I take a moment to look at her—really look at her. With her hair down in waves and minimal makeup on her face, there's no denying she's a beautiful woman. Her dress is elegant and classy, yet with the back completely bare and the front cut just low enough that the swells of her breasts peek out, it screams sexy and wild.

What Nick said about not knowing what's under the surface suddenly comes to the forefront of my mind. He's right, I won't talk about what happened, and too many times since I've met Giselle, I've thought there might be more to her than what meets the eye.

Before I can question what I'm doing, I step in front of her and extend my hand. She eyes it like it's covered in shit before she looks up, silently asking what I'm doing.

"Dance with me."

"Why?" she asks with a look of disgust.

"Because I'm paying you to," I hiss.

She flinches, and I curse myself because I suck at this shit.

Before I can apologize, she takes my hand and pulls me onto the dance floor. Her arms go around my neck and her eyes look anywhere but at me.

Encircling one arm around her waist, I use my other hand to steer her chin toward me, so she's forced to look at me. "I'm sorry."

"You have nothing to be sorry for. Everything you've said is the truth." Giselle diverts her eyes away.

"Hey," I murmur, "look at me, please." Her cold blue eyes meet mine and they're glossed over. "I didn't mean to make you cry. I'm sorry."

"Can you please just stop saying sorry?" She removes one hand from around my nape and swipes away the falling tear.

When she places her hand back, I feel the wetness of her touch, and it sends a chill through my body. I did this. I made her cry. I'm such a fucking asshole. "

I'm well aware of what I am and what I do for money," she murmurs. "I'm nothing more than a glorified prostitute."

It takes me a second, but her words hit me like a punch to the gut. "Hold up." I stop moving. "Do you have sex with the guys you go out with?"

Giselle looks at me incredulously, and I think she's going to tell me she doesn't. But instead, she glances around to make sure nobody heard me before she says, "Are you serious right now? You know I do!" she whisper-yells. "And don't go acting like you're better than me. I might get paid to fuck men, but you pay women to fuck you. There's no difference."

I open my mouth to argue but stop myself. She thinks I've hired her to get laid. I knew sex was an option with the escort service I use, the service she works for, but that's not why I use them.

"This is just a date," I tell her. "I have no intention of having sex with you."

Giselle rolls her eyes, misunderstanding the meaning behind my words. "Not up to your standards?" She eyes me up and down. "Don't worry, I have no intention of sleeping with you either." Her nose scrunches up in disgust.

"You would if I paid you to," I point out, and she glowers. *Jesus, have I always been such a dick?*

"I'm so—"

"Oh my god! If you say you're sorry one more time, I'm going to leave you here. How about you just stop talking for a while, so you won't have anything to apologize for?"

I nod once, and we go back to dancing in silence. One song flows into the next and eventually the awkward silence almost turns comfortable.

At one point, I think Giselle even forgets who she's dancing with because she lays her head down on my shoulder. A lump forms in my throat at the gesture, and I try to block out how good she feels in my arms.

She isn't my date.

She's here because she's getting paid to be.

A few songs in, the music comes to a stop and dinner is announced. Of course, we're seated at the same table as Olivia and Nick, Celeste and her date, and Olivia's parents. We eat and converse. Olivia and Nick speak on behalf of Touchdown for Reading and the Arts, and then they start to announce the winners of the auctions.

"...and the winner of the cruise for two donated by Global Yachts is...Giselle Winters with a bid of twelve thousand dollars. Thank you, Giselle."

Giselle's eyes bug out, but she stands to walk up to the podium, not wanting to cause a scene. "Thank you." She smiles nervously, takes the coupon, then sits back down.

Jokingly, when I filled out my bids, I put her name instead of mine. I thought it was funny at the time. Now, seeing her pissed off scowl, it doesn't seem quite as funny.

"Asshole," she hisses, slapping the paper on the table in front of me.

"It was just a joke," I whisper. "I didn't really think I would win any of them."

"You're paying for this." She glares my way.

"Obviously." I hand her back the coupon. "Global Yachts has beautiful ships. Take someone and have a good time."

"I don't want anything from you," she whispers, refusing to take the paper.

Not wanting to argue, I fold the paper and put it into my jacket pocket.

Once all the auction winners are announced, the deejay turns the music back on and several couples make their way back to the dance floor.

Since Giselle and I seemed to have found common ground while dancing earlier, I extend my hand and ask her to dance.

Once again, she eyes my hand and asks, "Why?"

This time, though, I don't answer her like I did before. Instead, I tell her the truth. "Because you look absolutely breathtaking tonight, and I enjoyed our last dance. I can't think of a better way to spend my evening than on the dance floor with you."

She appears stunned by my words but doesn't argue. Instead, she stands and takes my hand, so I can lead her out onto the dance floor, where I spend the next hour—with Giselle in my arms as we sway to the music.

The evening comes to a close, and after saying goodbye to Olivia and Nick, we step outside. My driver circles around to pick us up, and once we're in the car, he asks where we're headed.

"Brooklyn Heights, please," I say.

"Actually, if you could please drop me off at the subway station that would be great." Giselle glances down at her phone. "Grand Central off 42nd Street."

That's when I notice she has a duffle bag with her. She must've brought it with her when I picked her up, but I was too in shock over learning she was my date, I didn't notice.

"We can drop you off at home," I insist.

I know she got upset over the silent auction and some of the stuff I said, but after I apologized, we seemed to have an okay time.

"I'm not going home."

"Where are you going?"

"To the subway station."

The driver glances back at me and I shake my head.

"I saw that!" Giselle hisses. "What are you going to do, keep me hostage in your dumb limo?"

"Damn, first my Bugatti is stupid and ugly and now my limo is dumb? What have my vehicles ever done to you?" I laugh, and Giselle growls. "Tell me where you're going," I insist.

"To my mom's! And if you take me to Brooklyn, it will only make my trip longer."

"Leo," I say to my driver.

"Sir?"

"There's been a change of plans. Please stay here for a moment."

"Yes, Sir."

"Killian, I don't need you to take me. I can take myself," Giselle says, but I ignore her, stepping out of the vehicle. I dial Nick's number and he answers on the second ring.

"Did you drive here?"

"I did."

"Perfect, I need to borrow your car. I'll tell my driver to wait here for you."

"Okay, just let the valet know."

"Thanks, man."

We hang up, and I let my driver know the change in plans. Then I have the valet bring around Nick's car.

After arguing with Giselle for a good five minutes, I convince her to get in the car and then we're on our way to Rye, where her mom lives. It's a good forty-five-minute drive, but I make it in close to thirty.

"Thank you," Giselle says. "You can go. I'm spending the night."

"You're welcome."

She shocks me when she leans over and gives me a kiss on my cheek. "Despite the rocky start, I had a good time."

She grabs her bag from the backseat and gets out of the car.

As I wait for her to get safely inside, I check a couple text messages that came through while I was driving. I'm about to back out, when the door swings back open, and she comes running out.

"Killian, my phone is dead! Call 911 now!" She runs back inside without waiting for me, and I follow her in, doing as she said.

When the operator answers and asks what the emergency is, I'm not sure what to say. And then I see her. Giselle's mom lying on the bathroom floor with empty pill bottles surrounding her.

"We need an ambulance. Someone has overdosed on prescription drugs." I tell her the address then hang up.

Giselle's holding her mom in her arms and rocking her back and forth, begging her to wake up. She's completely still.

I google what to do when someone overdoses, and every website says to call for help and to make sure the person's airway isn't blocked.

"Open her mouth and turn her face to the side in case she chokes," I tell her.

She does what I say and then continues to rock her mom while begging her to wake up.

Finally, the paramedics arrive and take Giselle's mom out of her arms. Tears of devastation and fear are dripping down her cheeks as she quickly answers their questions.

I gather up the pill bottles and hand them to them, and then they're leaving with her mom on a gurney.

"Let's go," I say to Giselle, who is standing still in the driveway watching the ambulance leave.

"This is all my fault." Her voice is so soft, I almost don't hear her.

"Giselle, c'mon, we need to get to the hospital. I doubt it's your fault, but right now it really doesn't matter."

When she doesn't move, I walk around in front of her. Her cheeks are stained from her tears, and she looks almost as lifeless as her mom.

"I was supposed to be here." She shakes her head. "And then Bianca said if I didn't go tonight, I would be fired." Even in the darkness, I can see her throat move as she attempts to swallow her guilt down.

"I was on a date while she was trying to kill herself. I should've been here." She nods once to no one in particular then finally makes eye contact with me. "If you can let me use your phone, I can call for a cab. Thank you for calling the ambulance.

"When I found my mom, her phone was floating in the toilet. And when I tried to dial 911 from mine, it wouldn't even turn on. I didn't realize my phone was dead. I must've forgotten to charge it. I don't know what I would've done if you weren't still here."

"You don't have to thank me. I'm just glad I hadn't left yet. I'm not letting you call for a car. Let's go." Gently, I grip her wrist and guide her to Nick's BMW.

Thankfully, she gets in without arguing, and we head to the hospital.

120

Chapter Ten

GISELLE

THE ENTIRE DRIVE TO THE HOSPITAL IS SPENT with me silently working myself up. My mom is dead. How could she not be?

As I held her in my arms, I couldn't find a pulse. I couldn't feel any air coming from her nose.

Her body was limp, and she was white as a ghost. I don't work in the medical field, but it doesn't take a doctor to know the odds are stacked against her.

I have no idea how many pills she swallowed or how long ago she swallowed them. It'll be a miracle if I'm told she's alive.

I should call my sister and tell her what's going on, but I can't do it. Isn't telling your younger sister your mom is dead something that should be done in person?

This is all my fault. I should've gone straight to her the minute Dedra said she had to leave. It doesn't matter that she's been happier lately. Laughing and smiling. I know that at any given moment she can sink back into her depression. I shouldn't have chanced it.

Her life should've been more important than my job. More important than money.

But the job and the money are how you take care of her...

Killian parks Nick's car, and I jump out, heading straight through the emergency room entrance.

I find the front desk and give the nurse my mom's name. After she confirms who I am, I'm told she's been put into the system and is being worked on.

"She's not dead?" I ask.

The nurse's lips twist into something between a frown and a sad smile. "I'm not sure," she admits. "It doesn't give me any information. I've noted you're here, and as soon as there's any information, you'll be called."

I thank her and have a seat, and Killian sits next to me. I should tell him he can go, but I don't. As strange as it may seem, it feels nice having him here with me. He's the only person aside from my dad and sister who has seen my mom at her worst. And while he's said some pretty shitty stuff to me, he's never said a single mean thing about my mom.

I'm not sure how long we sit here, but at some point, his hand makes its way into mine and my head makes its way onto his shoulder.

My thoughts go back to last week when I wished for a man's shoulder to put my head on. My eyes close and my body shuts down temporarily, needing a tiny moment of reprieve from the onslaught of emotions that are weighing down on me.

"Giselle." I hear my name being whispered. I open my eyes and lift my head to find Killian softly smiling at me. "The doctor is here to speak to you."

My body shoots up too quickly and everything goes fuzzy. Killian's hands grip my waist, and I steady myself.

"Thank you," I whisper then step closer toward the doctor.

"Next of Kin to Sarah Winters?" he asks.

"Yes, I'm her daughter." I extend my hand to shake his and he takes it.

"I'm Dr. Goldberg. As I'm sure you're aware, your mother overdosed on prescription drugs. We were able to pump her stomach in time. We have her in a drug-induced coma and will slowly lower the dosage. I'm going to strongly suggest you have her Baker Acted."

"What's Baker Acted?" I ask.

"It's when you sign off on your mom to be held for up to seventy-two hours for involuntary examination."

"Like being committed?" I question.

"Yes, the doctors will be able to assess her more thoroughly. The form you filled out indicated she's been on several different types of prescriptions over the years.

"My guess is she's seen different psychiatrists who have diagnosed her to the best of their ability, but my recommendation is to have her evaluated more thoroughly.

"With this suicide attempt, plus the scars on her wrists, which indicate this isn't her first attempt to commit suicide—and add in the different diagnoses—they may even recommend she stay longer."

My initial thought is to ask how much this will all cost, but he's only the doctor, so he won't know anyway.

My next thought is that I'm a horrible fucking daughter to worry about the cost when my mom almost died. I will figure out how to cover whatever the cost is.

"Thank you. I will sign off to have her Baker Acted."

"Okay, I'll write up the referral to have her transferred." He flips through what looks like her chart. "It shows you're self-pay. I must warn you this is a private facility." This is exactly what I was afraid of. "They will bill you for the initial consultation, but if they decide to keep her after that, you will have to pay up front. You'll have a couple people come by so you can fill out and sign some forms, and they can go over everything with you."

I glance over to Killian who heard everything he said. "Can I go see her now?" I ask.

"Yes, but she's still unconscious."

I thank him one more time, and then he heads back to wherever he came from.

"You can go ahead and go," I tell Killian. "I have no clue how long I'm going to be here, but I imagine it will be a while. Thank you so much for everything you've done."

I pull him into a hug, and surprisingly he wraps his arms around my waist. My face presses against his chest, and for a moment, I revel in the scent that is Killian—a hint of cologne and a whole lot of just him—and then let out a deep cleansing breath. It's been a long time since I felt safe, but here in his arms, surprisingly, I feel just that.

"Are you sure?" he asks, concerned.

"Yes, thank you."

I'm used to dealing with this on my own, and I can't let a friendly gesture from Killian change that. All I can count on is myself and that's not going to change. I might not be able to stand on my own two feet when it comes to living on my own yet, but I've never once asked anyone to come to the rescue when it comes to the rest of my life.

Killian nods once. "All right, but if you need anything, please call me." He walks over to the front desk and comes back, handing me a piece of paper with his number on it. "Anything."

"I appreciate that."

I watch Killian walk away, then ask which room number my mom is in. The nurse directs me in the right direction, and I head back to her room.

I should probably call Adrianna and tell her what's going on, but I don't want to worry her. She needs to focus on her classes. She'll just want to drive down to be here when there's nothing she can do anyway.

My mom's room is quiet with only the sound of the machines monitoring her. Her color is starting to come back, and she looks so peaceful.

My heart clenches at the thought of her waking up.

Why can't the psychiatrists figure out what's wrong with her? She deserves to be happy, to live a healthy life. One where she doesn't think her only answer is to kill herself.

Chapter Eleven

GISELLE

"The quarterly earnings are projected to be up two hundred percent..." Paul, my date for the evening, drones on with his business partner over how much money they're expected to make this year.

I'm trying to focus on what he's saying, appear like I give a shit about whatever they're discussing, but I'm finding it hard to focus.

It's been four days since I signed for my mom to be committed to a mental health facility. I've applied to several insurance companies, but because of her situation, I keep getting denied. Nobody wants to take on someone with preexisting conditions, especially as extensive as my mom's.

Because she's still legally married to my father, she doesn't qualify for state assistance and the government offered insurance won't cover her stay.

I make a note to speak to an attorney about filing for divorce on my mother's behalf. If the house sells, I need to make sure my father doesn't get a dime of the money I make from the sale.

Paul's hand squeezes my thigh, and I look over to him, realizing I've been zoning out. I give him a smile, but his brows pinch together. He knows something is up.

We've been out enough times that he knows me well enough to know I'm not all here. He quirks one brow up, silently asking if I'm okay, and I give him another smile, then stand, excusing myself to the restroom.

Paul's business partner stops speaking and looks at his wife, Patricia, to see if she needs to use the restroom...because apparently women can't use the restroom on their own.

She stands as well and follows me down the hall.

After I do my business, I wash my hands, and while I'm drying them, I feel my phone vibrate in my clutch.

I pull it out to make sure it isn't Serenity calling—the behavioral health facility my mom's in.

UNKNOWN

"Have I gone mad?" "I'm afraid so. You're entirely bonkers. But I'll tell you a secret. All the best people are."

Glancing back, I see Patricia is still in the stall, so I text back.

ME

Who's this?

UNKNOWN

The Mad Hatter

I laugh to myself. I can't be positive, but something tells me this is Killian. He's the last person I spoke to about my love for Alice in Wonderland. Instead of asking if it's him, I go along with it.

ME

Funny. Enjoying the book?

UNKNOWN

Yep!

ME

Too bad that quote is from the movie...

I watch as the bubbles appear and disappear. Then, finally a response comes through.

UNKNOWN

You got me. And it's Killian.

ME

I figured...go read the book! A movie should never be a substitute. First read the book, then watch the movie. How did you get my number anyway?

I input Killian's name into my contacts while I wait for him to respond.

KILLIAN

In high school, the movie was always the perfect substitute ;) I got your number from Olivia. I hope that's okay. I just wanted to see how you're doing...how your mom is doing.

My heart rate picks up and tears prick my eyes. The truth is, I'm not doing well at all. I'm scared for my mom, tired from working fifteen-hour days to try to earn the money I'm going to need to pay for my mom's treatment.

I feel like I'm drowning. Every day feels like a struggle to breathe, to simply exist. But I don't tell him any of that. Instead, I text him back that I'm okay, and thank him for checking on my mom and me.

He responds with:

KILLIAN

What are you doing right now?

I reply with:

ME

Working

I regret typing the word as soon as I hit send. This late at night, there's only one job I could be at right now, and it's not Fresh Designs.

Less than ten seconds later, he responds.

KILLIAN

On a date?

I know what he's asking. Am I working as an escort?

I type back my response with a quote from *Alice's Adventures in Wonderland*—the book, not the movie.

ME

> If everyone minded their own business, the world would go around a great deal faster than it does.

I smirk as I watch the bubbles, which indicate he's typing. Then they stop. They start again. But then stop.

Immediately, I wonder if I offended him. I meant it as a joke, but even when it's put like that, in a quote from a children's book, it still means the same thing. *Mind your own business.*

And even if I meant what I wrote, I shouldn't be rude to Killian. What he did for my mom...he's the reason she's still alive. Had I taken the subway that night, I never would have gotten to her in time.

And once we arrived, it was his phone call that got the ambulance to her in time.

Before I can type back, a text comes in:

KILLIAN

> Off with her head.

I let out a soft giggle at his response, then reply:

ME

> I'm sorry, that was rude, Yes, I'm on a date...as an escort.

I throw my phone back in my clutch and make my way back out to the table. When I get there, I realize I left Patricia in the bathroom.

She walks up behind me and sits down, and for the next hour I try to focus better, participate in the conversation more, and earn my pay. When the bill is paid, we say our goodbyes, and part ways once the valet brings the cars around.

"You okay, Giselle?" Paul asks, glancing over at me as he drives us back to his place. He's a VIP client, which means his dates always include a 'nightcap.'

"I'm just a little tired," I tell him.

"Why don't I bring you home?" he suggests.

I want to tell him I appreciate that, but it will mean less money—and I need the money.

"That's okay." I give him a smile. "I'm good."

"No, you aren't," he argues. "If it's the money you're worried about, I'll note we had our nightcap."

"I appreciate that, but I couldn't let you do that. I promise I am good."

The last thing I want is another person taking pity on me.

Paul doesn't argue further. He takes me back to his place where we spend the next half-hour having sex.

When we're done, he thanks me for another wonderful evening and then calls his driver to take me home.

On the way, I check my messages. If I'm honest, I'm a bit disappointed to see Killian never texted me back. Not that I blame him. Why would he want to continue a conversation with a woman who's whoring herself out? Then again, he does hire women for the same services I provide.

Once I'm dropped off, I head upstairs. The place is dark and quiet, and I assume Olivia and Reed are at Nick's.

I take a hot shower, scrubbing the slut off me. It doesn't matter how much I clean myself, though. I know who I am and what I've become. I can't regret it, though. It's how I'm surviving. It's what pays my mom's mortgage, my sister's school, my school loan debt. It's how I'm going to get my mom healthy.

I don't have it in me to regret my choices. But even with all the justifying I do, it doesn't stop me from feeling gross and dirty.

After putting on my pajamas, I head out to the kitchen to get a bottle of water, when I hear something. I knock on Olivia's door, and she tells me to come in.

"I thought you were at Nick's," I say as I enter her room.

"I'm not feeling well," she whispers.

When I step closer, I can see she's been crying. Her eyes are puffy, and her cheeks and nose are blotchy. I crawl into bed with her, and she cuddles up next to me—her head landing on my chest. My fingers run through her long strands of hair.

"What's wrong?" I ask her.

"I—I'm not sure. I've just been really emotional lately, and the last few days I've been feeling nauseous. I threw up this morning."

My fingers still in her hair.

Emotional. Nauseous. Throwing up. She's pregnant. She knows it. I know it. She just doesn't want to admit it.

I could point it out to her, but it's obvious she's not ready to deal with it, so I'll let her remain in denial for a little longer.

If I were to guess, she's nervous to tell Nick, which is why she's home instead of with him. The last time she was pregnant, he didn't handle it well at all. Of course, he came around, but it makes sense that she would be nervous to tell him.

"I'm sure it's just a bug or something," I say.

"Yeah, maybe. Or maybe it's just nerves. Between the charity event and Nick getting injured, things have been crazy."

We lie in bed, not saying a word for several minutes. Then Olivia says, "I figured out the tattoo I want to get."

I stifle my laugh. She won't be getting a tattoo for at least the next nine months.

"Oh, yeah? What do you want to get?" I ask, going along with the conversation.

"I want to get 'And they lived happily ever after' written across my ribs with three hearts for Nick, Reed, and me."

"That will be beautiful."

But it will be four hearts and not three, I think, but don't say out loud.

"I miss you, Giselle," Olivia whispers.

"I miss you, too," I whisper back.

As we lie in bed, I consider telling her everything. She's my best friend, my sister. Olivia would never judge me. I know that. I could do no wrong in her eyes.

No, she wouldn't judge, but she would want to fix it. And the thought of her paying for anything, makes me feel sick.

She's done so much for me over the years. I can't let her fix this. But I also can't keep this from her any longer. It's destroying our friendship.

Just as I work up the courage to tell her what's been going on, Reed cries from his room.

"He's been teething," she says, getting up.

She brings him back into the room with us, and when he spots me, he gets excited.

"Gi Gi!" he exclaims in his cute little voice.

Olivia lays him between us, and he pulls on my hair with his chubby little fingers. He rolls from side to side getting comfortable. Once he's settled down, Olivia rubs his back and within minutes he's passed out.

"Do you have any plans tomorrow night?" Olivia asks.

I think for a minute. As of right now I'm not on the schedule.

"No."

"I was thinking we could do a girls' night out, and I can invite Celeste. We spoke a few days ago and she's been acting weird since the night of your birthday." I stifle a laugh for a second time. She's totally avoiding Nick. "We can go out for drinks."

"Or we can stay in and watch some chick flicks," I propose.

"Reed's been acting weird. My dad and Corrine will have to watch him here. He hasn't been wanting to sleep anywhere else lately."

"What about Nick?" I ask nonchalantly.

"His arm has been hurting. I don't want him to have to pick up Reed. He'll probably just hang out with Killian, play the PlayStation or whatever."

"Sounds good."

I let out a yawn at the same time Olivia does, and we both laugh.

Reed rolls over and his hand comes up to my cheek. His eyes stay closed, and I watch him for several minutes, realizing I never told Olivia anything I planned to tell her.

Tomorrow, I think to myself. I'll tell her tomorrow.

Tonight, I just want to pretend everything is right in my world.

Chapter Twelve

KILLIAN

"So, she's been avoiding you since you got injured?" I ask Nick, my eyes not leaving the television. The score's 28-35, and I need this touchdown to tie the game.

"Yep, I don't know why, man. Any other woman, I would say she's upset that I won't be a pro ball player anymore..." Nick's defensive team comes at my quarterback, and I throw the ball to one of my receivers.

"But this is Olivia," I say, finishing his sentence. "And the woman is richer than you are."

"Exactly," he agrees, "it doesn't make any sense. I thought she would be happy to have me home more."

My guy is tackled, and the time runs down. I throw the controller onto the coffee table, and Nick laughs.

"Where is she now?" I ask.

"Right above us." Nick looks toward the ceiling. "Girls' night. Coach and Corrine are watching Reed at her place. I think the moving back and forth is affecting him. He doesn't want to sleep anywhere but at her place." He frowns.

"Who all is up there?" I ask, attempting to sound nonchalant, when what I really want to know is if Giselle is up there.

The woman has been on my mind for days now. In a moment of weakness, I texted her to see how she was doing, only to learn she was out with another guy.

It shouldn't have affected me the way it did. I know what she does for a living. I know she dates and fucks men for money.

But it did affect me. And now I can't stop thinking about her. Everything doesn't add up. There's definitely more going on than she's allowing people to see, and I want to know what it is.

"Giselle and Celeste," Nick says, standing and heading to my kitchen. "Want a drink?" he calls out.

"Sure."

He comes back in and hands me a cold beer.

"If you're worried about Olivia avoiding you, you should go see her."

"Right now?"

"Yeah, she's upstairs, so she can't run." I shrug, and Nick gives me a curious glance.

"How did your date with Giselle go?"

"Fine." I take a long pull of my beer.

"Fine?" he parrots.

"It started out a bit rough. I may have said a few things that pissed her off..."

Nick groans.

"But I apologized, and by the end of the night, I have to admit, I was enjoying her company." I don't mention what happened with her mom and how it made me see Giselle in an entirely new light.

Nick eyes me warily. "Are you thinking about seeing her again?"

"What if I am?" I shoot him a *what the fuck* look. "Aren't you the one who said I should give her a chance?"

"Yeah, I did, but I don't want to see either of you get hurt. She never seems to last more than a couple of dates with the same guy. I think she just has a lot of shit going on. Her dad left, and from what I can see, she's paying for her sister's school and her mom's bills.

"She won't discuss it and she's never confirmed it, but it doesn't take a genius to figure out that when her dad left her mom, he stopped supporting his family."

I begin to do the math in my head: the mortgage, house bills, college can't be cheap. I remember that the doctor mentioned she was self-paying. Does she not have insurance? That bill would be thousands of dollars.

"You don't know shit, Killian. Don't you dare make assumptions or pretend to know anything about me or my life."

Jesus, is this why she's barely making ends meet even though she's living with Olivia rent-free? Why she's working as an escort, even though she has a job as an interior designer?

She's taken on an entire family in her father's absence. All the pieces finally fit together, and fuck if I don't feel like the biggest piece of shit.

"Why don't we go crash their girls' night? You know, so you can see how your fiancée is doing."

Nick laughs. "Okay, we'll blame it on me." We stand and head toward the door, but Nick stops me from opening it. "I know Giselle comes across tough, but this morning, when I was missing Olivia and Reed, I went over there to see them. I snuck in and saw Olivia, Reed, and Giselle all sleeping in Olivia's bed together. Olivia and Reed were both asleep. But Giselle...she wasn't asleep. She was watching them both... while crying.

"I think she's in over her head, Kill, but she won't let Olivia in. I know you don't understand why I won't push for Olivia and Reed to move out, but that woman was there for Olivia when I wasn't. I owe her. She's not just her best friend. She's her family, which means she's my family."

"Got it."

We get off on Nick's floor, and without knocking, walk into his condo. The girls are on the couch laughing and talking. Giselle and Celeste have a wine glass in their hand, and Olivia is drinking a bottle of water.

But the three of them stop speaking and laughing the second they see Nick and I enter. Celeste smirks, Giselle's eyes go wide and then she glares, and Olivia looks like she's nervous.

Celeste and Giselle both stand, setting down their drinks while Olivia stays seated.

"You don't have to leave on our account," Nick says to the two women. "I was just hoping to see my fiancée for a few minutes. She's been busy lately." He shoots her a pointed look, and Giselle giggles. My eyes swing to her, and she's grinning from ear-to-ear.

"I'm out of here," Giselle announces.

"Same," Celeste agrees.

"No, you aren't." Olivia stops them. "You've been drinking. Please spend the night. Nick has a spare room."

"It only has one twin bed," Nick says.

"Giselle's coming with me," I announce, making her eyes go wide. "We need to talk."

"Great!" Olivia exclaims. "Celeste, you can take the spare room."

Celeste and Giselle both look like they want to argue but for some reason, don't.

"Fine," Giselle says. "Let's go."

She gives Celeste and Olivia a hug, then, after grabbing her purse, follows me out.

Once we're in the elevator, before I can press the button to my floor, she presses the button for the ground floor.

"You agreed to come to my place. Like Olivia said, you've been drinking, and it's late." I press the button for my floor.

"I agreed because Olivia is hormonal and in denial. I didn't want to upset her."

I'm not sure what she means by that, but right now I need to focus on Giselle. Nick can handle his fiancée.

"Well, now I'm responsible for you."

The bell dings, indicating we've arrived, and the doors open.

Giselle crosses her arms over her chest in defiance, and I grin.

"You coming?" I ask, giving her one chance to come on her own.

"Nope." Her lips pop at the p, and I stifle my laugh at how adorable she is when she's been drinking.

"Fine."

I bend at the waist and throw her over my shoulder. She kicks and screams as I walk her down the hall to my condo.

With one hand, I unlock my door and walk us inside. When I get to my couch, I drop her, and she lands on the cushions with a huff.

"I want the truth," I demand. "Why are you an escort?"

Giselle glares my way, her invisible shield rising to protect her. "Because I love to fuck."

She stands and fills the gap between us. Then she runs her fingers down my chest and over my abs through my shirt. It's been a long time since I've been touched by a woman and my dick instantly takes notice.

"Do you love to fuck, Kill?" She licks her lips seductively. "I can fuck you." Her hand lands on my crotch and she squeezes my dick, and a groan escapes me. "I'm good at my job."

Her words are like ice water to a flame, knocking me out of my trance. "I don't want or need you to fuck me," I growl as I back up slightly. "Now, answer me. Why are you an escort?"

She flinches at my repeated question then steps forward into my personal space. "What do the other women have that I don't?" she questions, changing the subject. "You let Tabitha fuck you. I could please you. Just ask my other clients. They all come back wanting more."

I don't bother to tell her that Tabitha most definitely didn't fuck me.

Giselle encircles her arms around me and her lips press against the side of my neck. "Let me make you feel good," she murmurs.

My eyes close as I allow her to trail soft kisses up my neck and along my jaw. When her lips press against mine, I smell the wine, reminding me that she's been drinking.

I can't let this happen. I have rules and I'm not going to break them now. Especially for a woman who is treating me like I'm a paying client.

Gently, I push her away. "Giselle, I'm not your client. Stop avoiding my question. Why are you selling your body for money?"

Her arms cross over her chest in what looks like a defensive move. "Why did you bring me up here if you don't want to get laid?"

"I want to talk to you. Nick mentioned you're paying for your sister's school. Is that true?"

"Since when do you want to talk to me?" She snatches her purse off the couch. "It's not your business what I'm paying for."

"Wait, please." I grab her upper arm gently but firmly to hold her in place. "How's your mom doing?"

Giselle looks into my eyes for a beat before she lets out a deep breath. And then she shocks the shit out of me when she actually lets me in. "She's still being evaluated. I have to go tomorrow to speak to the doctors."

"Stay," I say. "Not to have sex, but to talk."

I don't know why I'm begging this woman to stay and talk. Maybe it's because I feel like it's possible we have something in common. We both carry secrets we aren't proud of, secrets we can't even tell our best friends and family.

"Why?" she asks, her voice small and vulnerable.

"I don't know," I tell her honestly. "Maybe it's because when I look at you, I see myself: broken and lonely." I let out a deep breath. "Stay the night and talk to me. Be broken and lonely with me."

I repeat the words to the song we heard on our way to her house the night of her birthday.

I've heard the song several times since that night and every damn time my thoughts go straight to Giselle.

Chapter Thirteen

GISELLE

I DON'T EVEN REALIZE I'M CRYING UNTIL KILLIAN swipes his thumb across my cheek. He presses the pad of his thumb to his lips and I'm almost positive he just tasted my tears.

Be broken and lonely with me.

Can I do that? Can I let him in? I practically threw myself at him to stop him from getting too close to me, and he refused to have sex with me.

Is it possible Killian Blake is just as broken and lonely as I am? I can't imagine what he's been through to feel that way, but then again, most wouldn't know what I'm going through.

Suddenly, a flashback hits me hard from the night of my birthday: the drive home. I drank way too much, and Killian made sure I got home safely.

"Do you ever feel broken and lonely, Killian?"
"Every damn day."

Unable to voice my answer, I nod once, and he nods back. Then, taking my hand, he leads me into his bedroom.

He opens up a drawer and pulls a couple items out, handing me a shirt and boxers. "So you're more comfortable." He shrugs. "My bathroom is through that door."

"Thank you," I tell him.

After changing out of my clothes and into his, I use the bathroom and wash my hands and face. This will be the first time since I was with Christian that I'm spending the night with a man.

Even the men I've been with, I never spend the night. My rule is midnight. Many have offered more money for me to break that rule, but I've never once done it.

It sounds stupid, but I never wanted to be that intimate with someone. It's one thing to have sex with them, but it's another to sleep and cuddle with them—to act like we're something we're not—something we'll never be.

When I exit the bathroom, Killian is dressed in a pair of New York Brewers sweats and a plain white T-shirt. I take a moment to look around his room. The walls are a soft beige, and the furniture is a dark chocolate brown. The four-poster bed is huge and placed directly in the middle of the wall.

"Would you like something to drink?" he asks. "Water? Tea?"

"Water would be great."

I stay standing in place as he walks out of the room. I can't believe of all places to be, I'm standing in the bedroom of Killian Blake. It wasn't too long ago the guy hated my guts—and the feeling was mutual. I guess the saying is true: there's a thin line between love and hate.

Not that this is love...

Never mind, ignore that last thought. I've clearly had too much to drink. There's a thick line—a very thick line—and we're nowhere near crossing it.

"Giselle," Killian calls out and I follow after him.

I find him in the kitchen grabbing two waters out of the fridge. He hands me one and I take a long sip. After taking a drink of his own water, he walks out of the kitchen and into the living room, sitting down on the sofa.

I study him for a long beat, confused as to how I got here. How we got here. And not just in his home, but the two of us, comfortable enough with each other that I'm wearing his boxers.

"I thought you hated me," I blurt out. "Why am I here?"

"Come and sit with me. Let's talk." He pats the cushion, and reluctantly, I join him.

"Why do you work as an escort?" he asks again, getting straight to the point. We both know he already knows why, but he wants to hear it from me.

"When my dad left my mom, he stopped paying the bills. I took over, but as an intern, I didn't make enough. I applied for assistance for my sister for school, but on every application they included my father's income. He didn't make a lot, but he made too much for her to get financial aid, and I couldn't let Adrianna take out loans. She would graduate and be thousands of dollars in debt like me.

"One night while I was out with Christian, I overheard his friends talking about the escort service they use. After I caught him cheating on me, in a desperate act to make some quick money to pay for my sister's semester of classes, I looked it up. I interviewed with Bianca and was hired."

My eyes close in embarrassment. Escorting has become a part of my life, but up until now, I've never discussed it with anyone. Saying what I do out loud makes it seem more real.

"My dad didn't just leave," I add. "He also quit his job."

"So, doesn't that mean you can get her financial aid?" Killian asks.

"It was already too late to apply. There's a deadline. And on top of that, because he's no longer employed, my mom's insurance was canceled. The medications she's on cost thousands a month. I'm trying to get her insured, but nobody wants to write a policy for a woman who has the preexisting conditions my mom has. And honestly, we don't even know the extent of her condition. She's been diagnosed a million times, but nobody seems to get it right. I've watched her struggle my entire life, and I have no idea how to help her. I'm hoping the doctors at Serenity—the mental health facility she's at—will be able to figure out something the others couldn't."

Killian stares at me for a few seconds before he says, "I'm so sorry, Giselle."

"I don't want your pity," I snap before I can stop myself.

"No." He shakes his head. "I'm not sorry for what you're going through. I mean, I am, but that's not why I'm apologizing. I'm sorry for the way I treated you. I assumed you were leeching off Olivia. And once I found out you were an escort, I assumed the worst. That you were loaded and choosing to let her pay your way." Killian takes my hand in his. "Please forgive me."

My head and heart are spinning. I've spent the last several months refusing to have any emotions, and now this man is pulling them out of me. I feel like I've been exposed and laid bare, meanwhile he hasn't given me anything.

"I'll forgive you on two conditions."

He nods for me to continue.

"One, you apologize to Celeste. You've been mean to her and she doesn't deserve it."

Killian nods. "Okay, and two?"

"The night of my birthday, you admitted you were broken and lonely..." When Killian doesn't deny it, I continue, "Then, when you asked me to stay with you tonight, you said 'Be broken and lonely with me.' Tell me your story."

Killian flinches but tries to quickly play it off with a small, nervous smile. "What you said about me paying escorts to have sex with me, you were wrong. I do pay them to go to events with me, but I don't have sex with them." He pauses for a moment, then surprises the hell out of me when he says, "I don't have sex at all."

I try to contain my shocked expression, but it must seep through my features because Killian laughs softly. "I'm not a virgin, if that's what you're thinking."

"Well, yeah, it kind of was," I admit.

"I haven't had sex in over ten years."

I have so many questions, but I remain silent and allow him to tell me his truth.

"I was popular in high school. Your typical varsity football player." Killian laughs but it's not a happy laugh. "I was even crowned homecoming king my senior year."

A giggle escapes me when I picture Killian wearing a crown.

"I definitely had no trouble getting laid. I slept around like most guys my age do. I wasn't a complete manwhore, but I had my fair share of women. When I started at the University of North Carolina, I continued as I had in high school, only I became even more popular. Girls would throw themselves at me, wanting to date a college athlete. Nick was the starting QB, and when we went out together, girls would flock to us.

"My sophomore year I met this girl, Melanie. She was in a sorority and a cheerleader. We hit it off. I took her out on a few dates and one of them led to us having sex. I really enjoyed her company, but I was young and immature. She wanted more..."

"To be your girlfriend," I say, and Killian nods.

"Playing college ball took up a lot of my time," he explains. "Between going to classes full-time and practice. Add in the away games. It was just too much. I wasn't in a place to commit to one person. She said she understood, and we continued to sleep together."

His eyes drop and my stomach tightens. Something in his voice tells me he's getting to the climax of the story.

"A few months later, Melanie got pregnant." He takes a shaky breath. I wait for him to continue, but instead he stands, and grabbing his water bottle, chucks it across the room. It hits a picture and knocks it to the ground.

"I'm sorry. I can't do this." He storms out of the living room and into his bedroom.

I wait a few minutes, unsure if I should go after him. Whatever happened can't be good. I consider leaving, but I make the decision to stay.

He started this. He asked me to be broken and lonely with him. I told him my truths and now it's time for him to tell me his. Judging by the way he's acting, if I had to guess, I would say he's never told anyone this before.

Standing, I head into the bedroom and find him coming out of the bathroom. He sits on the edge of the bed, his elbows landing on his knees, and his face falling into his hands.

"I have a spare room," he tells me. "I can take you to see your mom in the morning, so you don't have to ride the subway."

"Be broken and lonely with me," I say, repeating his words.

Killian looks up at me, and it's apparent from his bloodshot eyes that he was crying in the bathroom.

"Please," I add.

He stares at me for a long time, searching for what, I'm not sure, and then he nods once. I take that as my cue to sit next to him on the bed.

"Fuck, this is so hard." He closes his eyes and I take his hand in mine. I rub circles into his flesh with my thumb until he relaxes enough to reopen his eyes.

"When she found out she was pregnant, she came to me." His eyes close once more and a single tear falls. I watch as it makes its way down his cheek and lands on the front of his shirt.

"Fuck, Giselle." His voice cracks on my name. "She was scared and crying. She needed me to tell her everything would be okay."

He swallows loudly and then continues, "I had a game coming up, and finals, and I was exhausted. I freaked out. I told her I couldn't deal with it. She was on the pill. It shouldn't have happened.

"Looking back, I know shit happens and how she got pregnant shouldn't have mattered. Even if she was trying to trap me, it was my baby in her." He releases my hand and uses his to scrub his face.

I stay quiet, waiting to hear what happens next. Being as I've never heard of him having a kid, I have a sinking feeling his story doesn't have a happy ending.

"I left for my game without talking to her. I assumed she would be there when I got back. Only when I returned, she was gone."

I hear myself gasp.

"She dropped out of school and went to live with her aunt in Tennessee...after she had an abortion."

Tears of regret and devastation prick Killian's eyes, and before I can think about what I'm doing, I climb onto his lap, my legs straddling his muscular thighs, and give him a hug.

I wrap my arms around his neck and hold him tight. His shoulders shake up and down as he cries for the baby that was never born, the baby he blames himself for losing.

With his head buried in my chest, neither of us say a word. There's nothing I can say that will make this go away. His baby is gone, and he blames himself. He's spent the last ten years punishing himself over it.

When his body stops shaking, he looks up at me. His beautiful hazel eyes fall to my mouth and then he kisses me. Light, feather touches. His lips are strong yet gentle. The kiss is soft and has me melting around him like a pile of goo. It's been so long since I've been kissed like this. Like I'm something more than a whore who is getting paid to pleasure a man.

When he pulls back, he sees the tears brimming my lids, and he cocks his head to the side in a silent question. I'm not sure if it's that I need him to know it's not him but me, or if maybe I feel like after he's told me his deepest, darkest secret, I want him to know one of mine, but without a second thought, I tell him another one of my truths.

"It's been over seven years since I've been kissed like that," I admit. "I was eighteen years old. Christian kissed me goodbye as I boarded the plane to Paris."

"I thought you two got back together when you came back to the states with Olivia?" he questions.

"We did, but he had changed. The stardom had gotten to him. He was high or drunk all the time. We hooked up a couple times, but it wasn't good. Then I caught him cheating on me. Shortly after, I took the job at A Touch of Class."

"None of the guys you were with kissed you?"

I can tell from the sound of his voice that he isn't judging me but simply trying to understand. I go to climb off him, but his hands grip my hips, and he holds me in place.

"My job is to make it about them. Sometimes we kiss, but it isn't pure or sweet. It's filled with an agenda, a gateway to sex." Then I tell him something I haven't told anyone. "I've had sex with dozens of guys these last few months, but I've never once orgasmed."

"You've never orgasmed?" he asks incredulously.

"Of course, I have, but not by the men I've been with. It was always about them. I faked it every time just to quickly end it."

I cover my face with my hands in embarrassment, but Killian isn't having it because he moves them away. Then, holding onto me, he drags us up the bed.

He lays me down next to him and pulls me into his side. I lay my head down on his chest and wrap my arm around his front. He runs his fingers through my hair a few times before they move down to my back. My eyes close as I get lost in the feeling of his touch. I didn't realize how much I needed this, craved this. To be held and comforted.

And before I can second guess myself, I whisper one last truth. "It's not really the orgasms that are important," I admit. "It's the connection. I just want to feel connected to someone. I'm tired of feeling so alone."

Chapter Fourteen

KILLIAN

LAST NIGHT WITH GISELLE DIDN'T EXACTLY GO as planned—or maybe it did. I'm not sure what was going through my head when I brought her back to my place.

Maybe in the back of my mind I thought I would call her out on her shit, and she would open up to me about her money troubles.

I'm not sure what I was expecting to happen from there, but never did I imagine that with her legs wrapped around my waist, while hugging me, I would confide in her my deepest secret.

I never could've predicted she would hug and comfort me while I lost my shit and released all of the built-up guilt I've been holding onto for the last decade.

And then, in return, when Giselle admitted she hasn't been pleasured by a man in years, my first thought was to pull my boxers down her creamy thighs and eat her cunt until she was screaming my name while she orgasmed all over my tongue.

The only thing that stopped me was the fact that I knew it wasn't the right time. We were both too raw and emotional. When I pleasure her, I want it to be when she's of her right mind and not feeling exposed and vulnerable.

"I just want to feel connected to someone. I'm tired of feeling so alone."

While Giselle and I are different in many ways, we're actually similar in other ways. I understand exactly where Giselle is coming from. While I've spent years keeping women at arm's length, I have longed to have a deeper connection with someone.

I was so stuck in my way of not having casual sex until I was in a serious relationship, I never even unlocked the door to let a woman try to step through. I was afraid of their ill intentions, their hidden motives. Opening up to Giselle last night felt completely foreign, but at the same time it felt like it connected us.

Gently moving her body off mine, I get out of bed and go to the kitchen to start the coffee. While it's brewing, I hear the sound of feet padding across my wood floor.

Giselle appears in the doorway, still wearing my shirt and boxers. Her hair is messy from sleep, her face free of all makeup, and she looks gorgeous as hell.

She grants me a shy, nervous smile.

I know she wasn't drunk last night, but my guess is she's wondering if I regret everything we talked about. Needing her to know I don't regret anything, I grin back.

Her smile widens and then she throws her head back with a laugh, and fuck if it isn't the most beautiful sound I've ever heard.

"What?" I question.

"*We're all mad here. I'm mad. You're mad,*" she says through a fit of giggles, and the melodic sound has me grinning hard.

"An *Alice in Wonderland* quote?" I ask, even though I already know it is. After she told me to read the book, I googled '*Alice in Wonderland* quotes,' and came across several. Who knew the author of children's books could be so poetic?

"Yeah." She nods with a smile.

I pull a mug down from the cabinet and hand it to her. She goes to take it, but I don't let go. Instead, I use her grip on it to pull her closer to me.

Her body presses against mine, and I tilt my chin down to kiss her. Only she turns her head to the side at the last second and my lips land on her cheek.

Without letting go of her, I whisper, "I'm afraid we are mad. But I'll tell you a secret. All of the best people are." I have no idea if the quote is from the book or the movie. It's one of the ones I found when I googled, but I'm sure she'll tell me.

Giselle backs up and, shaking her head with a large grin splayed upon her face, says, "That's from the movie, and I'm pretty sure, you didn't even say it right. Read. The. Book."

Then, plucking the mug out of my hand, she goes about making her coffee.

I study her as she flits around my kitchen like she belongs here. She grabs the milk and sugar from the fridge and adds them both to her coffee.

Then she turns around and leans against the counter, her foot popping up against the cabinet, exposing her sexy thigh. She lifts the hot coffee to her lips and blows on it. Then her eyes come up slowly, peering up at me through her thick lashes.

"Thank you for last night," she says softly. "It felt really good to be able to talk to someone about everything without being judged."

I cut across the kitchen and encroach on her space. Then, taking the mug out of her hands, I set it on the counter.

She gives me a confused look, until my hands come down on either side of her, caging her in. With our faces only inches apart from each other, her look of confusion turns to nervousness.

"Why did you stop me from kissing you?" I murmur.

Giselle's lids flutter closed. She takes a deep breath, and when she reopens her eyes it's as if she's found her confidence. Her face takes on a look of determination.

"Kill...you're a pro ball player who uses escorts, so you don't have to have sex. I'm an escort who fucks guys for money, and I don't date athletes. Last night was exactly what

I needed. Someone to talk to. And I'd like to think it was what you needed as well. Someone to share what you went through all those years ago with. If you want to be friends, I can definitely use one. But that's all I can be. Your friend."

I stare at her for a minute, deciding where to begin first, because there's so much wrong with everything she just said. Finally, I start with her issue with athletes.

"Christian is a musician," I point out. "You mentioned you don't date athletes back in the Hamptons. Did one break your heart?"

Giselle shakes her head, then lifts my arm up and ducks underneath. She grabs her coffee off the counter and sashays across the kitchen. "No, I don't date musicians, athletes, pilots, traveling salesmen, doctors without borders...anyone who travels for their job." She shrugs and takes a sip of her coffee before she continues. "I'm not about to be cheated on again, and it's been proven more times than not, guys who travel, cheat. My dad traveled with his job, and he cheated on my mom. Christian cheated on me while on the road."

"Nick is an athlete, and he would never cheat on Olivia," I state matter-of-factly.

"Look, it doesn't matter. That's just one part of it. Did you not hear the part about me being an escort?"

"Yeah, I heard," I tell her. "But that's going to change. Even if you want to just be friends." I want to add *for now,* but I don't.

I'll take it slow with Giselle, but I'm not going to settle on just being friends with her. For the first time in years, I want to see where things can go with a woman, and I'm not about to let her stubbornness get in my way.

And yes, I'm fully aware just how much of a hypocrite I sound like, when just a few short weeks ago I was accusing her of living off Olivia. But that was before I took the time to find out the entire story. And now that I know, I'm going to make it up to Giselle. I'm not going to let her sell her body to take care of her family.

"That's not your decision to make." She takes another sip of her coffee. "I need to get going. I took the day off to meet with my mom's doctors." She pours the remaining coffee into the sink and rinses out the mug. Then she heads back into my bedroom.

Following her, I say, "This conversation isn't over."

She lifts her arms up in a *whatever you say* gesture.

I shower while she gets dressed and then we head down to the garage so I can take her home to get dressed. When I press the button on one of my fobs, the lights to my special edition Bugatti flicker on. It's a beautiful shiny black with accented green tones to match the Brewer's team colors.

"This is what we're taking?" Giselle laughs. "Aren't you afraid your precious car might get nicked?"

"I figured you needed to experience Betty yourself. You know, she was deeply offended when you called her ugly and stupid." I pout playfully, and Giselle doubles over in a fit of laughter.

"You named your car Betty? How cliché!" She laughs harder.

"Now you're dissing her name?" I tsk. "Get in. Once you get to know her, you'll regret the name-calling and apologize." I open the door for her to get in.

"Are we seriously taking this car? We're in New York! It's kind of a waste. Isn't it known for doing like zero-to-one hundred in thirty seconds? The only thing you'll be doing on the streets of New York is wearing out the brakes."

"Actually, it's zero-to-two hundred and forty-eight in forty-three seconds." I grin, and she rolls her eyes, completely unimpressed. "Now get in, so I can prove to you she's not only beautiful, but also smart."

Giselle shakes her head as she gets in. "She's not a person, you know."

"Shh, stop putting her down."

The truth is, I have only driven my special edition once, and she's right, driving this car in the city is a waste of its potential, but I can't *not* drive the cars I love simply because of where I live. Now that would be a waste.

Plus, fucking with her over her hatred of this car will be fun.

Once she's buckled in, I close the door and go around to my side to get in. It smells of new leather, and I can't help but inhale the scent, which has Giselle giggling.

"Feel the leather...the smoothness," I say as I run my fingers over the dashboard.

She snorts out a laugh, thinking I'm joking.

"Seriously," I say, "feel it." I take her hand in mine and run it across the material. She oohs and ahhs dramatically.

"Oh, yes, Killian, that leather feels so good!" She moans playfully.

I know she's only joking, but the sound she makes has me imagining what she'll sound like when a man finally makes her come. And holy fuck, do I want to be that man.

I let go of her hand and press the power button, and a moment later, it rumbles to life.

I smile over at her, and she groans. "I get it...It's powerful," she says dryly.

"Damn right it is."

As I back out, Giselle looks around, then asks, "Where's the radio?"

"There isn't one."

"Okay, stop," she demands, and I press the brakes. "I love Betty. She's sexy and beautiful and so very smart, but c'mon, Kill. We need a radio." She pouts. "We have like an hour drive to Serenity."

"Not in this car we don't. I'll get us there in fifteen minutes. And Betty doesn't need your fake praises. Soon enough, you'll be singing them for real."

She laughs. "Ugh! Fine!"

I grin wide and pull my phone out. It's already programmed for Bluetooth, so all I have to do is press play and the music surrounds us. "No radio, but there is music." I give her a playful wink.

Once we get to her place, she argues she can take the subway, but I'm not having it.

Thankfully, she picks her battles and lets me win this one.

Once she's showered and dressed in a new outfit, she gets back in the car, and we begin our trip to Rye.

We stop on the way to grab a couple croissants and Giselle gets another coffee. She groans when everyone stares at the car, but when a few guys ask if they can get a picture with it and me, she offers to take the pictures for them.

She fidgets as we drive through the city, messing with the music on my phone, but not saying a word.

She's obviously nervous about meeting with her mom's doctors. I want to discuss her finding another option aside from working at A Touch of Class, but now isn't the time. Instead, I go for a distraction.

When we hit the interstate, I make it a point to speed up. Giselle's back hits the seat as the car surges forward. She leans over to check the speed, and when she sees it's already at one hundred miles per hour, she gasps.

"Holy shit! It's like we're flying." She laughs as she turns the music up louder and raises her hands in the air. Her head goes back as she belts out the lyrics.

Not wanting to put her in danger—or get pulled over—when the car reaches one-twenty, I let my foot off the gas. It slowly descends until we're back to the speed limit.

She continues to play the music loud, singing along to each of the songs. Her voice is horrible, and she sings completely off tune, yet I find myself wanting to take a detour, so she'll keep singing for several more hours. I like this version of the woman next to me. The playful, outgoing, doesn't-have-a-care-in-the-world Giselle is how she should always be.

"So?" I prompt as we pull up. "Is she still ugly and stupid?"

"No! I love her! She's so fast and smooth. When I win the lottery one day, I'm going to get me one." She grins playfully.

"See! I told you she would grow on you."

"Yeah, yeah." She laughs. "You win."

I hand my keys to the valet and then walk around to open the door for Giselle. She tells me I don't have to join her, but when I give her a look that tells her to quit it, she simply nods.

After signing in, we're brought back to meet with her mom's doctors: Dr. Burns, who focuses on her mother's mental health, and Dr. Clay, who focuses on her physical health.

"After evaluating your mother for the last five days, my advisement is to admit her long term," Dr. Burns begins. "We've looked at her previous diagnoses, and while I've seen signs of depression, my thoughts are that there is more to it than that.

"Unfortunately, when it comes to diagnosing a patient, especially when dealing with medication, it's all trial and error. The brain doesn't send off a sure sign indicating the issue. It's not like cancer, for example. We can't do an MRI and have it find the mass."

Giselle listens intently, nodding as he speaks.

"If the patient isn't suicidal, we can have her see us as an outpatient."

"But my mom has tried to kill herself several times," Giselle says, finishing his sentence.

"Exactly. When we're working with someone as an outpatient, she would come in several times a week to determine what's working and what's not. Sometimes it's as little as finding the right medication and dose, while other times it's figuring out the diagnosis to begin treatment.

"In your mother's situation, it's best to have her under twenty-four-hour supervision. We have a team of highly-trained medical staff who can monitor her closely. That way if a medication isn't working, we will know right away. We can lower and raise the dosage and she'll be safe." Dr. Burns stops speaking and nods to Dr. Clay.

"Your mother has been evaluated completely, including extensive bloodwork, and physically, she's healthy. That leads us to believe what's wrong with her is a chemical imbalance of some sort.

"If you decide to keep her here, she will receive additional bloodwork to continue to rule out any physical issues. With any medication, there's a risk to the body. We will monitor her closely."

"Do you have any questions?" Dr. Burns asks.

Giselle looks over at me and gives me a small smile. "Would you mind if I speak to the doctors alone for a moment?"

Not wanting to argue, I nod once and stand. "I'll be outside if you need me."

"Thank you."

I walk outside the door, but when I see the receptionist isn't at her desk, I close the door and place my ear up to it. Her voice is soft, and I can barely hear what she's saying, but then one of the doctors speak and his baritone voice is loud enough that I can hear what he's saying.

"She could see a therapist, but as I said, I don't recommend it. She's clearly suicidal, and if left alone, we can't be sure she won't attempt it again, especially if she's on the wrong meds. If it's about money, we offer a private medically-needy loan. You can apply, and if you're approved, they will set up a payment plan."

The doctor stops talking, and Giselle starts. I can't hear what she's saying, but I don't need to. I've heard enough, and I know what I need to do.

GISELLE LOOKS AROUND, AND REALIZING WE aren't headed toward Brooklyn Heights, asks, "Where are we going?"

She's been quiet the entire drive back, and if it wasn't for her sniffling quietly every once in a while, I would've assumed she was sleeping.

When she walked outside an hour later from her meeting, I was sitting on the bench waiting for her. Under her eyes were puffy and her cheeks were stained pink. It was obvious she'd been crying. She told me they allowed her to visit her mom for a little while, which explained the tears. She mentioned her mom has forty-eight hours left in there and then she's going to have to make a decision.

"To get a late lunch," I tell her, answering her question. Then, before she can argue, I add, "And you already told me you took the day off, so I know you don't have to work." I shoot her a knowing smirk and she rolls her eyes.

I park my car in the garage, then get out and open Giselle's door for her.

"I thought you said we're going to lunch?" she asks.

"I said we're getting lunch, and we are. I'm going to have them deliver whatever we want to my place."

We take the elevator up, and once we're inside, I ask Giselle what she's in the mood for. She says she would love some soup and a sandwich, so I pull up the delivery app and order from the deli down the street.

Once I've placed our order, I have her join me on the couch. Figuring she's had enough of talking for one day, I turn on the TV and click on Netflix.

"What do you want to watch?" I ask.

She eyes me curiously. "I don't know. I can't even remember the last time I watched TV. I've been wanting to watch Sons of Anarchy for a while." She shrugs. "I've been on a huge MC romance kick lately. It drives Olivia nuts." She laughs.

"MC romance?" I question.

"Motorcycle club romance. The hero is a member of a club. Olivia prefers sports romance, but I love to read about a sexy tatted up biker."

"I'm tatted up," I say with a smirk.

169

"True, but do you ride a motorcycle?" She grins, and for a split second I consider buying one just so I can know how it feels to have her thighs wrapped around me from behind.

"Whatever. So, SOA?" I confirm.

"Sure!"

I've seen the entire series, but I don't tell her that. When you travel a lot for work and spend a good amount of time in hotels, Netflix becomes your good friend.

I click to start the first episode, and a few minutes into it, Giselle's head is on my shoulder as she snores softly.

Not wanting the food delivery to wake her up, I gently pick her up and bring her into my room. She must be absolutely exhausted because she doesn't even stir as I set her on the bed and pull the covers out from under her.

Once she's covered with my blankets, I quickly change into a pair of basketball shorts and a T-shirt to get more comfortable.

Closing the door behind me, I head back out to the living room and pause the show. When the buzzer goes off indicating the food is here, I open the door, so he doesn't have to knock. I thank him and place the food into the fridge for later. Then I spend the next few hours playing Madden on the PlayStation while I wait for Giselle to wake up.

I hear her cell phone go off a few times, so I dig through her purse and make sure it isn't her mom or sister. When I see it's neither one, I switch it to silent and put it back in her purse.

A couple minutes later, Nick calls me.

"What's up?"

"Did everything with Giselle go okay last night?" he asks without even saying hello.

"Well, hello to you too. It did. How's Olivia?" I ask, changing the subject.

"I think she's hiding something from me. She woke up this morning and ran out the door with Celeste to go shopping."

I laugh. "Olivia hates shopping."

"Exactly. We were invited to go to some grand opening of a new restaurant, and she used the excuse that she needs to buy a new dress. Anyway, I have Reed with me for the day. Want to join us at the park?"

My bedroom door creaks open and out walks Giselle. She's still wearing her outfit from earlier: silky black shorts that are the perfect mix of professional and sexy, and a midnight blue top that dips just low enough to show off the perfect swells of her breasts. Her lids are still hooded from sleeping, but she looks refreshed. A nap seems to have done the trick.

She comes over and sits down next to me. Her brows furrow slightly and her fleshy lips pucker. That's when I remember I'm on the phone with Nick.

"Let me call you back in a few minutes." I hang up without waiting for him to answer and throw my phone to the side. My only thoughts are that I need to kiss this woman again.

I lift Giselle onto my lap, and without giving her a chance to deny me, I grip the back of her head, her hair tangling in my fingers, as I pull her in for a kiss.

At first, she doesn't kiss me back, but when my tongue darts out, she shocks the shit out of me when she parts her soft lips and gives me access.

We kiss for several minutes. I forgot what it's like to taste a woman. I focus on the way her lips brush softly against mine, and the way her tongue duels with my own. Kissing this woman could easily become an addiction.

Giselle's silky shorts are thin, and the more heated our kiss gets, the more I feel her hot cunt grind against my pelvis. Her fingers pull at the little bit of hair I have, and it spurs me on to take more from her.

With one hand grabbing her ass, I use my other one to push aside her shorts and panties. They move easily, and I hesitate for a second, wondering if Giselle is going to stop me.

When she doesn't, I push a single digit into her. And holy fuck, the woman is soaking wet. I can't help the groan that escapes me as her wet heat surrounds my finger. It's been too damn long since I felt the inside of a woman.

I say a quick prayer to the man above that I don't make a fool out of myself. Then I stifle a laugh because let's be real here, God has more important prayers to answer than the one from a thirty-one-year-old man who's praying to remember how to give a woman an orgasm. The same man who might as well be a damn born-again virgin with no recent sexual experience.

Giselle moans into my mouth as she grinds down on my finger, trying to make herself come. I can't have that, though.

When she comes, it will be because of me—not of her own doing.

Adding another finger to the mix, I fingerfuck her as deep as I can go while we continue to kiss. My thumb finds her clit and I massage it in slow circles, applying just enough pressure to make her squirm in pleasure.

Giselle's breathing turns labored, her cunt grinding down on my hand as my thumb finds a good rhythm. And then she's coming all over my fingers. Her thighs shake as her orgasm overtakes her, and her juices drip down and soak my shorts.

She ends our kiss, and I take a second to look at her. Her lips are puffy and pink from my beard. Her face is flushed, and her lids are half-closed. I can't help the grin that spreads across my face. It's been quite a few years since I've made a woman come, and Giselle looks like she's high from the orgasm I gave her.

She stares at me for a long moment, and when she doesn't say anything, I have to ask, "What are you thinking?"

She gives me a shy smile. "I'm thinking that felt amazing." She backs up slightly and her hand grips my hard cock. My eyes drop down to see the wet spot she left behind. "And I'm also thinking it's only fair I return the favor."

The last thing I want is for her to think she has to reciprocate out of obligation.

"You don't owe me anything." I lift her off me and set her on the couch. "I need to go change."

When she frowns at my words, I add, "Nick is taking Reed to the park. Why don't we take our sandwiches to the park to join them?"

I don't want her to think I don't want her. I do. So fucking much. But only when she's sure I'm the guy she wants to get serious with, and not because she thinks I expect a tit for tat.

She gives me a confused look, but I ignore it as I stand and head into my room so I can change. When I come back out, she's put together—she must've used my guest bathroom—and checking her cell phone.

"You ready?" I ask.

"I actually need to get going," she says as she pulls her purse over her shoulder. "Thank you for taking me to see my mom today."

"Giselle, wait." I move in front of her so she can't run. "What happened a few minutes ago..." My eyes dart over to the couch.

"Was a mistake," she says, finishing my sentence for me.

She pushes against my chest to move me out of her way and saunters out of my apartment, closing the door behind her before I can even argue.

It takes me a few seconds to think about what just happened, but once I do, I run out my door and down the hallway to chase after her. Only, when I get to the elevator, she's already gone. I consider texting or calling her but decide it's best if I give her some space.

Chapter Fifteen

GISELLE

"You seem like you're somewhere else," Andrew, my date for the evening, points out.

We're finishing our dessert at a new French restaurant in the Upper East Side. The grand opening is tonight, and Andrew requested me to escort him to the event. It wasn't until right before he picked me up, I had a chance to read through the specifics and saw the line I was hoping wouldn't be there: nightcap.

"I'm okay," I tell him and then take another bite of my Gateau au Chocolat. I imagine it tastes delicious, but right now everything I put into my mouth tastes like cardboard.

The waiter comes over and asks if we would like anything else. Wanting to prolong the inevitable, I order a latte to go with my dessert. I feel Andrew's eyes on me, but I don't look at him. Instead, I focus on my dessert like it's the answer to all of life's biggest mysteries.

"Giselle?" I hear my name being called and my head shoots up. I would recognize that voice anywhere.

"Hey, I didn't know you would be here." Olivia's eyes dart back and forth between Andrew and me.

Nick doesn't say a word, but his glare is enough to tell me he either knows about me escorting or he knows about Killian and me. And I know Killian wouldn't share my secret, which means Killian told him something happened between us.

"I'm Andrew Parker, Giselle's date." Andrew stands and extends his hand to shake Olivia's and then Nick's. "I would invite you to join us, but we're actually just finishing up. The food is delicious."

"I'm Olivia, Giselle's best friend and roommate, and this is my fiancé, Nick. It's nice to meet you." I can tell she wants to say more, ask how long we've been dating, but before she can, the waiter comes over and hands me my latte then hands Andrew the check.

No longer wanting to be here, I ask the waiter if I can get the coffee to go. I feel three sets of eyes on me, so I excuse myself to the restroom. "I'll meet you out front," I say to Andrew, then give Olivia a quick hug. "I'll see you later," I whisper before I scurry away from the table and down the hall, closing and locking the door to the women's restroom.

After going pee and washing my hands, I unlock the door and exit, scouring the room to make sure I won't run into Olivia and Nick again on my way to the front door.

When I see the coast is clear, I hurry through the restaurant and out the door. I feel my phone vibrating in my purse, but I ignore it until I get inside the limo with Andrew.

Then I quickly check to make sure it's not my mom's doctors or my sister. When I see it's Olivia, I put the phone away. The ride to Andrew's place is quiet. Had we really been on a date, I'm sure he would have several questions for me, but we're not. I'm getting paid to go out with him. One of the main reasons men hire escorts is to keep things uncomplicated. That's why Killian hires them...

The thought of Killian has my stomach churning. Yesterday was a beyond shitty day. Finding out it's going to cost thousands of dollars to help my mom get better almost drove me into my own depression.

The entire drive home my brain wouldn't stop trying to figure out how to handle everything. But when we got back to Killian's place and he helped me focus on something else by watching television with me, I was able to breathe again.

And then when I fell asleep and woke up in his bed, my heart felt so full. I can't remember the last time someone took care of me the way he did. When he kissed me, everything around us faded, and for those few minutes while we made out and Killian pleasured me, I was able to just forget all of my problems and focus solely on him.

But all too soon, it ended. Because when I checked my phone and saw my schedule for tonight from Bianca, reality hit me directly in the face. I'm an escort, and right now more than ever I need the money my job brings in.

We arrive at Andrew's penthouse, and once we're inside, he doesn't waste any time. He pushes me up against the wall of the living room and his mouth goes straight to my neck. He sucks roughly on my skin, and I find myself pushing him away.

When he gives me a quizzical look, I say, "Please don't leave any marks." He nods once then focuses on unbuckling his belt. He undoes his pants and pushes them down to his ankles along with his briefs.

He doesn't even notice I'm standing here, immobile. I watch as he grips his cock and my heart speeds up. I can't do this. I can't have sex with him. My stomach tightens and I push him out of the way. I don't know where the bathroom is, so I run to the closest sink I can find—the one in the kitchen—and throw up my entire dinner and dessert.

"Jesus!" Andrew says with a tone of disgust. I glance up and his pants are back around his waist. "You okay?" he asks, but the look on his face tells me he's not really asking because he cares, but instead because he's not sure what else to do.

"No, maybe it was something I ate." I feel like the worst person for blaming it on the food when there was absolutely nothing wrong with it. I rinse out my mouth and wash my hands.

"I'm sorry. I think it's best if I go. If you call Bianca, she will give you a credit." I glance over at the microwave clock. "It's still early. I can see if she has someone else available. I'll let her know it's my fault."

Andrew waves me off. "It's fine. I'll have my driver bring you home."

When I get home, Corrine and Olivia's dad, Stephen, are watching TV. They must be babysitting Reed. Olivia mentioned he doesn't want to sleep anywhere but here.

"Hey honey." Corrine stands and gives me a hug. "How are you?"

"I'm good. If you guys want to head home, I can keep an eye on Reed. I'm home for the night."

"Sounds good. Thank you," Stephen says.

They both say goodbye, and once they're gone, I grab a quick shower to rinse off. When I get out, I check my cell phone to find a text from Killian.

KILLIAN

I'm taking you to see your mom tomorrow. Be ready at nine.

Olivia and Nick must not have had a chance to tell him they saw me on a date. Feeling guilty, I text him back.

ME

That's okay. I need to handle this on my own, but thank you.

When he doesn't respond, I put my phone to charge and head out to the living room. Any time I watch Reed, I have a tough time going to sleep. I know parents have to sleep when they have kids, but I feel like I need to be awake until his own parents are back with him.

I flip through Netflix and stop on Sons of Anarchy. I consider watching the rest of the episode I fell asleep during, but for some reason it feels wrong, like Killian should be here with me to watch it. *Well, in that case, I'm never going to finish the series...*

Needing a distraction, I grab my laptop and work on a couple proposals I'm presenting to potential clients this week. One is for an office being completely remodeled, and the other is for a couple who are moving in together and want to merge their homes into one.

I smile, remembering how cute they were when they explained they wanted to make sure their home felt like it was theirs instead of his or hers.

When an email pings through, I click on it and see it's the medical loan company I applied to yesterday. I was told I would know within twenty-four hours if I've been approved for the loan. I scroll through the email until I find their answer: Denied

Unsure of where to go from here, I set my laptop down and allow myself to cry. Of course, as I'm bawling my eyes out, Nick and Olivia walk through the door...and behind them is Killian.

"Giselle!" Olivia drops her purse and runs across the room to me. She throws her arms around me and hugs me tight. "What's wrong? Did your date end badly?"

My gaze flicks to Killian, who's standing next to Nick. His jaw is tight, and his eyes are shooting daggers straight at me.

"No," I tell her. "My mom...umm..." I don't usually talk about my money troubles with Olivia because I hate for her to feel bad and offer me money. "She needs long term treatment."

"Oh, sweetie. I'm so sorry. But that's good, right? They will help her get better."

"Yes," I agree. "But I was denied the loan." Liquid drops of defeat fall down my face as I come to terms with what I knew the other day when the doctors told me the cost of the facility. I can't afford it. And I couldn't possibly borrow that kind of money from Olivia. It's more than I make in a year. Hell, it's more than I make in two.

"Giselle..." Olivia's hands come up to my shoulders as she looks me in the eye.

"Please don't say it," I plead.

She sighs in frustration but nods.

"Can we talk?" Killian cuts in.

His words are formed as a question, but we both know he's not really giving me a choice.

"Sure," I say as I stand.

He heads down the hall toward my room, but before I follow him back, I stop and give Olivia a hug. "I love you. Thank you for not offering."

She gives me a sad smile of understanding.

When I get to my room, Killian is standing with his back to me. He turns around with my phone in his hand.

"I wasn't snooping," he says. "It went off a few times and I glanced at it to make sure it wasn't an emergency."

He hands me the phone, and I read the messages he saw. They're all from Bianca, and she's pissed.

BIANCA

This is the second date you've messed up! I'm taking it out of your pay.

> You're going out with Andrew again tomorrow night. You WILL make it up to him.

> I'll email you the information. A simple OK to confirm you've received my messages will suffice.

"So, let me get this straight. Not even twenty-four hours after I get you off, you're out with another man."

"I wasn't *out* with another man," I say. "I was working."

I set my phone down and look at Killian. The hurt in his eyes is exactly why I told him I could only be friends with him.

This is my fault. I shouldn't have let him kiss me. I should've stopped things when they got too heated. But it felt so good to be with a man who wasn't paying me to make it about him. Oh, no. Killian made sure it was all about me. Pleasuring me like it was his job.

And if I'm honest, it wasn't just the physical part I craved. Killian has done a complete one-eighty.

If he wasn't an athlete, and I wasn't an escort, I could see myself wanting more with him. Wanting to explore what could be between us.

Killian steps forward and takes my chin between his fingers. He lifts my face so I'm looking at him. And as if he can read my thoughts, he says, "I know you warned me we could only be friends, but I thought what happened between us yesterday changed things. Since I was in college and made my decision not to have casual sex, I haven't wanted to try again with someone until now. I assumed you felt the same way. That maybe you wanted to try too."

An involuntary whimper escapes my lips. I open my mouth to speak but the lump in my throat prevents the words from coming out. I swallow thickly and attempt to blink back the tears threatening to spill over.

"I'm sorry," I choke out. "In another life, if I wasn't...my mom..." I can't even form a damn sentence. I shake my head and the salty drops of devastation fall.

"It's okay," Killian says softly.

Then he leans over and gives me a kiss on my forehead. His lips linger on my flesh as the tears continue to roll down my cheeks. And then he releases me and walks out my door.

Chapter Sixteen

GISELLE

"KILLIAN! OPEN THE DOOR!"

I bang on his door with my fist. I was shocked when the security guard allowed me to go straight up, telling me I have permanent access. After I'm done with him, I can guarantee he won't be allowing me access.

My mind goes back to this morning at Serenity, where I learned someone paid for my mom's treatment.

"Everything is completely covered for the next sixty days while your mother undergoes treatment at this facility. Should any other charges occur, we have the credit card on file."

After my jaw dropped in shock, I picked it back up and demanded to know how it was all paid for and whose credit card was on file. Because it sure as hell wasn't mine. And I'd be damned if Olivia went behind my back and paid for my mom's medical expenses.

The woman in charge of the accounting department confirmed it was Killian. And are you ready for this? When I asked for him to be removed and to refund him his money, they told me it wasn't my decision! Because my mother approved it!

Needing answers, I asked to see my mom. I was then informed she isn't accepting visitors at this time, but she wrote me a letter.

The nurse gave me said letter and told me once my mom is up for visitors, she'll contact me.

I made the mistake of reading the letter on the subway while on my way home.

Giselle, my beautiful daughter,

I am sorry for everything I have put you and your sister through. I'm not sure how I will be feeling tomorrow or a week from now, but right now I am in a good place.

I had the pleasure of meeting your friend Killian, and he made me aware of your struggles. I've put so much weight on your shoulders, even from a young age. You are strong and independent, and I know you would go through hell to help me get better.

But he's offered to help, and I've accepted. He's assured me that when I'm better and have my life together, he'll accept my payments to him.

When the house sells, please use the money to get yourself a place. It's your time to shine. Focus on your future while I focus on mine.

My hope is when I get out of here, I will be healed. Maybe I'll even go back to teaching.

Please don't be upset that I'm not accepting visitors at this time. I just can't stand the thought of you worrying or seeing me during my bad days.

The next time I see you I want it to be on a good note. I love you. It's because of you I'm still alive and have this chance to get better. I'll be in touch soon. Please give Adrianna a hug and kiss from me. I love you both very much.

All my love,

Mom

So, here I am on Killian's doorstep. What am I hoping to accomplish? I'm not sure. But since I can't speak to my mom, he's next in line.

I can't decide if I'm grateful or pissed off for what he did. Right now, it's a combination of both.

I know my mom said she made the decision to allow him to help, but he knew what he was doing when he spoke to her! And God help him if he told her I'm a goddamn escort! He's going to pay for this. For taking the choice out of my hands.

And then an idea hits me.

Just as I'm about to give up on Killian answering the door, it swings open. And standing on the other side is the man I'm looking for...in nothing but a towel slung low around his waist. His hair is dripping wet, and for a moment, I'm frozen in place as I watch the tiny droplets of water run down his tattooed chest and over his delicious six pack of abs.

He clears his throat, and I force myself to look up. When my eyes meet his, he's smirking like a cocky fucking bastard. He knows exactly what he's doing. Well, two can play this game.

"Everything okay?" Killian asks in a concerned tone. "I was in the shower."

Wordlessly, I stroll past him and into his condo. I hear the door close behind him, and when I turn around, he's standing less than a foot away from me with his arms crossed over his chest.

I refuse to stare at his body, not wanting to get sidetracked. He might've started this damn game by going to my mom, but I'm going to win. I'm the ice queen when it comes to freezing out my emotions.

I've slept with numerous men in the last several months and not once felt a single thing toward any of them.

Not a single emotion.

Not a single orgasm.

Not a single ounce of pleasure.

Nothing.

And I can do it right now. Killian wants to treat me like a whore then I'll give him what he wants.

Stepping closer to him, I make sure my game face is on. The one that has men who are higher up than him falling to their knees and begging for me to pleasure them.

His emotions are written all over his face: nervous, wary, cautious. He's unsure of how I'm going to handle what he's done. And he should be all of those things because I'm not about to play fair.

"Everything okay?" he repeats.

My hand comes up to his neck and I pull his head down slightly until his mouth is only a breath away from mine. "Everything is perfect," I whisper against his lips before I kiss him softly.

He sighs, letting his guard down because he thinks he's won this game. Only he has no idea that he was never even a worthy opponent. He never stood a chance against me.

You don't date several multi-millionaires and billionaires for months at a time and not learn a thing or two about how to play the game.

Rule number one: make him believe you've thrown in the white flag.

I deepen our kiss for several seconds before I move my lips over to his cheek and across his jawline. I place kiss after kiss across his flesh, working my way down his neck.

When he lets out a low groan, I know I have him exactly where I want him. He thinks I'm thanking him for what he's done for me—for my mom. That I'm going to let go of the fact that he went behind my back. He spent thousands of dollars I didn't ask him to spend.

He thinks I'm going to forget he took my choices away. That I'll just accept I now owe him. Well, he better think again.

Rule number two: when he thinks he's won and his guard is down, get him off balance and bring him to his knees.

With my hand gripping his neck, I use my other hand to release the towel covering his bottom half. I feel his hard length bob up and hit the front of my thigh, and I wrap my fingers around his shaft, stroking him root to tip, making him even harder.

He lets out a growl of pleasure, and I grin on the inside that I'm about to bring Killian Blake straight to the ground.

Bending at my knees, I continue to stroke his cock as I guide him toward my mouth. I know from experience, the second my lips are wrapped around his shaft it'll be game over.

He said it's been years since he's been with a woman, yet it's only taken me less than a week for him to break every rule he's ever made.

Time to earn the money he gave my mom.

I guide his dick over to my mouth, wrap my lips around the head, and slowly take him all the way in. His shaft thickens as I wet his velvety flesh with my saliva.

Using my hand to pump the part of his cock my mouth can't reach, I simultaneously suck and stroke him. I can taste the saltiness of his precum.

Knowing he's close, I take his delicate balls into my hand and massage them gently.

Killian lets out a guttural groan, telling me he's close. But then his hand grabs mine—the one stroking his cock.

"Wait," he says breathlessly, his grip tight enough that it stops everything I'm doing.

My eyes glance up at him, his dick still in my mouth, and his face is contorted in what looks like unbearable pain.

"I can't do this." He shakes his head and pulls me into a standing position—his cock falling out of my mouth as I rise.

"You can," I murmur. "Let me make you feel good." My hand tries to grip his dick, but he stops me.

"I can't," he repeats. "You don't understand."

He backs up and scrubs his face with his hands, trying to get himself together. Then he picks up the towel on the floor and wraps it around his waist. "When I found out Melanie had an abortion, I made a promise to myself." He gives me a pleading look to understand. He thinks he's going to hurt my feelings by rejecting me.

"The next woman I have sex with will be the woman I plan to spend my life with. I never want what happened to Melanie to happen again. If we're in it for the long haul, she'll know I'm serious and won't run off and have an abortion."

My heart drops into my stomach at what I was just trying to do—seduce a man who isn't sexually active because he lives in fear of letting down another woman.

Jesus, if I'm not a fucking bitch.

Killian moves forward and I take a step back. He has no idea what my fucked-up intentions were. He doesn't have any idea what a horrible person I am.

He's good. And I'm not. I need to walk away. Leave him alone. He deserves better than anything I'm capable of giving him. I might be broken, but Killian's not. He's just a little bent.

"Have you ever thought about seeing where Melanie is now?" I ask. Killian gives me a quizzical look, so I elaborate. "You've been punishing yourself over something that happened over ten years ago. Yes, it's true, you might not have handled it well, but you didn't demand she have an abortion. She chose to run. She chose to have an abortion."

Killian frowns but doesn't say anything, so I continue, "You both were so young. Maybe it's time you find her. See how she's doing. Has she moved on? Is she married with kids? Apologize to her and hear her out as well."

I walk past Killian to the front door. "You're a good guy, Kill. Stop punishing yourself. Get closure and then find a sweet girl to love the hell out of."

With a small smile, I open the door and walk out of his apartment. I barely make it halfway to the elevator when I hear his door open.

"Giselle, wait," he demands.

I stop in my place, but I don't turn around. I know what's coming.

"Don't leave, please. You're right. I should go see her and get closure. I'm sorry for rejecting you. I just...Well, I..." He can't seem to word what he's trying to say, and it would almost be comical if our situation wasn't so fucked up.

"Can you turn around and talk to me, please?" His voice is closer. His hand lands on my shoulder and he turns me around to face him. "Why did you come over? Did you see your mom today?"

"She wouldn't let me see her, but I know what you did," I tell him. "I came over here to seduce you. To get you to break your rules."

He cocks his head to the side. For a guy who has had his guard up for so long, you'd think he would be able to spot a manipulative woman from a mile away.

GOING DEEP

"You paid for my mom's medical expenses," I hiss. "So I came over here to pay you back."

His eyes widen in understanding. "You thought I would let you whore yourself out because I helped your mom?"

"Why not?" I throw my arms up in the air. "You gave my family thousands of dollars. It's not like I can afford to pay you back. But I am a whore, so I can at least offer you my services."

Killian flinches. "I told your mom I don't want you guys to pay me back. I did it so she would get better. So you could quit escorting. It's the reason you keep pushing me away."

When I don't say anything, he adds, "You're going to quit, right?"

"No, I'm not going to quit!" I yell in frustration.

I know it's not logical, but fuck! He took my options away. He can say I don't owe him, but I do. My mom does. He shouldn't have done what he did no matter how good his intentions were.

"Giselle," he says my name slowly, "please don't do this. I'm sorry for not talking to you first, but you wouldn't have agreed."

"Damn right, I wouldn't have. I don't want or need your help!"

I turn on my heel, but Killian's next words stop me in my place.

"If you walk away, I'm going to tell Olivia. I'm not going to let you continue to sell your body when you have people in your life who are willing to help you. Stop being stubborn and accept our help, please."

I press the button to the elevator, which thankfully opens right away. When I get inside, he's still standing in the hallway, barefoot and in only a towel. His eyes are pleading, but I ignore them, glaring at him in a way that I hope conveys he better not say a word to my best friend.

After catching a cab, I head straight home. I'm walking in the door when my email pings. It's from Bianca. I click on my schedule and almost drop my phone when I see what's written: Killian Blake...every goddamned night this week.

"That motherfucker!" I shout, slamming the door behind me.

"Who?" Olivia asks, making me jump. Lost in myself, I didn't realize she was home. And then I spot Reed sitting in his highchair, eating. And I just said the F word in front of him.

"Shit...I mean shoot! I didn't mean to curse." I walk over to Reed and give him a kiss on top of his forehead. "Hey handsome," I coo, and he grins wide.

"Who were you cursing about?" Olivia asks again.

"It doesn't even matter." I wave her off. "I was just having a bad moment."

My phone dings again and I consider throwing it off our balcony. I glance at it and see it's from Bianca confirming I received my schedule since I have a date tonight.

"I need to get going," I tell Olivia. "I just came home to change."

"Another date?" she asks.

"Yep," I say as I head down the hall to my room.

I quickly change out of my jeans and into a more professional outfit. I'm going to have to go speak to Bianca regarding Killian. There's no way I'm going to spend every damn night with the man. And to top it off, if he's on the schedule, he's paying for my services! That only means he's spending more money on me.

As I'm reapplying my deodorant, I hear a man's voice and recognize it as Nick's. I didn't realize he was here.

"There's something you need to know about Giselle," he says, and my blood rushes downward. *Motherfucker told Nick!*

I hear Olivia say okay, and then Nick says, "Killian said he paid—"

"Don't you dare finish that sentence!" I yell, cutting him off.

Just as the words come out and Nick and Olivia look at me, the front door opens and in walks Killian—without fucking knocking.

"This is none of your business," I say to Nick. I give him a hard stare then turn my glare to the man who's blowing my world apart.

"Somebody, tell me what's going on, please," Olivia demands.

"Either you tell her, or I will," Killian says in a tone that tells me he will make good on his threat.

"I hate you!" I shout at him. And that's when I realize tears are raining down my face at lightning speed.

"No, you don't," he says back, "but if you continue this, you're going to hate yourself."

"I already do," I whisper before I run out the door.

Chapter Seventeen

KILLIAN

I KNEW TELLING NICK WOULD UPSET GISELLE, but she left me no other choice. I can't just sit by while she continues to allow men to fuck her for a paycheck.

I understand why she's doing it. I really do. I once thought Giselle was dependent on Olivia. I thought she was living with her because it's rent-free and she was taking advantage of her best friend.

But I was wrong. Fuck, was I wrong.

When I went to the billing department at Serenity, where Giselle's mom, Sarah, is staying at, they told me they couldn't allow me to pay for anything without Giselle or her mom's consent.

The doctor confirmed her mom is sane enough to make decisions. She has a chemical imbalance of some sort that affects her moods—they obviously aren't sure yet what exactly, hence her being there—but she's able to make decisions for herself.

While Giselle signed for her mom to be committed, her mom actually signed for herself to be treated.

The doctor wasn't keen on me meeting with Sarah, but he gave her the choice, and thankfully she met with me.

It was during our conversation I learned just how rough it's been for their family over the years. Sarah's depression affected her job, which ultimately led to her being fired and their family being dependent on Giselle's dad's income.

It also affected her marriage as well as her relationship with her daughters. She wasn't able to be the mom they deserved, and because of her absence, Giselle stepped into the role.

Sarah also confirmed what Giselle mentioned the other night: because their father walked out on his family, Giselle is not only paying for her own student loans but is also paying for her sister's college. And that's on top of covering all of the household bills and her mother's medical expenses.

The woman is working two full-time jobs and is still struggling to make ends meet. Something has to give. I didn't tell Sarah about Giselle's "career path," but I did make it clear Giselle needs some relief, and I'm here to help. I could see it in Sarah's eyes that she didn't want to accept my help. She's been burned by a man—her own husband—someone who promised for better or worse. But she agreed because she knew it was the right thing to do for her daughter.

"Killian, what's going on?" Olivia asks.

Reed screeches to be let out of his highchair, and Nick picks him up.

"Giselle..." Fuck, now that I'm standing here, I feel like such an asshole for telling Nick Giselle's business. I just didn't know what else to do. The woman is beyond stubborn. I thought if I told Nick and he told Olivia, she could talk to Giselle. I clearly didn't think this through.

"Killian, tell me!" Olivia demands. "My best friend just ran out the door crying. Is she sick? What's going on?"

Remembering Giselle left, I say, "I'll let Nick tell you. I need to go find Giselle."

I run out the door and take the elevator down. I have no clue where Giselle even went, but I can't just sit here and do nothing.

When I exit the front entrance, I hear her voice. She's sitting on a bench against the building and talking on the phone.

"I understand I need the money, but I have the right to pick who my clients are."

She must be talking to her boss, and my guess is that it isn't the one at the design firm.

"Bianca, you don't understand..." She pauses to listen to whatever she's saying. "Okay, I understand. Goodbye."

She presses end on the phone call, shoves her phone into her back pocket, and lets her head hit the back of the wall with a loud sigh.

I want to be mad at her stubbornness, but if I'm honest, it's a damn turn on. Any other woman would've gladly taken my money. Not Giselle, though. She has a ton of baggage sitting on her shoulders and she's hell-bent on holding it all up herself.

I sit on the bench next to her, and she glances over at me. She doesn't even look mad anymore. She looks defeated.

"So, does my best friend know I'm a whore?" Her voice is too calm, too even. She's definitely reached her breaking point.

"You're not a whore. You took a job to support your family, to pay for your baby sister's school."

"Maybe so, but it doesn't change the fact that I spread my legs for money." She looks down at her gloved hands, wringing them nervously. "Did you tell my mom when you spoke to her?" she whispers.

"No."

I wouldn't do that to her. I want to help her, not humiliate her. Plus, it would only hurt her mom to know what her daughter has resorted to, in order to pick up the slack in her absence.

I only told Nick in hopes that Olivia would convince her to stop. I know Olivia wouldn't judge her. She doesn't have a judgmental bone in her body. Hell, she's even become good friends with Nick's ex-fiancée for God's sake.

She nods once. "It's not your job to take care of me and my family. That's my job, and I don't need or want your money, so you can stop wasting your money in an attempt to take care of me."

I thought it was obvious I didn't just hire her to take care of her, but I'm not going to assume anything. My assumptions are what caused me to take months to get to know the real Giselle.

"I didn't hire you to take care of you. I hired you because I enjoy spending time with you."

Her chest rises and falls with a soft laugh.

"I like you, Giselle, and I want to get to know you more. But I can't do that if you're being forced to be with other guys. You won't quit, so I fixed the problem."

"Apparently fixing problems is your thing," she says dryly.

I'm about to tell her it's just money, but I stop myself. To someone like me, who earns millions of dollars a year, it's just money, but to someone in Giselle's position, there's nothing *just* about it. It's been ten years since I was picked up by the NFL, and it's easy to forget where I came from.

Giselle wraps her coat around herself and shivers. It's February in New York, and today, while it's a bit warmer, it's still in the high thirties. "So, what are we doing tonight?" she asks. "Whatever it is, can it be indoors?"

She lifts the hood of her jacket up as small flecks of snow fall down around us, and I smile at how adorable she looks. Her cheeks and button nose are a beautiful shade of pink. She looks like one of those porcelain dolls my mom has from her childhood.

"You tell me." I stand. "What would you like to do?"

"You're the one paying." She shrugs. "It's your date." She stands. "And to be honest, in all the years I've lived here, I've never really taken the time to experience New York. I was either taking care of my mom and sister or going to school.

Then I moved to Paris for six years." She smiles at her mention of Paris. "And since I've been back, I've been working."

I love that she just told me all that. It doesn't seem like a lot, but even with her not thrilled with me, she's still opening up to me.

"There has to be one thing you enjoy doing in this city," I say.

"People watching." She laughs. "Adrianna and I would go to Washington State Park and people watch for hours." Her grin lights up her face.

"Then let's go people watch." I take her hand in mine.

"It's too cold!" She laughs some more.

"I have an idea." Still holding her hand, I pull her down the street to flag a cab. When I ran after her earlier, it was quicker to take a cab than my own car. Driving your own vehicle in New York is only done when necessary.

I pull up the place I'm going to take her to on my GPS and get the address, then I give it to the driver.

About ten minutes later, we're getting out in front of Seward Park. Across the street is one of my favorite coffee shops. We enter the shop and Giselle eyes me quizzically.

"Sit and I'll get us coffee." I point toward the tables that are lined up along the big, open window, and Giselle smiles.

The coffee shop is small, but the entire front is made up of one giant window, where you can drink your coffee and, as Giselle said, *people watch*. I don't sit in the coffee shop often, as I get recognized when I'm out, but I grab coffee from here a lot. Today, though, Giselle and I will people watch.

After I order two lattes and a couple pastries, I bring everything over to the table Giselle found. She's staring out the window with her chin in her hand, and the happy look on her face has me wanting to purchase this coffee shop so she can stare out the window like this for the rest of her life.

But something tells me if I want to stay on her good side, that's not the way to do it.

I hand her a latte and a pastry, and she thanks me. When she takes a sip, her face lights up. "This is delicious."

We stare out the window for several minutes, drinking our coffees and eating our pastries. When she lets out a cute giggle, I look around to see what has her laughing.

"What are you looking at?" I ask when I don't see anything out of the norm.

"I'm watching those kids over there."

She points to a bench directly across the street. It's facing the park. There's a guy and a girl sitting next to each other. It's hard to tell how old they are, but from their side-profiles, they're at least in their teens. The guy's arm is resting on the back of the bench, but every few seconds he lifts it in an attempt to put his arm around her.

Giselle giggles again. "Guys act so tough, yet you place them in front of a pretty girl and they get scared and turn to mush."

She gives me a playful side-eye, and that's when I notice that my arm is halfway over her chair. I laugh along with her. Then, gripping her shoulder, I pull her into my side.

"I'm manly enough to admit I might turn into mush around you, but I'm not scared."

Giselle rolls her eyes, but as she turns back to watch the couple, I see a small smile splayed upon her lips.

We watch the couple for a few minutes, and the kid finally gets enough guts to slink his arm around the girl. She turns toward him, and you can see it from a mile away, he's going to go in for a kiss.

Completely invested in this couple, Giselle leans in closer to the window. "It's like watching a love story play out," she murmurs. "Will he do it? Will he kiss her? Will she let him? Will she kiss him back?"

Giselle's grin widens as the kid leans in, and when his lips press against the girl's and she doesn't back away, Giselle cheers like she's watching a football game and the receiver just scored a touchdown.

She glances around her, cringing slightly when she remembers she's in a quiet coffee shop, and then goes back to watching the couple make out.

"Oh! Look!" She smacks my chest to get my attention, and I realize I've been watching her the past few minutes. "It's a horse drawn carriage!"

"It's like thirty-five degrees outside," I point out.

"So what! It's romantic, and they're bundled up in blankets." She sighs. "I should take a picture to show Olivia. It looks like Cinderella. She could do this for her wedding." She snaps a photo and sends it to her friend. "I wonder if he's going to propose, or maybe it's just a romantic evening out."

As I listen to her talk about how romantic it all is, it's clear that while she may be tough, she obviously has a soft spot in her that loves the idea of a romantic fairytale. She sighs in contentment as she watches the carriage go by, and I realize the key to her heart just may be through romance.

And then it hits me that I want the key to her heart.

"Oh my god! Kill, look!" Giselle squeals, throwing her head back in laughter. The couple, who was sitting on the park bench, is now running and ducking behind the bench as several kids throw snowballs at them. With the bench being used as a shield, they gather snow and make their own snowballs to throw back.

"Let's join them!" I say, standing and grabbing Giselle's hand.

She looks at me in shock, then grins devilishly. "Okay!"

We run across the street, and the two of us start gathering up snow to make balls out of. The kids are still engaged in a snowball fight, and they don't see us coming.

With a few icy cold balls in each of our hands, we step out into the line of fire. Giselle throws the first ball. It hits one of the kids in the arm and gets all of the kids' attention. They all turn to look at us.

"You want in?" the kid she hit, who can't be more than ten, yells. "Better watch out!" He grabs a snowball from his pile and throws it right at us. We both duck and it misses.

"You need to take some throwing lessons!" I shout before I throw a ball at him. It hits him directly in the chest, and his eyes widen in shock.

The other kids start laughing, and everyone goes back to their snowball fight. Giselle and I run all over the park with the kids for who knows how long. We get hit several times, and we definitely get a lot of good hits in.

When I notice Giselle's cheeks are a deep pink from the cold, and she's nearly out of breath from running, I take her hand in mine and raise our arms in defeat.

"We're out!" I say, waving the metaphorical white flag.

The kids all laugh.

"Hey! Are you...aren't you Killian Blake?" one of the kids asks.

Giselle's eyes widen, afraid I'm worried about getting caught. I'm not, though. It's part of the job.

"I am," I admit.

"Holy shit!" another kid yells. "We just threw snowballs at Killian Blake."

This time Giselle laughs.

"Don't use that language around here," I admonish. There are tons of little kids running around. The kid has the decency to look sorry. "And you did. What's your name?"

"I'm Drake and this is my brother Dean." He points to the kid next to him. "That's my sister, Dana." He points to the girl who was making out with the boy earlier. They're standing next to each other and holding hands. "And that's her boyfriend, Mark." Drake scrunches up his nose in disgust.

"Nice to meet you." I shake their hands. "This is my friend, Giselle." I put my arm around Giselle, and she smiles softly at me.

"You have a good arm," I say to Drake, whose face lights up at my words. "You play ball?"

"I do! All of us do...Well, not my sister." He shrugs. "I want to be a quarterback just like Nick Shaw...no offense."

"None taken," I tell him. "Nick's my best friend and a very talented quarterback."

"It sucks he's retiring," Drake states.

"Yeah, well, he wants to go back to school. He loves reading and writing," I say.

"That's cool, I guess." He shrugs.

"I can't believe you're here," Dean cuts in. "And my ball is at home. I can't even have you sign it." He shakes his head in regret. "Damn it." He glances at me. "I mean, darn it."

"How about this? I'll write down the email of my publicist. She's the lady who is in charge of my life. Have your parents email her, and she'll give you passes to the first home game next season, and I'll make sure to sign whatever you bring then."

"Are you fu—are you serious?" Drake yells. "Heck yes!"

The kids all cheer. I ask a woman nearby for a pen and scrap piece of paper and write down Amber's email address. Using the kids' cell phones, Giselle takes a few pictures of me with them and then we say goodbye.

"That was very sweet of you," Giselle says as we walk toward Broadway to catch a cab.

"It's part of the job."

"No, catching a ball is part of your job. What you did back there isn't a requirement."

"Those kids are why I have a job. They watch the games and buy my jersey," I tell her honestly, then change the subject. "So, what's next?"

I glance at my watch. It's still relatively early, and I'm not ready to say goodnight to Giselle yet. The past couple hours we've put aside all the drama from the outside world and have had a really good time.

She blows out a harsh breath. "I don't know...that snowball fight exhausted me." She grins playfully. "I can't remember the last time I used that many of my muscles at once."

"I think the last time I was part of a snowball fight was as a kid in North Carolina." I smile as I remember my childhood growing up.

"Is that where you're from?" she asks.

We continue to walk down the street, and since she hasn't mentioned wanting or needing to go home, I go with it.

"Yeah, I was born and raised in North Carolina. I received a scholarship to the University of North Carolina and that's where I met Nick. My parents still live there. I have one brother, Dylan, but he lives here in New York."

"I've met your brother," Giselle admits. "Your brother and his wife were at the game where Nick was injured. He seems nice."

"He is. He used to be a family attorney back in North Carolina, but he didn't love it. So, he moved here and opened up his own firm focusing on sports law. Shortly after, he met his wife, Christina, who was a model. They got married and settled down and gave me my niece, Julia. She's an awesome kid."

We stop walking and I realize we're standing in front of my building. "Want to come up?" I ask. "We can order in..."

Giselle flinches, but quickly covers it with a tight smile. "Or if you're tired, I can call you a cab."

"I am a bit tired," she admits. "I worked all day then had to take the trip up to see my mom's doctors, but I'm okay. We can go up to your place."

"You sure?" I ask just to make sure.

"Yeah." She smiles, but it isn't the same one she had earlier. I want that smile back on her face.

When we get up to my place, I tell Giselle she can have a seat in the living room while I pull out a few takeout menus from the drawer in the kitchen and grab us each a bottle of water.

When I walk back into the living room, Giselle is sitting on the couch. She's removed her jacket and gloves. She's wearing a pair of black slacks and her pink top is see-through, but I think it's the way it's made. Her bra underneath is the same color pink. She's checking something on her phone, but when she hears me, she sets it to the side.

"If you don't see anything you like, we can order something else," I tell her, handing her the stack of menus and sitting next to her. She takes them from me and sets them aside.

"I'm not really hungry," she says. "I was thinking we could get right to the nightcap." She takes the bottom of my hoodie in her hands and lifts it up. I help her by lifting my arms and removing it from my body. She lifts my shirt next. This time I stop her.

"Giselle..." I say slowly. I don't want to offend her, but we've talked about this.

"What?" she asks, sounding genuinely confused.

"I told you I don't want to be sexual with anyone until I'm in a serious relationship."

She frowns. "You requested a nightcap. I thought you changed your mind."

"I requested a what?"

And then it hits me. The different options with A Touch of Class. A nightcap means coming back to the client's place for sex.

When I called Bianca earlier today on my way to Giselle's place, I told her I wanted Giselle every day and night she's available for the foreseeable future.

At first, she gave me shit, saying she already has regular clients booked, but once I offered to pay double, she gave in. She must've marked me for a nightcap.

"Your boss must've included it by mistake," I tell her. "I wouldn't pay you to fuck me."

As soon as the words are out of my mouth, I regret saying them. I didn't mean it like it came out.

"Oh," she says. "Well, make sure you get that fixed. It's a waste of money to pay for it and not get it." She laughs, but it sounds off.

She opens the top of her water bottle and takes a sip, then sets it down and laughs softly. "I understand you not wanting to have sex, but you do know you can't get a woman pregnant from oral, right?"

I let out a loud laugh that has her grinning, and it's the one I love to see on her face.

"Yeah, I know, but oral is a gateway to sex. When I first started my NFL career, I was young, and women would throw themselves at me.

At first, I thought maybe they were doing it because they liked me. I'd meet a girl at a party and we would make out. Sometimes it would lead to more. Her giving me head or me going down on her. I would stop it there, though, not wanting to continue until I knew there could be a future with us. The girls would get pissed."

I shake my head thinking about how many times a girl would accuse me of being gay.

"As I got older, I realized most women wanted me because I was a professional athlete with money in the bank. While many made it clear they would be more than happy to commit, they weren't what I was looking for. Because I didn't want to lead them on or put myself in a position where I would have to explain why I wasn't going to have sex with them, I eventually stopped being with them in any capacity.

"I told myself I was going to wait until I found a woman I could see myself having a baby with, but it never happened. Every woman I came across I just couldn't imagine creating a family with." I shrug. "Look at Nick and Olivia. Sure, it worked out for them, but what if she didn't attend the football game? He would've never known he was a father. She would've had to raise their baby fatherless. I guess I've just never been willing to risk it..."

Until now, I find myself thinking.

"That makes sense." She nods in understanding then stands. "But you did give me an orgasm." Her cheeks burn pink.

"I did," I agree, remembering how fucking good she felt as she came around my fingers and the fact that I wasn't the least bit concerned about where it would lead to.

"I should probably get going," she says. "I have to work tomorrow and..."

Before she can finish her sentence, I lean over and kiss her. Our lips curl against each other and we kiss for several minutes. She tastes like the vanilla latte she drank, and fuck if I don't want more.

When we finally separate, I don't give her a chance to say whatever negative thing I'm sure is going to come out of her mouth.

"Stay the night with me." Her eyes go wide. "Not for sex. Let's have dinner, watch some crappy television, and when we're tired, we'll go to sleep."

"Why?" she asks.

"Because when you're around I don't feel so broken or lonely."

Chapter Eighteen

GISELLE

KILLIAN'S HANDS MASSAGE MY BREASTS AS I MOAN in pleasure. His fingers tweak my nipples, and my back arches, needing more of his touch. "More, please," I beg. "Suck on my nipples, Kill," I plead.

I'm so close to coming...

"You sure you want this?" Killian asks.

"Yes!" I demand. A little more and I'm going to explode. "Suck on my nipples, please!" I beg again.

He doesn't listen, though. He just continues what he's doing—massaging and pinching.

My hands move to his head to force him to wrap those full lips around my nipples, only his head isn't anywhere near my breasts.

Then who's touching my breasts? Am I dreaming?

My eyes shoot open. My gaze goes to where Killian's face really is—between my leg—and I glance around at my surroundings.

I'm in Killian's room, in his bed. I look down and notice the hands that are on me aren't Killian's—they're mine! My hands are massaging my breasts. My fingers are pinching my nipples.

Killian's hands are holding onto the insides of my thighs as he licks and sucks on my clit. I don't even have time to ask him what is going on before I'm coming so hard my butt lifts off the bed.

"Jesus, woman," Killian murmurs, "that was so fucking hot."

He sits up and lifts the bottom of his T-shirt to wipe his mouth, his perfect set of abs peeking out just enough to give me a tease.

I take a second to slow down my breathing and then ask, "Did you just make me come while I was sleeping?"

He gives me a quizzical look. "I'm pretty sure you begging for more indicated you were awake."

"I thought I was dreaming!"

I pull my shirt down and sit against the headboard. I glance down and notice the boxers I borrowed from Killian last night are no longer on me but instead on the floor.

"Giselle, did you have more to drink last night other than the one glass of wine with dinner?"

He stands and picks his boxers up from the floor and throws them to me.

"I thought you said you wouldn't pay to touch me!"

"No," he says, "I said I wouldn't pay to fuck you, and I wouldn't. However, it's eight in the morning. I paid for you from five p.m. until midnight, which means you're off the clock. Plus, you came on my tongue and fingers, not my dick."

"What happened to oral being the gateway to sex? This is the second time in a week you've made me come!"

"You woke up this morning begging for me to make you come. A man only has so much restraint." Killian tilts his head to the side. "Wait a second...when you were begging me, you were asleep?"

"I—" I clear my throat. "I think so..." I try to remember begging Killian to make me come, but I can't.

Killian smirks. "So that means that while you were sleeping, you were dreaming of me making you come?" His grin grows wider. "I haven't had sex in over ten years, yet I'm pleasing you while you're awake *and* in your dreams."

Cocky. Fucking. Bastard.

Grabbing his boxers, I slip them on and get out of bed to go pee. When I'm done, I change back into my clothes I left in the bathroom. I'll need to stop at home to shower and get dressed before I go into work. Shit! Work! It's already eight and I have a client meeting at ten.

I step out of the bathroom and Killian is changing his clothes. His shirt is off, and his back muscles are on display. My goodness, no man should be this good-looking.

He turns around and grants me a sexy lop-sided grin, and I just about melt into a pile of goo.

"You've made me come twice," I blurt out. Killian's smile grows bigger. "When are you going to let me reciprocate?"

His smile deflates slightly, but it's still there. "When you make the choice to want me." He shoots me a wink. "Now, let's get going, so you're not late to work. I have a meeting I need to get to and can't be late."

The entire drive to my place, I think about what Killian said. *When you make the choice to want me.*

Last night, despite only hanging out with him because I was getting paid to, was a lot of fun.

Until we got back to his place, I don't think I once thought about the fact that I was getting paid.

It was also the first time I spent the night at a client's place, but the truth is, I didn't view Killian as a client. After he told me he didn't mean to request the nightcap, I could've gone home. Without a nightcap, a client only has until nine o'clock, unless he pays extra because of an event that will run later. I stayed because I wanted to.

Killian parks in front of my building and I get out, but before I close the door, I lean into the car, so I can look at him while I speak. "Just so you know, I've never spent the night with a client." His eyes widen in understanding. "Last night, when I spent the night, I made the choice to."

I close the door and head upstairs. I take a quick shower and get dressed for work. When I come out, Olivia is sitting on the couch reading a book to Reed.

"Morning," she says cautiously.

"Morning," I reply.

"Giselle."

"Livi."

We laugh at having said each other's names at the same time. Reed has no idea why we're laughing, but he joins in, which only has us laughing harder.

"You go first," she says.

"I'm sorry for hiding so much from you." I open my arms and Olivia stands and gives me a hug. "I love you."

"I love you too," she says.

"I know things have been crazy, but I'm ready to talk."

"Good!" Olivia exclaims. "How about tonight? Nick and I have some news to share. We can go to dinner and afterward Nick can take Reed for the night while you and I talk."

"That sounds great." But then I remember I have to work. I'm about to tell her tonight won't work after all, when I remember it's Killian who's hired me. "Is Killian invited too?" I ask.

"We were planning to invite him. Is that okay?"

"It is." I smile, and Olivia gives me a questioning look. I'm sure while I'm at work she'll be writing down a list of questions to ask me tonight. The first one starting with what's going on with Killian.

"Great," she says. "I'll text you the time and location."

I give Reed a kiss goodbye and head out. It's already after nine o'clock, and if I don't haul ass, I'm going to be late to my meeting.

Figuring it will be quicker to take a cab—even though it's more expensive—I start to head toward where they all wait, when I see Killian's car still in the same spot with him in it. At least today he's being more practical by driving a Dodge Challenger. I wonder just how many cars this man has. I mean, we live in New York. You barely need one.

He lowers his window. "Let's go."

"You waited for me?"

"Yeah, I figured you could use a ride to work." He shoots me that damn panty-dropping wink. "Plus, that means I get you to myself for a little longer."

"I thought you had a meeting," I say.

"I do, now get in before we're both late to our meetings!" He laughs.

"Fine!"

We stop at a coffee shop on the way and Killian buys us both a coffee and a breakfast sandwich. We arrive at the building I work in with ten minutes to spare, and I tell him he can just drop me off in front of the building, but he insists on finding a parking spot.

"Thank you," I tell him. "I totally would've been late."

"No problem. I told you I have a meeting as well."

"Oh!" I say, remembering Olivia's and my conversation. "Olivia and Nick want to have dinner tonight with us. They have an announcement to make."

"Sounds good." He turns off the car and gets out, and then we both make our way toward the building. "Do you know what they're announcement is? Nick said she's been a bit off lately."

I roll my eyes. I probably shouldn't tell him, but he'll find out tonight anyway. "Olivia hasn't told me yet, but she's pregnant."

Killian stops in his place. "Really? Well, damn. She must not have told Nick yet, because he would've told me."

"I think she was living in denial for a little while." I laugh. "Good thing they're getting married in a few months."

Killian laughs as well. "They're going to need a bigger place for their growing football team." He presses the button for the elevator.

"I put my mom's house up for sale," I admit. "I told Olivia I'm moving out as soon as it sells."

The elevator doors open and we get in. I press the button to the floor I need to go to.

The doors close and Killian corners me. "I'm sorry about all the shit I said to you about living off Olivia. I didn't know, Giselle. I really am fucking sorry." He runs his finger down the side of my face. It's such a simple yet intimate gesture.

"It's okay, you were right. I need to stand on my own two feet." I give him a small smile, so he knows I really don't hold a grudge over what he said.

"Stand on your own two feet?" He eyes me incredulously. "I don't even know how you stand at all with all that damn weight on your shoulders."

"I'm handling it," I tell him. "I'm hoping if I prove myself at work, I'll get a promotion sooner rather than later. And once I do, it will mean better pay and benefits."

The elevator dings and the doors open. I check and it's my floor.

"And if you get it, are you going to quit your other job?" he asks as we step off the elevator.

"I would like to say yes, but I have to see how much I'll be making," I tell him honestly. "Even if I sell my mom's house, I'll still have to pay for another place to live, plus my sister's school and my student loans." I sigh. "Thank you for what you did for my mom. I don't like that you went behind my back, but the truth is, I don't know what I would've done. I got denied the loan."

I open the door to my small office that my boss, Lydia, has given me and have a seat. Killian sits across from me.

"You're welcome," he says.

I pull my laptop out of my bag and open it up. It makes the sound indicating it's starting up. I type my password in and pull up my calendar since it has all the details I need for my client who is due to arrive any minute.

And that's when I notice Killian is sitting in my office. With me. I was so focused on our conversation, I didn't even think about the fact that he didn't just drop me off. He got out and followed me in.

"Umm, Kill, you're in my office," I say dumbly.

Of course, he laughs. "I know. I told you I have a meeting."

"Okay, well, I do too. And..." I click on this morning's agenda. "Mr. Blake is due to arrive here any second."

Killian nods, and I gasp.

Mr. Blake.

Killian Blake.

Killian is my ten o'clock appointment.

Motherfucker.

"Why are you on my calendar?" I hiss. "This is not the place to play these games."

"What games?" he says, sounding genuinely confused. "I made an appointment with the receptionist yesterday. She told me you had a last-minute cancelation."

"Kill," I snap.

Then I stand and walk over to the door to close it, so nobody hears our conversation.

"What?"

"This is my place of employment. I am trying to establish a career here." I don't understand why he's doing this. "This isn't A Touch of Class."

"I know...it's Fresh Designs." He nods once. "I've decided it's time to have my condo professionally decorated. I'm tired of the whole bachelor look."

"You're serious?" I ask.

"I am."

"You're just doing this to find another way to give me money, but I work under Lydia, Kill. I don't get paid commission."

"I'm not doing this to give you money." He grins. "Now, treat me like any other client. Where do we begin?"

I fall into my chair and take a deep breath. This man is encroaching himself in every part of my life. And if I'm honest with myself, I kind of like it.

"How did you know I was pregnant and I didn't?" Olivia laughs.

"Maybe because I know you." I grin and give her a hug, but when I pull away, she's frowning. "What's wrong?"

"Nothing, it's just...you know me so well, yet I had no idea you were—" Olivia looks around and whispers "—working every night. I'm such a horrible friend." Tears pool in her lids and fall down, and I pull her in for another hug.

"Stop it. I kept it a secret from everyone. You couldn't have known."

"Known what?" Celeste asks.

Olivia's eyes go wide, and she gives me an apologetic look.

"That Giselle and I are dating," Killian says, pulling me into his arms. "We were hiding it for a while."

Celeste's face contorts into a look of disbelief. "Really? I thought you hated her almost as much as you hate me."

"I don't hate you," Killian says. "And I definitely don't hate Giselle." He grabs my face and kisses me hard, his tongue quickly delving into my mouth.

When we break from our kiss, he gives me a wink and a smile, and butterflies attack my belly.

"Okay, on that strange note..." Celeste stands. "I need to get going. I'm heading to Paris tomorrow morning."

"You'll be back for Reed's baptism, though, right?" Olivia asks.

"Of course." She makes her way around the table, giving everyone—besides Killian—a kiss on their cheek.

"Don't you have something to say to her?" I nudge Killian.

"Hey Celeste, wait." Killian stands and approaches Celeste. "I just wanted to say I'm sorry for the shit I've said to you. You might be friends with Nick, but I never took the time to get to know you. Maybe we can change that."

Celeste gives him an incredulous look like she's waiting for the punchline.

But when it doesn't come, she says, "Okay...well, thank you...yeah..." She gives me a soft smile before she turns to leave.

Nick and Olivia are both staring at Killian, stunned as he walks back over and sits next to me.

"You ready to go?" he whispers into my ear.

We spent the day going over what he wants done to his condo. We went to lunch and to several stores so he could show me what his tastes are.

His likes: whatever I like.

His dislikes: whatever I don't like.

When Olivia texted that we were meeting for dinner at six o'clock, and it was already five, Killian insisted on us driving together.

"Actually, I made plans for tonight," I tell him.

His jaw visibly ticks.

"Tonight is my night with you," he comments.

"Until nine o'clock," I counter and stand. "Reed, come give your favorite aunt some loving."

I pick up my sweet soon-to-be-godson and pepper kisses all over his face. He giggles and my heart melts.

"You ready?" Olivia asks me.

"Yep," I answer her. Then I give Nick a smile. "Congratulations, soon-to-be-daddy of two. Tag, you're it."

He gives me a confused look.

"You weren't around when your fiancée was pregnant the first time. The cravings, the night sweats, the freaking out if she was gaining the right amount of weight. Waking me up in the middle of the night to go out and buy her orange juice because she read it will make the baby move more."

Nick laughs and Olivia groans.

"I can't wait for every damn minute of it," Nick says and gives Olivia a kiss. "I will gladly buy you orange juice at midnight, Brown-Eyes."

Olivia grins at the nickname he's called her since the day they became reacquainted.

Then Nick pulls me into a hug. "In case I haven't told you enough, thank you for being there for her."

"You don't have to thank me. She's my best friend."

"You're more than that to her...to us...you're family," Nick points out.

"Thank you," I say, trying not to get choked up.

I start walking toward the exit when a hand grips my arm. I feel a hard body against my back, and then I smell the sweet yet masculine scent that is all Killian. "You made me think you were going out with another guy," he growls into my ear.

"You assumed that," I say.

He chuckles. "I want you in my bed tonight." My body stiffens at his words, and then he adds, "To sleep, Giselle. Just to sleep."

I make sure not to react to what he's said, but inside, I'm not sure whether to smile that he enjoys my company enough to just want to simply spend time with me, or pout that deep down I was hoping he wanted to have sex with me. Because if he did, that would mean he wants me on a deeper level. One that allows him to be with me in a way that he hasn't been with anyone in over ten years.

Yet, at the same time the thought of him wanting me scares the ever-loving shit out of me because I'm not in a place to want that. I can't want that.

"I can't," I say. "I'm hanging out with Olivia tonight."

"All right," he concedes. "But my bed will miss having you in it."

I release a giggle. "Your bed or you?"

"Me...definitely me."

Olivia and I end up riding back with Killian since we're going to Nick's place and Nick is staying at our place with Reed.

I told Olivia we could hang out on the patio, but she said if we were there, Nick or Reed might interrupt us and she wants some time with me alone.

Once we're inside, we change into comfier clothes Olivia has here. I head out onto Nick's balcony with a thick down comforter for us to bundle up in, and Olivia follows, bringing me out a glass of wine and her a bottle of water.

"Okay, start from the beginning," she says, and I do.

I tell her everything, beginning with my mom and her illness. I tell her about my paying for everything since my dad left us. And then I tell her about Killian being with me when my mom tried to commit suicide and how he went behind my back to help my mom get the treatment I couldn't afford.

"I've only known Killian for a short time," she says, "but I've never seen him so smitten before." She giggles. "Nick thought maybe he was gay but didn't want anyone to know."

My thoughts go back to this morning when I woke up to Killian expertly eating me out. The way he fingerfucked me like it was his job, one he took seriously. My cheeks heat up and I'm thankful we're sitting in the dark, so she can't see just how affected I am.

"Trust me, Killian is not gay."

Olivia giggles. "So, what are you going to do?"

"With what?"

"With your second job. You can't date Killian *and* escort."

"We're not dating."

Olivia gives me an *oh please* look.

We head back inside, and Olivia's phone goes off. She smiles and shows me the text. It's of Nick and Reed lying in bed together blowing her a kiss.

"You should go home," I tell her.

"What? No." She shakes her head.

"Yes. Go home and be with your boys. I'll call you a car, so you don't have to catch a cab."

"Wait, you aren't coming?" she asks. Then she slowly nods her head. "You're totally going to see Killian, aren't you?"

"Your car will be here in ten minutes," I say, not answering her question.

A few minutes later, Olivia locks up Nick's place, and I walk her down and wait until she's safely in the car. Then I head back up to Killian's place.

I knock once, and he opens the door, his eyes slowly raking down my body. "Are you here to invite me to your sleepover?" He smirks playfully.

I glance down and groan when I see I'm still wearing Olivia's Victoria's Secret Pink hoodie and sweats.

"Olivia went home. I was wondering if...uh...if you're up for company?" I ask nervously, suddenly second-guessing my idea of inviting myself over.

But then Killian grants me a sexy lop-sided grin and says, "I'm always up for your company," and my nerves are instantly calmed.

"Sons of Anarchy?" I suggest.

"Sounds good."

We go straight to Killian's room. He folds his comforter down and throws me a pillow, and then we climb into bed, but neither of us turn the television on.

"Did everything go okay with Olivia?" he asks.

A few strands of my hair fall out of my bun, and Killian reaches over and tucks them behind my ear.

"It went good. We're good."

"I'm glad."

"I guess I have you to thank." I scoot closer to Killian. "Ever since you came into my life, it feels like everything has been turned upside down...in a good way."

"I haven't really done anything," he begins to say, but I stop him.

"You took me to see my mom the day my dad left, you were there the day she tried to kill herself. It was your phone that saved her life. You sat with me in the hospital, you paid for her treatment. You even hired me so I wouldn't have to have sex with other guys." I lay my head down on Killian's chest and my arm goes around his torso as I let out an exhausted yawn.

"When you can't look on the bright side, I will sit with you in the dark," Killian murmurs, and even though I can't see him, I know he's smiling.

"That's very sweet," I tell him, "but it's not from the book."

"Damn it." He laughs. "Google keeps failing me."

"Read. The. Book."

Those are the last words I say before I fall asleep in Killian's arms, feeling safer and more content than I've ever felt in my life.

I WAKE UP TO AN EMPTY BED. WHEN I OPEN MY eyes, I notice there's a note.

Good morning, beautiful,

Going to the gym with Nick. There's coffee waiting for you. I'll be back soon.

Xo Killian

After my heart picks up speed and the butterflies in my belly attack my insides, I roll over and grab my phone to check the time. It's eight a.m. on a Sunday and I have no plans.

Before I get out of bed to make myself a cup of coffee, I click on my emails to see if there's anything new. There's one from Bianca, confirming the upcoming week's schedule. Of course, my entire week consists of Killian. I smile at the thought of getting to spend my evenings with him. Whether I want to admit it or not, the man is growing on me.

I click out of it and send my sister a text, asking how she's doing and suggest we get together soon. Then I send one to my mom's doctor to ask if there are any updates and when he thinks she might be up for company.

I climb out of bed and use the bathroom, and as I'm walking to the kitchen, the front door opens.

"Home already?" I yell. "I hope you brought me breakfast."

I'm only joking, but if he really did, brownie points for him.

"Uncle Killian," a tiny voice calls out, making me stop in my tracks to look down and make sure I'm decent. I woke up in the middle of the night, warm from Killian being wrapped around me, and took off my sweats, leaving me in only a shirt that barely covers my ass.

"I'm so sorry!" Killian's sister-in-law, Christina, says. "We didn't realize Killian wasn't here."

"Or that he would actually have a woman over," Dylan adds.

Christina shoots him a glare, and I laugh through my embarrassment.

"It's—it's not like that...we're not."

"We're not what?"

My eyes dart over to Killian, who is standing in the doorway in a pair of basketball shorts with his shirt slung around his neck. His entire upper half is covered in sweat. When he notices I'm ogling him, he smirks.

"Your family is here," I say, tilting my head toward them.

His eyes move to them and widen, and when he sees his niece, he grabs his shirt from around his neck and puts it back on.

"Sorry, I thought Giselle was on the phone...or talking to herself."

Dylan and Christina laugh, and I glare. "Isn't it a little chilly outside to be running around half-naked?"

"I could say the same for you." He chuckles. My cheeks heat up in embarrassment, and it only makes him laugh harder. Throwing his arm over my shoulders, he pulls me into his side and kisses my temple. "I was at the gym downstairs," he clarifies.

"Uncle Killian, you're so gross and sweaty!" his niece yells, her nose scrunched up in disgust.

Killian looks around at everyone standing in his condo then curses under his breath. "I'm watching Julia today, aren't I?"

"If you have plans, we can bring her with us," Dylan says, his gaze darting from me to Killian, who still has me in his hold.

"No!" Julia pouts. "We're going ice skating and to the zoo, right, Uncle Killian?"

"Right," he confirms. Then he looks over at me. "Join us."

"Yeah!" Julia exclaims. "Join us." She skips over to me and extends her hand. "I'm Julia Blake."

"Nice to meet you. I'm Giselle Winters." I shake her hand.

She grins wide then runs over to the TV, clicking it on and changing the channel. She's clearly been here before, which makes sense since she's Killian's niece.

"I need to go home. I don't have any clothes here," I tell Killian quietly, not wanting to have this conversation in front of other people, especially his family.

Killian, on the other hand, doesn't seem to care who's here. "Maybe you should keep some stuff here, so we don't have to drive across the bridge all the time to get your clothes."

My gaze bounces between him and his brother and wife. They look more shocked than I do, but Killian doesn't notice. He removes his arm from around me and walks into the kitchen. He makes a cup of coffee then hands it to me—kissing my cheek as he does.

"I'm going to jump in the shower. Why don't you just grab another outfit of Olivia's? We can get some of your stuff to keep here later." Without waiting for my answer, he says to his brother and Christina, "You guys can go. I got Julia." Then he says to Julia, "Once I'm out of the shower, and Giselle is ready, we'll go."

Chapter Nineteen

GISELLE

I'M SWIPING THROUGH MY PHOTO ALBUM ON MY phone, trying to find a particular couch I know I took a picture of when my finger stops on a photo of Killian and me at the zoo in front of the tiger exhibit last weekend with his niece.

After I took a picture of Julia with Killian, she insisted on taking one of us. Unable to tell her no, I handed her my phone and stood next to Killian.

He wrapped me up in his arms and kissed me on my cheek as Julia took the picture. She laughed and said to smile nice. So, Killian did as she asked and smiled for the camera.

I can't even remember the last time I enjoyed myself as much as I did that day.

I swipe to the next photo of Killian devouring an ice cream. He didn't care how cold it was outside. He said when you go to the zoo, you have to eat ice cream.

The next photo is one of him and Julia. My heart squeezes at how good he is with her. Had Melanie not have gotten an abortion, I know deep down in my heart, Killian would have done the right thing, and he would've been a damn good dad.

I keep scrolling through picture after picture of Killian's and my time together the last couple weeks. From the snowball fight with the kids at the park, to our visit to the Belvedere castle and Shakespearian Theatre, to the Alice in Wonderland statues I never knew existed in Central Park until the other day when Killian took me to see them. The man has made it his life goal to show me a little bit of New York every day, ever since I told him I've lived here most of my life but have never really seen it.

As I stare at each of the pictures, an idea begins to form for what I can get Killian for Valentine's Day.

Grabbing my purse, I let the receptionist know I'm leaving for my lunch. I'm not sure if I'll be able to pull this off since *today* is Valentine's Day, but I have to try.

I find the store I'm looking for and explain to the associate what I would like done. An hour later and my gift for Killian is wrapped in pretty red and black wrapping paper.

At six o'clock on the dot, there's a knock on my office door. Killian is standing in the doorway, dressed to the nines in a three-piece suit that fits every inch of his body to perfection.

"You ready to go?" he asks.

"Yep!" Grabbing my jacket, I throw it on over my outfit. "You're all dressed up," I tell him when I get closer. "You look very handsome." I pat his crimson-colored tie. He gives me a chaste kiss on my lips—an intimate act that has become the norm between us.

"Thank you. The place we're going to for dinner has a dress code."

I glance down at my outfit. I'm not in jeans, but I'm not exactly dressed to go anywhere that requires a black tie, either. "Can we stop by my place on the way?" I ask.

"I have you covered." Killian pulls a box out from behind him that I didn't notice before. "Olivia gave me your size."

"You didn't have to do that," I tell him.

"I know, but I wanted to."

I take the box into the women's restroom and open it. Inside is a beautiful, crimson-colored dress—that matches Killian's tie—and black heels.

When I pull them out, I notice the dress is a well-known designer and the heels are donning the signature red soles. This outfit probably cost more than I make as an intern here in a month.

And suddenly, the gift sitting inside my purse feels childish and stupid. What was I thinking? I should've bought him a watch or something. *Right, like I could actually afford one a guy like Killian would wear.*

When Killian and I woke up this morning, he had a dozen roses and a box of chocolates waiting for me. He had also run to the coffee shop and picked us up coffee and adorable heart-shaped donuts. When he dropped me off at work on his way to the gym, he told me he would be back at six o'clock to take me out to dinner.

Until he walked through the door, I thought I got him the perfect gift. I mean, what do you even get for the man who's paying you to date him and redecorate his home? The man you're slowly falling in love with but are afraid to tell him? Candy? Flowers?

Sure, he got me both of those, but he can also afford to buy me anything he wants if he desires to do so. Killian is a professional athlete who makes millions of dollars a year. There isn't anything he can't afford to buy himself.

I put the dress and heels on and place the outfit I was wearing inside the box. I apply a light layer of lip gloss and then fix my hair the best I can.

My mood has plummeted, but I remember Killian is paying me to go out with him, which makes this about him and not me.

So, I plaster a smile on my face and head out of the bathroom.

"Jesus, Giselle. You look stunning," he murmurs as I enter the lobby where he's waiting for me. "Everything fits perfect." He lifts my chin with his fingers and gives me a soft kiss to my lips.

"Thank you," I tell him, forcing my smile to remain on my face.

He gives me a concerned look but lets it go.

The ride to the restaurant is quiet. Killian has gone all out and rented a car and driver for the night. It reminds me of the first night when we went to the charity gala. Instead of enjoying Killian's company, the entire drive I'm stuck in my own thoughts and insecurities.

I know he can tell something is wrong because he's holding my hand a little tighter than usual. He keeps glancing at me like he wants to say something, but he's not sure what to say. I need to snap out of this. It's not worth it to ruin tonight over a stupid outfit I can't afford, and a gift I've already decided Killian will never see. I've escorted tons of rich men. I never cared before.

That's because Killian is different, I remind myself.

When we arrive at the restaurant, we're shown to our table immediately. I have a seat and Killian sits across from me. He orders us a bottle of wine. Once the waiter leaves, he turns toward me. "What's going on?" he asks, getting straight to the point.

"Nothing," I say, already knowing he's not going to accept my answer but not knowing what else to say.

"Talk to me, please."

I hate that I'm ruining our date. Killian deserves better than this. Knowing he'll need some type of explanation from me, I go with a half-truth. "I don't like that you spent a lot of money on me," I admit. "It's bad enough you're paying to take me out."

Killian frowns. "I'm not paying to take you out."

"Yes, you are. You're on the schedule for tonight. If you weren't, I would be on a date with another guy."

Killian flinches at my words.

"I'm sorry," I add, "I didn't mean it like that. I just hate that you're wasting your money on me."

"Let's just enjoy our night, okay?" He takes my hand in his. "The reasons we're here together don't matter. The only thing that matters is that on Valentine's Day I'm out to dinner with the most beautiful woman in New York."

"Just New York, huh?" I joke.

Killian laughs. "I was trying to be romantic without sounding too over the top."

"Ah...okay, then you nailed it. Just the perfect amount of romantic."

The waiter brings us over our drinks. We order our food and then we're left alone again.

"I worked on some ideas for your condo today," I tell him. "Want to see?"

"I want to say no because we shouldn't be discussing work at dinner, but something tells me you're going to show me anyway."

"I am." I laugh, grabbing my purse, which is draped over the back of my chair, to pull out my phone.

My purse strap gets stuck on the ear of the chair and then falls to the ground—several items falling out.

Killian jumps into action, helping me pick up everything that rolled every which way. Luckily, we're seated in the back of the restaurant, away from other people.

"What's this?" Killian asks, holding up the wrapped gift.

"Nothing." I try to grab it from him, but he moves it out of my reach at the last second.

"Is it for me?" He grins like a little boy.

"It was, but I'm not giving it to you anymore." I try to reach for it again, but Killian takes it with him back to his seat.

"You bought me something for Valentine's Day?" His face is lit up like a damn Christmas tree as he shakes it like one does with their gifts on Christmas morning.

Boy, is he about to be disappointed.

"It's nothing much," I tell him.

"I bought you something too." He pulls a small box out of his pocket and sets it on the table. Of course, he bought me jewelry.

"You shouldn't have done that." I nod toward the imposing item now sitting on the table between us.

"Stop saying that. Open it."

Reluctantly, I pick up the box and open the lid.

Inside is a white gold—maybe platinum—necklace. The chain itself is delicate. In the center of the necklace is a charm in the shape of a heart with a crack going down the middle, accented with tiny diamonds. It's beautiful, but as I lift the necklace out of the box, I'm confused as to why he bought me a broken heart.

"Turn it over," Killian murmurs, so I do. And engraved on the back is a quote, that if I wasn't already sitting, would have me falling to my knees.

She made broken look beautiful and strong look invincible.

"Killian," I whisper, my throat clogged with heavy emotion.

"Everybody is broken, Giselle," he says, "but not everybody handles it with such strength and beauty."

He stands and comes around behind me, taking the necklace from my hand and placing it around my neck.

Now that I've seen what he's given me, I'm especially terrified of him seeing my gift. I can't even imagine how much this cost him.

"Thank you," I say. "It's beautiful and perfect." I eye my gift in his hand. "Is there any way I can convince you not to open your gift?"

"What? Why?" Killian asks, confused.

"Well, for one, it probably cost less than the box this necklace came in." I laugh humorlessly through my tears.

"I don't give a fuck how much your gift cost," Killian says seriously. "You should know me better than that."

"No, I know. It's just that you spent so much money on me, and..." I let out a deep sigh of defeat. "Well, whatever. Just open it. Let's get this over with."

Killian eyes me curiously then proceeds to open his gift. He opens the flat box and inside is a book.

"It's a coffee table book."

A lot of clients like to have one on their coffee table. It makes for a pretty center piece. They're usually of something they enjoy, like architecture or art. The one Killian is holding is of him—of us.

I had several photos printed that we've taken on our phones over the last couple weeks. I also had Nick and Olivia send over some they had of him. And I reached out to his sister-in-law, who was more than happy to send some over.

There are some from the games he's played. One from the Super Bowl he won last year. They're all in dated order. The last image is of us. I wrote a note on that one: *Thank you for being broken and lonely with me.*

"Giselle," Killian whispers, "you weren't going to give me this? Why?"

"Well, because it only cost me like twenty bucks to make. I just had the photos printed. Like I said, it's a coffee table book. You leave it on the coffee table as decoration." I shrug. "You bought me this beautiful necklace and outfit. It really isn't comparable."

Killian's eyes meet mine, and if I'm not mistaken, they're a tad glossy. "I love...it. I love it. Thank you."

He reaches over and pulls me into a hug. "I'm going to use the restroom. I'll be right back."

He sets the book down on the table and stands, walking in the direction toward the restrooms.

My phone pings with a new email. I still have it out because I never showed him the items I found for his condo. When I check it, I see it's from Bianca. I click on the schedule, and once again, it's filled with an entire week of Killian. My heart drops at the thought of him spending all this money on me. He might be able to afford it, but that doesn't mean he should have to. I glance toward the restrooms and notice Killian is still gone.

I dial Bianca's number, and she answers on the first ring.

"Giselle, how can I help you?"

"We need to talk. I can't allow Killian to pay to see me anymore."

Chapter Twenty

KILLIAN

I need a moment to breathe. To think.

When I opened the gift Giselle gave me, I almost told her I loved her. I had to walk away before I did something that would push her away.

I'm falling hard for this woman, but we aren't quite in sync yet. I'm sprinting down the field toward the end zone, waiting for her to throw me the ball. I'm completely open and ready, but she isn't. She doesn't trust us enough yet. She's scared of not making a complete pass, so instead she keeps throwing it out of bounds.

That's okay, though, because I'm willing to wait until she trusts in us enough to make the play, and when she does, I'll be right here ready to catch whatever she throws. And I can assure you, it will most definitely be a fucking touchdown.

As I stand in the bathroom, rinsing my face off, my phone rings. It's Bianca, Giselle's boss. Confused as to why she would be calling, I answer the call.

"Killian, this is Bianca. I'm calling to let you know Giselle is no longer available to escort you. If you would like to see the women who are available, I can have my assistant send you over their profiles."

Shocked by this turn of events, it takes me a second before I respond. "Giselle is who I choose. We spoke about this."

"Giselle is no longer available to you effective immediately. I'm sorry for the inconvenience, but as I said, I can send over—"

I cut her off. "I don't want anyone else. If she isn't available to me, who is she available to?"

There's a slight pause, and then Bianca says, "I am not at liberty to disclose my employee's clients with you."

Without responding, I hang up.

This can't be fucking happening.

For the last ten years, I've focused on my career, my family, my friends. This is the first Valentine's Day where I've actually taken a woman out.

I'm aware that, up until right now, I was technically paying for her to escort me places, but these last couple weeks haven't been about her job. They've been about us.

She wasn't paid to spend her nights with me in my bed, tucked into my side. She wasn't paid to take her lunch break with me. She definitely wasn't paid to go with my niece and me skating and to the zoo. She's been doing all of those things because she wants to.

Giselle has come to mean so much to me in such a short amount of time. She isn't just some woman I want to help or date. She's important to me. We have fun together. We laugh and joke and we have a lot in common.

I saw the gift she gave me. That wasn't from a woman who doesn't want to be around me. She wouldn't do this. She wouldn't refuse to see me anymore, only to see other men.

But she also isn't in a place to quit her job...

Not wanting to cause a scene, I decide not to bring up Bianca's phone call while we're at dinner. We will definitely talk about this, but it will be later.

I adjust my suit then head back out to our table. The food has arrived, but Giselle is waiting for me to eat. I lift my fork and knife to cut my steak, but then Giselle looks up at me and smiles sweetly, and my earlier decision flies straight out the window.

My blood boils at the idea I was so inconsequential to her she could just walk away from us and smile at me like nothing has happened—like nothing has changed.

My utensils clatter against my plate, and Giselle gives me a concerned look. Did she really think I wouldn't care? Maybe she was hoping I wouldn't find out until after dinner. After I took her home.

Does that mean she wasn't planning to spend the night?

Bianca said effective immediately.

This time tomorrow Giselle will be out with another man. She will accompany him to an event of some sort. He will parade her around on his arm like a trophy he's won. One he doesn't deserve. He'll treat her like an object. He won't pay attention to whether she's happy. Whether she's satisfied. He'll be undeserving of her, but still, she'll give herself to him.

My thoughts go back to her confession a couple weeks ago: *"I just want to feel connected to someone. I'm tired of feeling so alone."*

If that's what she craves then why is she pushing me away?

"Was I not enough for you?" I ask before I can stop myself.

Giselle's brows furrow together in confusion at my question. "Excuse me?"

"Was. I. Not. Enough. For. You?" I repeat slower. "Was it because I wouldn't fuck you?"

"Killian," she hisses, looking around at the other patrons, "what are you talking about?"

"You know what I'm talking about, don't play stupid. I know you called Bianca and told her to take me off your schedule."

Giselle goes pale. "Can we please talk about this in private?"

She glances around at the couples near us, clearly embarrassed. I feel like shit for calling her out right now, but fuck if with one phone call she didn't go and break my goddamn heart. The thought of her with other men tears me apart.

"Please," she whispers, and it's then I notice her eyes are glossed over as if she's about to cry.

Why would she cry? She's the one who has ended us, not me.

"Fine." I stand, our meal disregarded. "Let's go."

It isn't as if we're going to sit here and eat our food now anyway. Giselle stands as well, and the light hits the necklace I gave her. I want to turn the clock back to ten minutes ago, when I was still ignorant to the decision she made about us behind my back.

Grabbing the book she gave me, I stalk out of the restaurant with Giselle trailing behind. We're at a restaurant where I have an account on file, so the meal will be paid for.

I text the driver, and a few minutes later he pulls around. Once we're in the car, I give him my address and then press the button for the privacy partition.

The second it's closed, Giselle turns to face me and says, "I did call Bianca." Several tears fly down her pink cheeks. Has she been crying since we were inside? I was so hellbent on not looking at her, I didn't notice her tears actually fell. "I told her I couldn't continue to let you pay for my services. That when you fall in love with a man..." She chokes on a sob. "When you fall in love with a man, you don't request payment from him."

It takes a second for what she said to soak into my brain...

Fuck. Me.

She quit her job.

For me.

She's fallen in love with me.

Needing to touch her, to feel her against me, I grab her hips and pull her onto my lap. She squeals in surprise and wipes the tears from her eyes.

"Giselle, baby, I just...I assumed you were tired of waiting for me to get my shit together. I can't even tell you how sorry I am. God, I am such a jackass."

Lifting her chin, I look into her beautiful, soulful eyes. The same ones I had once mistaken for being cold, but in actuality were broken and lonely—like me. "Please forgive me. I was a damn fool. A fool who was too blinded by his love for you to see that you were always mine."

"You love me too?" she whispers.

A single tear escapes down her cheek and I use my thumb to wipe it away. "I do. I love you, baby."

Her breath hitches and then our mouths crash against each other. Our lips molding, our tongues swirling. We kiss fervently as Giselle undoes my pants.

I glide my hands up her creamy thighs to find she's wearing a silk thong, then palm the globes of her perfect ass.

She lifts slightly and pulls my dick out of my boxers, stroking it a few times before she pushes the thin material to the side and guides me into her slick cunt.

A throaty groan escapes as she begins to ride me with abandon. Our kiss doesn't once stop, instead it gets harder, rougher. Her fingers tug on the strands of my hair as she grinds against me, pelvis to pelvis. Up and down. She feels so damn good.

Hot. Wet. Tight.

And then I'm coming.

Like a motherfucking virgin.

I break our kiss, embarrassed as fuck. My head drops to Giselle's chest. She's breathing heavily from doing all the work, yet she didn't even get off.

"That's not how I wanted this to go down," I mutter as her body shakes with laughter.

I look up at her to see she's smiling down at me, and I shake my head in frustration. "I wanted to make love to you, not fuck you in the backseat of a town car and blow my load in ten fucking seconds like a horny teenager."

Giselle giggles. Fucking giggles.

"Actually," she says, "it was me who was fucking you."

I groan and close my eyes, and she giggles some more.

"It's not funny. You didn't even get off."

I go to lift her off me, but her thighs clench around mine, my now-flaccid dick still inside her.

"Hey," she murmurs. When I don't open my eyes, I feel her cold palms against my cheeks. "Look at me, Kill." I do, and fuck if she isn't the most stunning woman I've ever met. Her hair is tousled, her lip gloss is smeared. Her cheeks are a light pink. She's fucking gorgeous.

"We have all night," she says. "Once we get back to your place and your dick recuperates, you can fuck me."

"I don't want to fuck you," I say, repeating my earlier words. "I want to make love to you."

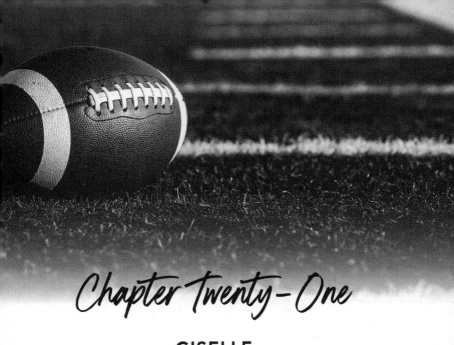

Chapter Twenty-One

GISELLE

"Take that dress off now," Killian demands when we enter his condo. I watch as he pulls at his tie until it comes loose, then he drops it to the floor along with his jacket. He unbuttons his shirt and drops it haphazardly, then kicks his shoes into the corner before he removes his pants and boxers.

I follow him into the bathroom—enjoying the view of his tight, muscular ass—where he turns the water on in his spacious shower. He looks at me and frowns. "Giselle, clothes."

I giggle—because apparently a man telling me he loves me leads to me turning into a teenage girl—and unzip my dress.

It falls to the marble floor and pools around my high-heeled feet. I step out of it and am left in a pink and black satin bra and panty set and my heels. I didn't plan on Killian seeing me in this, but when I woke up this morning and remembered it was Valentine's Day, I wore it to feel pretty. Now, based on the way Killian is looking at me, I'm very glad I did.

I unlatch my bra and let it fall to the ground, my nipples pebbling from the slight chill in the air. Then, I hook the sides of my panties with my index fingers and slowly lower them down my legs until they reach my heels. I step out of them, fully aware that I'm putting on a show for Killian.

"Fuck me," he groans as he eye-fucks his way down my now-naked body while I stand in front of him in only the heels he bought me.

He stalks over and lifts me up, placing me onto the counter. The granite is cool against my overheated body, and it causes me to shiver.

His lips land on my neck, and he peppers kisses downward, stopping along the way to suck and lick my overheated flesh.

My fingers pull on his hair, demanding more while my heels wrap around his bare ass, pulling him into me.

His dick, once again hard, teases my clit, and I pull him in closer, guide him into me.

Killian groans, biting down on my shoulder, as our bodies connect.

"Fuck me," I beg, and he does. His hips thrust powerfully as he fucks me harder than I've ever been fucked in my life. My head lulls back and hits the mirror as I moan in pleasure.

His lips go to my breasts, sucking on my nipples, as his dick, thick and long, hits my G-spot over and over again.

And unlike last time, I come completely undone. My entire body shakes, my vaginal walls clench, and I orgasm around Killian's cock as his warm seed fills me.

"Jesus fucking Christ, woman!" he growls. "I can't control myself with you."

I laugh at his words. "Well, at least we're getting closer to the bed," I point out. "What's the saying? Third time's a charm?"

"Shower, now," he grunts, and I laugh some more.

"Yes, caveman."

He glares playfully then pulls out of me. When he backs up farther, his eyes go wide, and I follow his gaze downward to see what he's looking at.

Shit! We didn't use protection.

Both times.

I'm about to tell him I'm on birth control when he says, "That's the sexiest fucking thing I've ever seen in my life."

"What?" I look down, confused. I waxed recently, but surely he's seen a hairless pussy before.

"My seed dripping out of your cunt and running down the inside of your thigh."

His words have me wanting him back inside me, but I know he needs time to recuperate. "C'mon, dirty boy, I want to soap you up."

I jump down and kick my heels off. The water is still on and the bathroom is now all fogged up. I step into the hot water and moan as it rains down on my body. Killian joins me, pulling my body against his and laying a hard kiss to my lips.

"Thank you," he murmurs. When I give him a puzzled look, he elaborates. "For quitting your job. For taking a chance on us. For opening your heart and letting me in. I will do everything in my power to make sure you never regret it."

A lump forms in my throat and my eyes become blurry through my tears. I'm thankful we're in the shower so he can't tell I'm crying again. This man. He's quickly come to mean so damn much to me.

Pulling his head down, I kiss him softly. "You don't have to thank me, Kill," I whisper against his lips. "You loving me, broken and all, is everything."

MY EYES FLUTTER OPEN. THE ROOM IS DARK. IT must still be nighttime. Why am I awake?

Then I feel it...Killian's strong yet firm lips on my flesh.

Kiss behind my ear.

The front of his body is pressed against my back. We fell asleep naked with his dick nestled between my ass cheeks.

Kiss to my neck.

His rough hand makes its way down my arm and over my bare hip. I wiggle my ass to tease him and his cock twitches slightly.

Kiss on my shoulder.

He rolls me onto my back. Spreading my legs, he situates himself between my thighs. His fingers thread with mine, our hands landing on the pillow over my head. Then, he pushes slowly into me, his wide girth stretching me deliciously.

He doesn't thrust.

No.

He glides.

In and out of me.

Like my body was made for him.

His lips meet mine and he kisses me softly.

And for the first time, I know what it feels like for a man to make love to me.

Chapter Twenty-Two

GISELLE

"Wow! This dress is exquisite! You're going to be the most beautiful bride," Corrine, Olivia's stepmom, gushes as Olivia turns in a full circle.

"It's perfect," Olivia agrees. "I'm just glad there's room for growth and we're getting married soon, or I would have to buy a different dress."

"It would be worth it," Corrine says. "You're bringing another little miracle into this world."

"I know. I just can't wait to finally marry Nick and move into our new home." She smiles into the mirror and our eyes lock. Her lips turn down, and I hate that she's putting her future off because of me.

"You could move into the house now," I suggest. "It's practically move-in ready. You don't have to wait until you're married." When she looks like she's going to argue, I add, "I could keep an eye on our place until it sells."

"I haven't put it up for sale." She frowns.

"Not yet, but you are, right?"

"Well..."

"Olivia, we've gone over this." I stand and turn her around so we're facing each other. "I love you. You're the best friend a woman could ever have. But it's time to put yourself first. It's only a matter of time until my mom's house sells. Move in with your fiancé and put your place up for sale."

"Okay." She nods but still looks unsure.

"It's not a request. I'm demanding, as your best friend, that you move in with Nick now."

"Okay." She smiles softly. And then her eyes glance down and spot my necklace. "This is beautiful. Who gave this to you?" She fingers the heart and flips it over to read the inscription. "Oh, Giselle."

"Killian gave it to me for Valentine's Day," I admit.

"You two are together?"

"We are." I can't help the grin that lights up my face, and Olivia's smile widens as well.

"Oh my god! I'm going to need all the details."

I laugh. "Okay, but first, let's finish our fitting."

"Fine!" Olivia pouts playfully.

"I'm very happy for you, Giselle," Corrine says, pulling both of us into a hug. "I'm so glad you two have found love."

"Thank you."

After we finish at the bridal boutique, we head out to brunch. While we're there, my friend Tabitha texts me with some info I was waiting on. I excuse myself for a moment and make the call.

"Good afternoon, may I please speak to Benjamin Fields? My name is Giselle."

I'm put on a brief hold, and then a baritone voice appears over the line. "This is Benjamin Fields. How can I help you?"

I explain to him that Tabitha gave me his info and I'm looking for an evening job—one where I don't sell my body—or soul—for money. Because I hold several of the qualifications he's looking for, he agrees to meet with me tomorrow night.

After thanking him, we hang up and I see a text from Killian.

> No wise fish would go anywhere without a porpoise.

I let out a soft laugh at his, for once, correct Alice in Wonderland quote, then text him back.

> Google finally got it right.

Another text from him immediately comes through. It's a picture of a hard covered copy of Alice's Adventures in Wonderland.

I text him back a big smiley face, loving that he picked up the book simply because he knows I love it.

A few seconds later, his response comes through.

> What time will you be done?

It's been a little over a week since Valentine's Day and every night has been spent in his arms. He picks me up from work every day, and we either go to dinner or order in.

Today is Saturday, so I'm off, and I know he was hoping to spend the day together. But then I remembered Olivia made an appointment for us to get fitted for our dresses for her wedding.

Killian pouted as I left this morning, but I promised we would spend the rest of the weekend together. I'm not sure how I'm going to explain it to him if I get this job. It will mean once again working evenings.

I text him back I'll be done in a little while, and he responds that he'll be here to pick me up. For a man who's never been in a serious relationship, he sure makes it look like he's an expert.

After lunch, we step outside, and sure enough Killian is waiting on the sidewalk, only he's standing against the light post and not in his car.

He smiles when he spots me, then he stalks over, picking me up and twirling me around while kissing me like he didn't just see me this morning. It reminds me of the shit you see in those cheesy Hallmark movies.

I crack up laughing when he puts me down, and Olivia and Corrine both swoon. I guess that's why you see stuff like that in those movies...

"Ladies," Killian says as he bends at the waist and bows. "Do you need a ride anywhere?"

Olivia giggles but shakes her head. "Nope, I drove. You two have fun, but not too much." She mock glares and then she and Corrine head to her car.

"Your place?" I ask.

Killian takes my hand in his. "Actually, I have a surprise for you." He opens the car door for me and I get in. He doesn't tell me where we're going but when we get onto the interstate, I have an idea. Forty minutes later, we pull up to the facility my mother is staying at.

"She's accepting visitors?" I ask, hopeful.

"She is, and she would like to see you."

I throw my arms around him. "Thank you."

"Your sister is here too. We're going to meet with the doctors and go over her diagnosis, and then your sister and you will have some time with your mom."

We're greeted by the receptionist who walks us back to the office, and Adrianna is already in there.

"Addy!" I run into the room and give my sister a hug. It's been too long since we've seen each other. "Oh, Addy," I murmur, "I've missed you."

"I've missed you more." She smiles brightly. "Thank you for making sure mom is getting the best care. I hate that I can't do anything..."

"Hey, stop," I say. "Your job is to go to school. I peeked at your grades the other day, and you're doing phenomenal."

"Thank you."

She glances over at Killian and gives him a knowing smile. "It's nice to see you again."

The one and only time they met was the day my dad left my mom.

Now they're meeting for the second time to discuss my mother's mental health. *Can you say dysfunctional family?*

Adrianna extends her hand to shake his, and he takes it. While chatting with my sister the last couple weeks, I've mentioned Killian a few times, and while I haven't come out and said what we are to each other—hell, I'm not even sure we know—the grin my sister's currently sporting tells me she's drawn her own conclusion, which means she's imagining us married and with kids in the near future.

"Killian is actually the one who—" I begin to tell her he's the reason our mom is getting the help she needs, but Killian cuts me off.

"I'm the one who made sure your sister got to this appointment on time."

I give him a confused look, but then it clicks. He doesn't want my sister to know I needed his help for our mom. And just like that, my heart expands at his selflessness.

The doctors come in and introduce themselves since it's their first time meeting Adrianna, and then in walks my mother.

"Mom!" Adrianna and I both jump up and give her a hug.

"Oh, girls, I'm so happy to see you both," our mom coos.

Killian pulls a chair up, so she can sit between Adrianna and me. "Killian, it's good to see you, again." She gives him a hug.

"You too, Mrs. Winters. You look good."

"Oh, thank you." My mom blushes, and I stifle my laugh.

Killian seems to have that kind of effect on all the Winters women—even the one who's gay.

Dr. Burns begins, "We wanted your mom to be in this meeting because it is her health we're discussing. After the last few weeks of close evaluation, we have determined your mother was in fact misdiagnosed. It's actually something that is very common, especially since the symptoms are alike.

"Looking at her history, the different psychiatrists diagnosed her with MDD: Major Depressive Disorder. What we've determined is your mother actually has bipolar disorder. While the symptoms are similar, the medications are not."

Dr. Clay continues, "Oftentimes you might've thought your mother's medications were working. She would have good days, and you probably assumed it was because of the medications. But then when she would have bad days, you thought they weren't working, and so you did what most people do. You took her to a new doctor to get reevaluated."

My heart plummets in my chest as I listen to them. They're describing exactly what we went through, and what we did the last fifteen years.

"I see the look on your face," Dr. Clay says. "Don't do that. Don't feel like you've let her down. She doesn't feel that way. Do you, Sarah?"

Everyone turns to my mom. "If it weren't for my daughters, I wouldn't even be alive right now." Tears fill her lids. "Nobody could've known. I didn't even understand it myself. The highs, the lows. The depression. I hate that my daughters spent their childhood without the kind of mother they deserved."

"Oh, Mom, we love you. We just want you better," I tell her.

"And I appreciate that, but now that I'm able to see things more clearly, I need to take responsibility. I failed my family."

"Mrs. Winters," Dr. Clay says, "have you spoken to your counselor about your feelings regarding this matter?"

"I have," Mom says. "We're agreeing to disagree at the moment."

Dr. Clay laughs. "Okay, please make sure you continue to speak your thoughts. While accepting responsibility is a good thing, you weren't aware of what was wrong and didn't understand what was happening. I don't like you using the word failed."

Mom nods in understanding.

"So, what now?" Adrianna asks.

"Now that we have a firm grasp on your mother's situation, we continue to treat her," the doctor says. "We're going to keep her here for at least another few weeks. Bipolar is treatable, but it's also about learning how to live with it. She will continue to see her counselor here and be monitored closely.

"Once she's discharged, in the beginning, she will need to see a counselor several times a week. She'll need to live a life free of as much stress as possible. We want her to work on figuring out how she can accomplish this. Bipolar isn't something that will just go away. It's something she will have to be aware of and manage every day.

My stomach knots at the thought of my mom having to deal with this forever. I was so sure her being here would mean she would be fixed. But from what they're saying, the only thing they can offer her are heavy duty Band-Aids. She's going to have to deal with this for the rest of her life.

"Mom, how are you feeling?" I ask her.

"I feel really good," she says with a confidence I don't think I've ever heard from her before. "I feel calm and less anxious. I'm beginning to feel like my body and my head are actually my own."

I reach over and place my hand on top of hers and squeeze it. She gives me a watery smile and I vow once she gets out of here, I'm going to make sure she never loses her smile again.

I'm going to sell the house and find us a place to live, and I'm going to make sure she takes her meds and sees a counselor. The last fifteen plus years were a rollercoaster between heaven and hell, and I will never let her get back on that ride again.

The doctors continue to explain the diagnosis and treatment plan some more, and when they're done, they let us know we can spend some time with our mom in the visiting room.

"Dr. Burns, can I ask you a question in private?" I ask as everyone stands.

"Sure," he says.

Everyone steps out of the room while we remain inside. "I was just wondering...bipolar disorder, is it...can it be genetic?"

The doctor gives me a quizzical look, so I elaborate. "My mom wasn't always like this. I can remember the good times from when I was little. There weren't many, but there were enough to think she wasn't born like this."

"Bipolar is a brain disorder which can develop any time," he begins. "Some people are born with the vulnerability to the disorder, which means they have a higher chance of eventually developing the disorder.

"In your mom's case that's probably what happened. She might've had the symptoms when she was younger, but nobody knew to pay attention to them."

"Can my sister and I have this...vulnerability?"

"Some studies have shown it can run in families, but just because your mom has it doesn't mean you will. It's important for you to pay attention to the symptoms we've discussed, and if you feel you're experiencing them, see a counselor immediately. Bipolar Disorder isn't a death sentence. You saw your mom today. She is doing well. The key is to monitor her and teach her how to live with the disorder. Many people with Bipolar live a normal life."

A normal life. My mind goes to all the years my father tried to love my mom but couldn't handle it. To the years my sister and I practically raised ourselves. Nothing was normal about any of that.

I know it was before she got help, but who's to say once she gets out we'll ever have a *normal* relationship with our mom.

The medications are working for now, but what happens when they don't? Yes, this facility is one of the best, but like the doctors said, it's all trial and error to find a way to manage the disorder.

"Thank you, Dr. Burns."

After spending some time with Mom, we all say our goodbyes. Adrianna heads back to Boston, and Killian and I head back to his place.

While he's driving, I make the mistake of looking up my mom's condition. Of course, there are a million and one horror stories—from patients having a higher chance of suffering from substance abuse, to a higher risk of suicide.

So even if my mom's medication works, and for the most part she's okay, there's still a chance of things going wrong.

Just as I'm about to click on another page, my phone rings. It's the realtor.

"I have some good news," she tells me. "An offer has been put in for the house."

"Oh, thank God." My entire body relaxes.

"It was actually placed a few hours ago, but I had to type up the contract. It's a cash offer and they have agreed to your asking price."

"Really? They didn't even try to counter?"

Weird...I'm asking for what the going rate of the homes in the area are, but still...

"All you need to do is have your dad sign the papers, and since you have the power-of-attorney for your mom, you'll need to sign them as well, and then we'll get the deal done."

Shit! My dad. I'm going to have to find him and get him to sign the damn papers.

"Giselle...that won't be a problem, will it?"

"No, I just need to find my dad."

We hang up and Killian glances over at me. "Your mom's house?"

"It sold. A cash deal. This is perfect timing."

And then it hits me. The timing is too perfect.

"I told Olivia today to move into her new house with Nick. You don't think she bought the house, do you?"

Killian's eyes flit back and forth between the road and me. "I don't think she would do that," he says.

"You're right. She knows how upset I would be. Now I just need to find my dad."

"I can have my brother search for him."

"Thank you."

"So, what did you want to talk to the doctor about alone?" he asks.

"I asked him if Bipolar is genetic."

"And?"

"It can be, and I've made a decision." One that was cemented the minute I viewed all those posts online. "I don't want to have any children."

Killian glances over at me then back to the road. "Giselle, what you went through growing up was because your mother wasn't diagnosed properly. You heard the doctor. Your mother will live a normal life."

"There's that word again...*normal*. Nothing was normal about what Addy and I went through. I can't imagine ever putting my children through that. The physical and emotional abuse. I won't do it. And who's to say this time will work?"

"Maybe take some time and think about it. It's not like you have to decide right now."

"There's nothing to think about. I won't put my family through that. The doctor said it can develop at any time."

"So, what? You just won't have a family? You won't get married?"

"It's one thing to get married. I'm not saying I'm going to not have a life. But had my parents not had kids, when my mom got sick, they wouldn't have had to deal with us."

"I can't speak for your father, but I don't believe your mother would view it as *dealing* with you. She was so happy to finally feel good. You heard her when we were talking to her afterward. She's excited to start this next phase of her life with her daughters."

Killian pulls into the parking garage and parks in his spot, then he turns to me. "I feel like I'm finally living again, and you're the reason why. Please don't stop what's happening between us out of fear."

I take a second to assess his features. His messy chocolate-brown hair and deep mesmerizing hazel eyes. The way he smiles at me like I'm everything. He's the perfect mix of sexy and beautiful and perfect. And I know exactly what he means, because it wasn't until he entered my life, I felt like I was finally really living. I don't want to stop living. I just don't want my living to negatively affect those around me.

"I don't want to stop anything between us. But Killian, I have to ask, and I know it's too early to even mention children, but would you be okay with...I mean..." I take a deep breath. "I don't want to have kids.

"I know it sounds like overkill, but you weren't there when I was growing up. You didn't see what we went through because of my mother's illness. You didn't read the articles I read. I want to live my life and love you.

"But I don't want you to feel you have to stay with me out of obligation, if what happened to my mom, happens to me. My dad sucks, but I believe that a lot of the reason why he stayed with my mom all those years was because of my sister and me. I don't think it's a coincidence that he left once Addy went away to college.

"I don't ever want you to feel you *have* to be with me. And I don't ever want to put my children in the position that Addy and I were put in. I'm not trying to blame my mom. I know she didn't know. But I do know. And it would be irresponsible of me to have kids knowing there's a chance that at some point I might not be able to be the mother they deserve. Are you okay with it just being the two of us?"

"Shit, baby," he says. "I know what you went through was rough, but I would never leave you. Whatever happens in life we will face it together. And you can't go by all the crap on the internet."

"It wasn't just crap," I argue. "Many of those sites are credible. Did you know people with Bipolar run a higher risk of committing suicide? Of becoming addicted to drugs? Is that what you want to potentially expose our kids to? I found my mom on the floor half-dead. I would never wish that on another person."

Killian stares at me for a long moment, and I don't even realize I'm holding my breath until he nods once. "I just want you, Giselle. Whatever it is you want or don't want I'm okay with. But I think you should speak to someone."

"Like a counselor?"

"Yeah, I can go with you if you want. I just think it would be a good idea to speak to someone about how you're feeling."

"Okay," I agree.

We get inside and Killian gives his brother a call, and not even twenty minutes later, he calls back with an address for my dad.

"That was fast."

"My brother has connections." Killian winks playfully.

"Will you go with me to see him?"

"Of course. When?"

"Now? The address isn't too far from here. We can swing by and get the papers from the realtor and take them to him to sign and get notarized."

WE PULL UP TO AN OLDER YET STILL BEAUTIFUL brownstone in Chelsea. I'm not a real estate expert, but if I had to guess, the place is worth a few million. "Are you sure this is the address?" I ask Killian.

He double checks the information his brother sent over. "Yeah."

We get out and walk up to the front door. I ring the doorbell and immediately hear the sound of children's laughter. The door swings open and, standing there is a young, gorgeous blond-haired woman of maybe thirty. Based on how she's dressed and the way she presents herself, it's obvious this woman has money. Two little boys who can't be any older than five peek out from behind her, giggling.

"I'm sorry. I think I have the wrong address. I'm looking for Craig Winters."

The woman smiles softly. "You have the right address." She turns her head back toward the inside of her home. "Craig, honey, someone is here for you." My stomach lurches at the term of endearment, and Killian's hand finds mine. Something isn't right here.

My dad steps forward, and when he realizes it's me, his face pales. "Giselle..."

"Dad."

"Craig," the woman says, "why is she calling you 'Dad'?"

"Heather, give us a moment, please." My dad steps outside, shutting the door behind him.

"Is she...are they..." I can't even finish my sentence. I'm in shock. Killian's grip on my hand tightens.

"She is, and they are," my dad murmurs softly.

Oh my god! He has two kids by a woman who isn't my mom—his wife. "But you're still married to mom!"

"Heather and I aren't married. We're engaged, though. I was waiting for your mom to get out of the facility before giving her the papers."

"You knew she was in a facility?" I shout. "Those little boys aren't babies! And that woman doesn't even know you have a daughter!"

"Giselle, please let me explain."

"No! Fuck you, *Dad*!" I'm about to storm away when I remember the papers I need him to sign. I turn back around and push the contract into his chest. "The house sold. You need to sign these papers, and don't you dare even think for a second you're getting a penny. Did you take out the second loan on the mortgage to purchase this place?"

"No, Heather has her own money."

I notice he doesn't explain what he did take the money out for. At this point, though, it doesn't matter. I just need him to sign these damn papers so I can deal with what he left behind.

"Just sign the papers," I tell him.

He nods once.

Knowing how upset I am, Killian goes with my dad to get the papers notarized while I wait in his car.

When they return, my dad tries to speak to me, but I refuse. He made his choice, and clearly he's having no problem living with it.

"Do not bring those divorce papers to mom to sign," I say before he walks away. "Send them to me, and when she's healthy enough, I'll tell her the man she married is a lying, cheating, asshole."

Dad looks like he wants to say something, but I don't give him a chance. "Don't ever contact any of us again. As far as I'm concerned you're no longer part of our family—not that you've been for a long time." I roll up my window and wait for Killian to get in.

I try to tell him I'd like to be dropped off at my place, but in typical Killian-fashion, he ignores me completely.

Once we're inside his place and changed into comfier clothes, he pulls me into his side on the couch.

"It feels like today has been the never-ending day." I laugh humorlessly.

He lifts me into his lap and kisses me tenderly. "How about I make you forget about today?"

"That sounds like a damn good idea to me."

Killian kisses me harder this time, his fingers reaching up and pinching my nipples, while my fingers thread through the strands of his hair.

We kiss for God knows how long, getting lost in each other. Eventually, he carries me into his room and lays me on the bed.

We remove each other's clothes and then he spreads my legs and enters me slowly.

And as he makes love to me several times, he successfully makes me forget the craziness of today.

Chapter Twenty-Three

KILLIAN

"Damn, I don't want to pat my own back, but this sleeve is going to look fresh as hell when it's done. Shit, it already does."

Jase turns the gun off and the buzzing sound immediately stops. He brings a handheld mirror down to my arm so I can see the new work he's added, and he's right, it looks damn good.

What started out as a tattoo of my college team football helmet has turned into an entire collage of my career. From my NFL team logo to the numerals from the super bowl we won last year.

Today, though, I had him add in something more personal. The quote on the back of the heart I gave Giselle on Valentine's Day has been artfully wrapped around my bicep and woven through several of my other tattoos. I know it's only been a couple weeks since we made this thing we have going on between us official, but I can feel it. She's it for me.

My phone rings, so I pull it out of my pocket while Jase rubs Vaseline across the new artwork. The caller ID shows it's my brother.

"Hey, bro, what's up?"

"I have news on Melanie."

Damn, straight to the point. The other night while lying in bed, Giselle mentioned again that maybe I should find Melanie to get some closure.

So, the following night when she said she had to work late and couldn't come over, I went over to my brother's place for dinner and told him everything. And like I knew he would, he agreed I needed closure and told me he would get Melanie's contact info.

"All right."

"She's living in North Carolina. Cedar Wood Acres."

"She's back living where we went to school?"

It would make sense since she once told me she grew up there, but it's weird to imagine her back after she made it a point to run away from that very same place all those years ago.

She even went as far as to drop out of school just to get away.

"Yep," Dylan confirms.

"Is she married? Have kids?"

"I didn't tell him to find anything out. I have a phone number and an address. I'll text it to you. I think if you want to know about her, it's best if you find out from her yourself."

"You're right," I agree. "I'll give her a call and see if she's up to meet with me. I can even visit Mom and Dad while I'm there."

"Good idea," he says. "Are you going alone?"

He knows Giselle and I are dating. I didn't tell him about her old job as an escort, but he knows things are serious between us. I try to imagine flying to North Carolina by myself, but I can't picture it. I'd love to introduce her to my parents and show her where I grew up.

"I'm going to ask Giselle to go with me."

"All right, cool. Let me know if you need anything. Don't forget your niece's birthday is next weekend."

"I won't. I'll talk to you later."

We hang up and I text Giselle.

> Dinner tonight? I can pick you up from work.

She responds immediately.

> Can't. I'm sorry. Working late. Rain check?

Shoving my phone into my pocket, I head out to the main lobby of Forbidden Ink. This is the third time this week she's asked for a rain check because of work.

My only thought is that maybe because of the lack of paycheck from A Touch of Class, she's asked for more hours at Fresh Designs.

I hate to think she's struggling now to make ends meet because of me, but it makes sense. She needed that income and now it's gone.

"Sorry about that," I say to Jase. "My brother called. The addition looks amazing."

I slide my card across the counter, and he takes it to ring me up.

"No worries." He hands me the receipt to fill out. "So, uh, have you seen Celeste lately?"

My gaze leaves the receipt and lands on Jase. Why the hell is he asking about Celeste? And then I remember the night of Giselle's birthday and the awkward as fuck vibes Jase and Celeste gave off.

"Here and there. I think she said something about Paris."

I shrug, and he nods, trying to appear nonchalant, but his eyes are darting all over the place like he's nervous.

"You don't like her, do you?"

I'm well aware I sound like a gossipy teenage girl.

"Nah." He shakes his head emphatically and clears his throat.

"You sure?" I ask while I fill out the tip and sign my name.

"Yeah, man. The last time I saw her she left a bit pissed, and I was just wondering how she's doing. Forget I asked."

He takes the receipt from me and hands me back my card.

And that's when I remember something. "You know Celeste..." Jase's face doesn't give anything away. "When I was in college, you came to the campus looking for her."

It was a good ten years ago, but now that I'm thinking about it, it was clear that day he not only knew Celeste but was really upset.

"That was a long time ago," Jase says. "And to be honest, I don't think I ever knew her."

"She doesn't seem to let a lot of people in," I tell him.

A few weeks ago, I would've told him she's a gold-digging bitch and to run, but now, after seeing how wrong I was about Giselle, I'm done assuming the worst in every female.

Giselle, Olivia, and Nick are good people and all three of them like and care about Celeste, so that has to mean something.

"From what Nick's said over the years, Celeste's upbringing caused her to keep most people at arm's length. I don't know what happened between you two, but I wouldn't take it personally. Celeste's sole focus has always been on her career."

I'm not putting her down, just being honest. The woman came from nothing and has made it her life mission to make herself into something, and she's done just that. If nothing else, Celeste Leblanc is determined.

Jase flinches but doesn't respond. He extends his hand and we shake. "Thanks for the heads up."

"Sure thing."

"Quinn isn't here right now, but you can give her a call when you're ready to set up your next appointment."

"Sounds good, man."

I head out and jump into my car. I check my phone and remember I never texted Giselle back. It's already after six, and an idea hits me. S

he mentioned working late, but she needs to eat. She might be stuck in the office, but I can bring dinner to her.

Stopping by the deli, I order us some soups and sandwiches, then drive over to Giselle's office.

When I get to her floor, the place, for the most part, is empty.

"May I help you?" an older woman asks, stepping out of what I assume is her office.

"I'm looking for Giselle."

The woman's brows furrow slightly, then she must remember her manners because she smiles and introduces herself. "I'm Lydia, Giselle's boss."

"Nice to meet you. I'm Killian, her boyfriend." The title rolls off my tongue easily. We haven't discussed labels, but giving myself that title feels right.

Lydia looks confused but quickly composes herself. "It's nice to meet you as well," she says, but it's obvious Giselle hasn't mentioned me. "Unfortunately, Giselle isn't here. Our office closes at six."

"Is it possible she stayed late to work?" I eye the hallway which leads to her office.

"Occasionally she does, but tonight she actually left a few minutes early, so no, it's not possible."

A sinking feeling hits me hard.

I thank her and head back to the elevator.

GOING DEEP

When I get back in my car, I text Giselle.

> Where are you?

A few minutes later, she texts back.

> I told you I'm working.

There's no way she lied to me, right? She wouldn't tell me she quit working for A Touch of Class and it not be true.

Not wanting to play games, I go for the truth.

> I'm at your office and you're not here.

The bubbles indicating she's typing appear and then disappear. This happens several times before they disappear for good, and then minute later my phone rings.

"You're at Fresh Designs?" she asks, sounding out of breath.

"Yes, and you're not."

"You came to check up on me?" Accusation drips in her words.

"I came to bring you dinner."

She sighs. "I'm not there."

"I know."

Another sigh.

"Giselle, talk to me, baby."

I don't know what's going on, but whatever it is we'll figure it out.

"Promise me you'll listen before you react." Jesus, fuck.

"Giselle..."

"A friend of mine who works at A Touch of Class mentioned a popular nightclub recently opened, so for the hell of it I applied." I notice she doesn't name the club. "I didn't think I would get hired, but I did."

"And that's why you haven't been able to hang out." The pieces are slowly coming together.

"Yes, because I've been working evenings."

"When did you get hired?"

"Umm, like two weeks ago."

I do the math in my head. The day after we met with her mom and went to her dad's place, she mentioned she had an appointment. Several times since then she's canceled our plans. She must've been working and didn't tell me.

"Giselle, what club are you working at?"

I close my eyes and wait for the blow. The one I know is coming.

"Assets," she whispers.

Fuck! The goddamned strip club. A high class one no less, but still a strip club.

"I'm not stripping," she rushes out.

"Then what are you doing there?" I try to keep my voice composed, but fuck, this woman is going to be the death of me.

"I'm waitressing and working the bar. I worked the bar throughout college." We're both silent for a beat, and then Giselle adds, "Please don't be mad."

"I'm coming to get you."

"Kill, please. I searched all over New York for a job! You don't understand how hard it is to find a job that will pay me enough to cover my sister's school *and* my school loans.

"Sure, the house being sold helps, but I still need to find a place to live and rent isn't cheap. I have a masters in interior freaking design. I might as well not even have a college degree. The tips I make here are more than I make working at Fresh Designs."

I put my car in drive and peel out. "I get it, babe. I do. But you're not working there. I'll be there in ten minutes. You can come out willingly or I'll carry your ass out."

Giselle gasps. "You wouldn't."

"I would."

"There's no way my boss—"

"Benjamin Fields?" I laugh humorlessly. "Trust me, he won't do a damn thing about it."

"You know him?" she shrieks. "Of course, you do! You're a goddamned NFL player. You know everybody!"

"Eight minutes, Giselle," I warn.

"Kill, please! I'm on break. I took it just to call you."

"And now you're clocking out. Seven minutes."

I click end on the call and throw my phone into the center console. Damn woman is testing my patience. I'm pissed as hell she'd get a job at a fucking strip club without telling me, but at the same time, it's what I love about her.

She's hellbent on being independent, and she's determined to take care of her mom and sister.

While I'm furious, I'm also pretty sure I just fell even more in love with her.

I pull up to the valet and park my car. "I'll only be a minute," I yell to the guy.

When I get up to the front, the bouncer who scans in the VIP members immediately recognizes me. Assets is a newer club but already well-known. Several of my teammates have VIP memberships here.

"Killian, how are you?"

"Good. You?"

"Can't complain."

"I didn't know you were a VIP member." He types away on his iPad.

Before I can correct him and explain why I'm here, out walks Giselle from the side door. Her hair is in a high, tight ponytail. Her makeup way overdone. She's wearing sweats and a hoodie, which means she changed out of whatever the uniform is.

I expect her to be mad, furious even, but she's not. She's frowning and her eyes appear to be glassed over like she's about to cry.

"I'm not," I tell the bouncer. "I'm just here to pick up my girlfriend." I wrap my arm around Giselle's shoulders and kiss her cheek. "You ready?" I ask her, and she nods wordlessly.

The ride home is quiet, and once we're inside, Giselle excuses herself to shower. I consider joining her, but figure she needs some time to herself.

I reheat the soups and place the sandwiches on plates. I pour us both something to drink then wait for her to get done.

When she comes out, she's in my boxers and Henley. Her hair is in a messy bun and her face is makeup-free.

She's back to looking fucking gorgeous.

She sits across from me at the table and thanks me for the food before she starts to eat. We eat in silence for a few minutes, and then she finally speaks. "I'm in debt with over a hundred thousand dollars in student loans. The interest accrues every month."

I set my spoon down to give her my full attention.

"My mom's house sold, but because of the second loan my dad took out on it, which was probably to help out his *other* family, I only got so much from the sale, and now I need to find a place to live. My mom is due to get out in a few weeks. She needs somewhere to go."

I nod in understanding.

"Right now, my sister has zero financial aid, which means I have to cover her tuition, room, board, books, and food card, plus her car insurance, which comes out to over sixty thousand dollars a year. And even once she applies for financial aid in the fall, it won't cover everything."

She continues, "You paid for my mom's care at the facility, but once she gets out, she will need to see a psychiatrist several times a week. And then there's her medications. Right now, she has no insurance, and the quotes I've been given, due to her condition, are over ten thousand a year."

I do the math in my head, unsure how this woman hasn't collapsed from the weight she's been forced to carry.

"I make pennies at Fresh Designs. I'm busting my ass and Lydia keeps telling me that soon I'll be hired on as a regular employee with benefits, but even if or when that happens, it will only put a dent in the money I need to shell out."

Giselle stands and comes around to my side of the table. She climbs into my lap and straddles me, and I back up slightly to give us room.

"I love you," she tells me. "Tonight, when you called me your girlfriend to the bouncer, it felt like my heart leapt right out of my chest."

"You are my girlfriend," I tell her. "I love you, baby." I give her a kiss.

"Tell me a job where I can make enough to pay for everything I need to pay for."

I don't need to think about it. I know there isn't one that doesn't require her to fuck someone or at the very least take her clothes off.

"The NFL," I joke, and she glares, but there's a hint of a smile threatening to come out.

"Killian, I'm serious."

"I am too. I make enough money to pay for all of that. I get you want to be independent, but let me help you, please."

There's no way she's going to agree, but I have to try.

She wraps her arms around my neck and hugs me tightly. Her face nuzzles into the crook of my neck, and her lips kiss my flesh softly.

"I can't let you do that, Kill. I love you for offering, but we've barely even started dating."

"We'll figure it out, Giselle," I murmur. "But please don't work at Assets."

She lifts her head and eyes me. "Are you actually *asking* me not to work there and not demanding it?"

"I was mad, baby. Shocked. But we both know I can't force you not to work somewhere."

She nods and gives me a chaste kiss. "Thank you for not demanding it. I told Benjamin I made a mistake and quit."

My body sags in relief.

"My brother found Melanie," I tell her, changing the subject. "She's in Cedar Wood Acres, North Carolina. It's only about twenty minutes from where we went to college. I grew up in the next town over."

"Are you going to go see her?"

"I am, and I was hoping you would come with me."

Her face lights up, telling me I made the right decision by asking her to join me. "I would love to."

"How about this weekend? I know it's last minute, but maybe you could take a day or two off work. We could take an early flight and make a long weekend out of it. I would love for you to meet my parents while we're there."

"I have a few personal days left I can use," she says. "Let's do it."

"And when we get back, we'll figure out your financial situation," I add.

She nods, but her smile loses its brightness.

"Okay," she agrees.

Chapter Twenty-Four

GISELLE

"THIS WAS MY LOCKER." KILLIAN POINTS TO THE half-rusted metal rectangle, and his face lights up like it's a box that once held all of his hopes and dreams. "And this is where my coach told me I had a shot at playing in the NFL." He walks us over to a tiny office with a big smile.

On our way here, he mentioned this is his first time showing a woman around where he went to school. I love that I get to be that woman. He knows so much about me, and I love every time I learn more about what makes Killian who he is.

After speaking with Lydia, who assured me she was okay with me taking a few personal days—after I promised to work remotely—we took an early flight out of JFK to Charlotte.

We're going to check into our hotel this afternoon, and Killian has spoken to Melanie, who has agreed to meet him for dinner this evening.

Tomorrow, the plan is to spend the day with his parents. But this morning, Killian is showing me some of his favorite spots, starting with the University of North Carolina.

We've seen the football field, the cafeteria, and he even convinced the kid currently residing in his old dorm to let him show me around.

Of course, once the kid recognized Killian as one of the wide receivers for the New York Brewers, he practically gave him the room.

Right now, we're currently standing in a smelly locker room he's showing me around.

While I'd rather not be in here, where it's clear football players aren't aware of the benefits of deodorant, the prideful look on his face and the twinkle in his eye as he speaks makes it all worth it.

We spend the next hour catching up with his old coaches, and they share some funny stories of Killian as a college football player. A few of the players are in the locker room for a Saturday practice, so Killian talks to them about working hard and making sure to take school seriously.

I learn Killian has a business degree, and had he not made it into the NFL, he planned to get his MBA. When Killian tells them we need to get going, his old coaches make us promise not to be strangers.

"New York is where you were drafted to?" I ask as we walk out of the locker room and head to our rental car.

North Carolina is so different from NYC. It's quiet, low-key, and people are actually friendly. It's hard to imagine Killian being happy here and then moving to New York.

"Yep, I've been there for ten years."

He opens my door for me, and I get in.

Once he's inside, I ask, "Do you think you will retire in New York?"

"Yeah," he says. "At this point in my career, if they made the decision to trade me, I would retire before I would move."

"Even if it meant not playing?" I ask, curiously.

"Most wide receivers retire by the age of thirty. I'm almost thirty-two. I've had a damn good career. I've even won a Super Bowl, something most can't say. Every year I play now is just a bonus." He glances over at me and his hand goes to my jean-clad thigh, squeezing it gently.

"Kind of ironic...you're at an age of retirement and I'm still trying to get a real job in my chosen profession." I laugh.

"You'll get there, Giselle. You're hard-working and motivated."

"I know, it just seems like we're at different points in our lives."

I'm not sure why I say that. Even to my own ears I can hear doubt creeping in. The differences between us. Wondering how this is all going to work. Maybe it's knowing he's going to meet with Melanie today. Maybe I'm scared that once he sees her and gets his closure, he'll question why he's with me.

He asked to be broken and lonely with me, but what happens once he's healed? When he's no longer broken? Will he still want me when he's fixed and whole and perfect while I'm still damaged?

"Look at the bright side, when we have kids, I can be a stay-at-home dad." He winks flirtatiously, and my stomach does some weird flip-flop thing at the thought of having kids with Killian, and then it sinks like a body in a lake being tied down by a heavy stone.

My breaths turn labored, and then Killian's eyes land on me.

"Shit, Giselle. I'm sorry!" Killian says, realizing his slip. "It was meant as a joke. Fuck. It just came out."

"It's okay," I tell him, trying to calm my breathing. "But maybe that slip…"

He's already healing, while I'm still broken. Soon I'll be lonely once again.

"No, don't you dare go there. I told you I'm okay with us not having kids, and I meant it." He scrubs his face in frustration. I know he feels bad for what he said, but that doesn't mean he didn't mean it. "I really am sorry," he says again.

"It's okay," I promise, my tone betraying my words.

We arrive at The Ritz Carlton, where Killian has booked us the penthouse suite, even though I told him any old hotel will do. But he said it's near his parents, which prevented me from continuing the argument.

After we check in, he suggests we hang out and order lunch in, since he'll be leaving in a few hours to meet Melanie.

When he originally made the plans with her, he asked if I would like to go. I told him I appreciated him wanting to include me but felt this is something he needs to do on his own. I'll be here when he gets back.

After we eat lunch, we settle on the couch, and I wait for Killian to grab the remote, but he surprises me when he pulls out *Alice's Adventures in Wonderland* and insists on reading the next chapter to me. I'm shocked to learn he's already on chapter eleven: Who Stole the Tarts?

Less than ten minutes into him reading, though, my eyes slowly shut, and I pass out in Killian's arms, dreaming of hearts instead of tarts being stolen.

Chapter Twenty-Five

KILLIAN

I ARRIVE AT THE RESTAURANT MELANIE suggested and let the hostess know there'll be two people. It's a small hole-in-the-wall place that if it wasn't for how good it smells, I'd be a bit concerned.

I'm sitting on the bench when Melanie walks in. She looks the same as she did twelve years ago, only a bit older. Her blond hair is a tad lighter and instead of her glasses, she must be wearing contacts. Her body has transformed from a teenager to a woman.

She smiles shyly at me, and I pull her into a friendly hug.

"Killian," she murmurs into my ear, her voice thick with emotion. "I never thought I would see you again." She pulls back, her eyes filled with unshed tears.

"You mean you don't watch football?" I joke, and she laughs. The tears spill over and she quickly wipes them away.

"My husband does," she says with a soft smile.

The hostess comes over and lets us know our table is ready. We sit and each order a Coke.

"So, you're married?" I ask, not sure how to start a conversation I requested to have.

"I am. His name is Brian. We'll be married for six years in August..." She looks like she's about to say more, so I don't say anything. And then she adds, "And we have two daughters: Brenda and Bridgette."

"How old?" I ask, unsure of what else to say.

"They're actually twins." She laughs softly. "They just turned three."

"I'm happy for you, Mel," I tell her truthfully, because I am. Regardless of what happened, I'm glad she's found happiness.

The waiter delivers our drinks and we place our food order. Based on the menu, this place is known for their seafood, so I order the Salmon and Melanie orders a Mahi sandwich.

"Killian, I need to apologize to you," Melanie says once the waiter leaves.

"I'm the one who should be apologizing to you," I argue.

"Just let me go first, please," she requests, so I do. "When I found out I was pregnant, I was scared and I went to you, hoping that you would comfort me, but I didn't even give you a chance. I had known I was pregnant for weeks. I had time to process and scream and cry and curse the world and everything else, but I didn't even give you ten minutes to process."

A loud sob escapes her, and she covers her face with shaking hands. I'm not sure if I should comfort her or wait for her to speak again. I'm so far out of my comfort zone here. Grabbing a napkin, I hand it to her so she can wipe her face.

"Thank you." She smiles sadly. "I was a teenager and scared, and I should've given you more time, but instead I ran and had an abortion, and for that I am truly sorry." Her lips tremble as she cries. "Every day I have regretted my decision. I often wonder if it would've been a boy or a girl. If she would've had my eyes or if he would've been an athlete like you."

A flood of new tears gush down her ashen cheeks. "Every day that I look at my beautiful daughters, I ask God to forgive me for not giving our baby a chance in this world. I'm..." She chokes on a sob. "I'm so sorry."

My heart aches over her words. She doesn't blame me. She's given me an out, but I don't want one.

"I shouldn't have pushed you away, Mel," I tell her. "I should've pulled you into my dorm and told you it would all be okay. Had I not pushed you away our baby would be here with us."

She shakes her head. "No, you did what anyone would do. You reacted out of shock. We were both so young. Just babies ourselves. I struggle every day with being thankful for my life because had I had our baby, I wouldn't have my two beautiful daughters." More tears race down her face. "I just hate myself for..." Killing our baby. She wants to say it, but she can't even get the words out.

"I know," I tell her, giving her an out.

I don't need to hear the words. I've felt them every day for the last decade. While I've been being eaten up by guilt all these years, I can't even possibly fathom what this woman has been feeling, knowing she's the one who ultimately had to make that decision.

It wasn't my body the baby was in. I didn't have a choice in the matter. I want to be mad at her for not choosing to keep our baby. I want to be mad at myself for not reacting the right way quicker. But she's right. We were just babies, and we both made decisions we have to live with.

I thought coming here, I would tell her that for the last ten years I haven't had sex so I could never put myself in that position again, that I wanted our baby and would've loved him or her, but I decide against it. She already feels guilty. She doesn't need more weight added to her load.

So, instead, I say the only thing that's left to say, "I forgive you, Melanie, and I hope you can forgive me too."

Fresh tears escape her lids. "Thank you, Killian." She sniffles loudly. "And just so you know, I forgave you a long time ago."

I stand and give her a hug. "Don't ever feel bad for the beautiful family you have," I whisper. "One choice shouldn't dictate the rest of your life. You deserve to be happy."

I sit back down, and a few minutes later, our food is brought out. We eat, mostly in silence. And when the waiter brings me the bill, I pay and walk Melanie out.

"Thank you for asking to meet up," she says when we get to her car. "I didn't realize how much I needed your forgiveness."

"Probably as much as I needed yours." I give her one last hug. "Have a good life, Mel."

"You too, Kill."

As I get in my car and think about everything we discussed, my mind goes to what Melanie said about struggling to be thankful for her family, knowing they came at the cost of our baby.

It's time for both of us to move forward. We can't change what happened, and while I would give anything to have a chance to raise our baby, my mind goes to Giselle, and I have to wonder if maybe everything happens for a reason. If Giselle is my reason.

When I wouldn't let any other woman into my heart or bed, I let her in. I didn't even ask if she was on birth control when we finally had sex. It just felt right with her.

It's because she's the one.

Even if she sticks with her decision to never want children, I know she's the woman I want to spend my life with. Just simply being with her is enough for me.

Instead of going back to the hotel, I take a detour into the city. There's somewhere I need to stop first.

When I get back to the hotel, Giselle is sleeping. Only this time, she's lying in bed with her laptop still open, which tells me she woke up and later fell back asleep.

My poor woman is working herself to death. I'm not sure how much longer she can keep going like this.

When I move the laptop from the bed to set it on the nightstand, it comes to life. On the screen are online classified ads. She was looking for another job. To the left of the website is a digital notepad with a list of the jobs she's found so far: maid services at a couple different hotels, a nighttime cleaning position for a law office.

I scroll farther and see a few waitress positions at a few different diners. My eyes flit to Giselle, who is snuggled up in her blanket. She's dealing with this because of me. I know she wants to take on the world alone, but she can't do it all.

And if it wasn't for her loving me, she wouldn't have to deal with this.

I'm sure she's going to give me shit for this later, but I'll deal with it when the time comes. Taking her laptop out to the main room, I search for her usernames and passwords.

Once I find them, I forward them to my email then delete it in her sent mail. I close her laptop and set it on the counter. Then I pull up the email on my phone and get to work.

I'm just finishing up when I hear Giselle's feet padding out of the room. "You're back."

She stops in front of the couch I'm sitting on and gives me a concerned smile.

"I am. I didn't want to wake you."

I open my arms and she fills the void, her arms wrapping around my torso and her head landing on my chest as I inhale her sweet scent.

"I prefer waking up next to you," she murmurs.

"How would you feel about waking up next to me for the rest of your life?" I ask, and Giselle stills.

Then she sits up, and I immediately want her back against me.

"Killian..." She stares at me as I sit up and reach into my pocket. I pull out the ring box and get down on one knee.

I hadn't planned on proposing tonight, but it feels like it's the right time.

Giselle's hands cover her mouth. "Killian," she says again.

"I know some would say what's happening between us, this relationship, is probably moving too fast." She nods slowly, and I laugh. "As you know, I'm a wide receiver. My job is to catch the ball." She laughs out loud, calming my nerves. "There's a phrase in football. Going Deep. Have you ever heard of it?"

She shakes her head.

"It's when you run down the field for a long pass. You're serious. Committed. Unstoppable. I'm in this *deep* with you, Giselle. I'm serious. Committed. There's no stopping what I feel for you. I'm running down the field to catch the ball, and I just need you to throw it."

I open the ring box and pluck the engagement ring from the felt that's holding it in place.

After leaving Melanie, I went to a few jewelers in the area my mom recommended. After the third one, I found the ring I knew was meant for Giselle. A three-carat halo cut diamond on a simple platinum band.

"Will you throw the ball to me, baby?" I ask her, holding the ring up for her to see.

Tears leak from her eyes, and I'm not sure if they're happy or sad. And then she says in a voice, so quiet I can barely hear her, "You're healed."

"What?"

I heard what she said, but I'm unsure what she means.

"Be broken and lonely with me." She repeats the words I said to her before. "You're no longer broken." She swipes a falling tear. "But Killian, I still am."

It takes me a second, but when I piece together what she's saying, it all clicks. She thinks by me meeting with Melanie, I've been healed.

"Giselle..." I set the box down on the table and take her hands in mine. "Yes, meeting with Melanie helped me find closure, but she didn't fix me. I'm still broken, baby, but I'm no longer lonely.

"Since the day you stepped into that limo, I haven't felt lonely. Nobody is perfect. We're all broken, filled with imperfections, scars from the wounds life has inflicted on us.

"Being with you has shown me that it's not about trying to fix the broken, but finding the person you can be broken with. Be broken with me, baby. I can't play in this game alone. My arms and heart are open. The ball is in your hands. Will you throw it to me?"

Tears fall harder down her beautiful face as she begins to nod, slowly at first and then quicker.

Finally, she speaks. "Okay...Yes! I'll throw the ball to you. I mean, I have no clue how to throw a damn ball, but you've won a Super Bowl, so surely you can catch just about any pass I throw, right?"

I laugh loudly, loving that my woman just went along with my football analogy.

Standing, I take her hand in mine and slide the ring onto her finger. I wasn't sure her size, so I called Olivia and she was spot on. Giselle eyes the ring for a second before she throws her arms around me and kisses me hard.

"Let's get married now," I suggest, shocking the hell out of both of us.

"Now?" she squeaks.

"Yeah, we can meet with my parents for breakfast and then take off somewhere to get married. Just the two of us. I don't want to wait. I want you to be my wife."

"Okay," she agrees, excitedly. "Let's do this!"

WE'RE LYING IN BED AFTER CELEBRATING OUR engagement for the second time tonight—with me balls-deep in my gorgeous fiancée.

Giselle is drawing letters and pictures across my torso and chest with her sexy thigh draped over the top of my legs and her head in the crook of my shoulder.

We haven't discussed my dinner with Melanie yet, but we need to. I need to. I don't want to ruin the moment, but Giselle assumed by my meeting with Melanie everything is now perfect, when in fact it's not.

"Melanie's married with twin daughters," I say, and Giselle's finger stills. "She apologized for having the abortion."

"I'm glad you two finally talked. It was long overdue," she murmurs.

"She felt the same way. She lives with a lot of guilt over the decision she made, and she said she doesn't blame me."

Giselle sighs softly. "I can't imagine having an abortion at any age is an easy thing to do, but as a teenager, it must've been absolutely traumatizing."

"Yeah," I agree. "She told me she should've given me more time to process."

"If she would've, the baby would be here," Giselle states.

"Maybe, but we can't look at it like that. What's done is done. She's happily married with her two daughters, and I'm about to marry you. Everything is the way it should be."

Giselle nods into my chest. "I love you, Kill. If it meant you'd get to raise the baby you never had the chance to meet, I would give you up, but since that's not possible, I'm really glad all the situations out of our control lined up and gave me you."

Chapter Twenty-Six

GISELLE

"You seriously got married without me?" Olivia yells into the phone.

Killian is lying next to me under our umbrella by the pool. We're currently enjoying the sunshine as husband and wife at the Cozumel Palace in Mexico, where just a few short hours ago we said our 'I do's' in a tiny church with a priest, who barely spoke English, and two witnesses, who work for the church and didn't say anything but grinned with twinkles in their eyes.

I'm not exactly sure *all* of what the priest said, but I know what Killian said:

"I, Killian Blake, promise to be your best friend, your lover, your protector, your partner. I will cherish you and love you and do everything in my power to make sure you're happy

and never feel lonely. I promise to be broken with you every day for the rest of our lives."

It was in that moment it really hit me. I was marrying Killian, and everything he was promising to do, he had already been doing since the day I let him in.

I might be broken, but every day spent with Killian has been far from lonely. I feel loved, cherished, and if I'm honest, a little less damaged when I'm with him.

He loves and embraces every part of me: the good, the bad, and the ugly.

"Giselle!" Olivia shouts, reminding me she's still on the phone, pissed off because like the chicken shit I am, I texted Olivia a picture of our wedding rings instead of calling her.

"I'm here, sorry, I was..."

"In newly-wed bliss?" she screeches. "When Killian asked for your ring size, I knew he was going to propose, but nowhere in our conversation did he mention eloping."

Her tone has gone from mad to hurt.

"I'm sorry, Livi. It wasn't really planned. He proposed and I said yes, and then we decided not to wait."

"Yet, you went to breakfast with his parents..."

She's got me there. When we told his parents we were engaged, they were thrilled. And then Killian told them we were planning to elope.

I thought for sure his mom would be upset she wouldn't get to see her son get married, but I think she was so sure he would never get married, she was just happy to know it was actually happening.

We agreed to go to dinner in a couple weeks to celebrate since they'll be flying in for the birth of Christina and Dylan's baby.

"Livi, I know you're upset, but you know I'm not into being the center of attention like that. Plus, my mom is still getting better and my sister is crazy busy with school. I have nobody from my family to even attend a wedding."

"I'm your family," Olivia whispers, and my heart breaks, tears stinging my eyes.

When Killian notices, he flies out of his chair to my side. I put my hand up to stop him from taking the phone, but he reaches around and grabs it anyway.

"Olivia, this is Killian. I understand you're upset you weren't there for the wedding, but here's the thing. Everything Giselle has done has been about other people. She moved here for you. She takes care of her mom and sister. This wedding, this marriage, it was about us."

My heart squeezes at Killian's words.

He couldn't have worded it better, and if I'm honest, I didn't even think about any of that.

For the first time, I wanted something for me and I went after it. I didn't think about anyone else but me, and I'm not going to feel bad for that.

Olivia says something I can't hear and Killian grins. "Okay," he says. I hear Olivia reply, but I can't hear what she's saying. When she stops talking, Killian says, "You have my word."

He hands me back the phone and leans in to kiss me. "I love you, Mrs. Blake," he murmurs.

I put the phone back up to my ear, swooning so damn hard. "Hello." My voice is breathy, and Olivia notices.

"My God, you have it bad." She laughs. "I'm sorry for freaking out. Killian is right. This was about you two. You deserve to get married how and where you want. I love you, Giselle, and I'm so happy for you."

"Thank you." I'm shocked she's suddenly so okay with this.

"You're welcome. Plus, Killian told me I can throw you guys a party when you return," she says, triumphantly.

"Oh, well, actually, his parents are coming to New York in a few weeks and we're just going to go to dinner."

"Sounds fun! But I'm still throwing you a party! Enjoy your honeymoon! Bye!" She ends the call before I can argue.

AFTER SPENDING THE DAY SWITCHING BETWEEN the pool and the beach, Killian and I head up to our room.

Although, 'room' doesn't do the place we're staying in justice. How Killian managed to pull everything together in such a short amount of time baffles me, but at the same time, it shouldn't surprise me. Money talks.

While Killian is showering, I pull out my laptop to do some work. Killian doesn't know it yet, but when we return tomorrow night, his condo will be done. I left the key with Olivia so she could let the workers in. While working remotely isn't as easy as being there in person, with technology, it makes it possible.

After confirming the painters have arrived and are working, I go through my emails. I notice one from Adrianna and click on it. It's a forwarded email from her school. Any time I pay the bill, it goes to her school email, so she forwards them to me to keep on record. It's a receipt indicating the remaining balance on her food card, and it's enough to feed her until graduation.

I click on the email and sign into her account. Why the hell is there so much money in there? Did she somehow get approved for some type of financial aid I didn't know about? I click through the account. Everything was paid, and her denial of financial aid hasn't changed.

I click on the next semester and there's a positive balance. This doesn't make sense.

I pull up my bank account. If they took all that money from me by accident, my account must be in the negatives! I do a double take when I see the number of zeros in the balance of my checking account. Something is wrong here. Even with the sale of the house, I shouldn't have this much money. I scroll down and find the deposit. Killian Blake. *Motherfucker.*

I sign in to my student loans, and sure enough, everything is paid off. My credit cards. Paid. I am one hundred percent debt free.

"Killian!" I scream across the massive suite, which is more like a small mansion than a hotel room.

Instead of responding, he comes out of the bathroom, a worried look on his face.

For a second, as he stands there in nothing but a towel hung low around his waist with beads of water clinging to his tanned, perfect body, I forget how pissed I am at what he did behind my back.

My eyes fall to the brightly colored tattoos and land on one in particular, so I stand and walk toward him to get a closer look. It's shinier than the others. Newer. How did I not notice this before?

He glances down and grins, knowing which one has gotten my attention. My fingers trace the same quote that is on the back of the heart he gave me.

He had it tattooed on his body.

The quote.

The heart.

It's permanent.

Tears burn my eyes as I stare at the words. I want to be mad over the money, but I can't muster up the anger. My heart is just too damn full.

"When did you get this done?" I whisper.

"Right before we left for North Carolina."

Gently, I wipe the water off it so I can get a better look at it. "It's beautiful," I tell him, leaning in and kissing the broken heart, the one identical to mine. His skin is chilled from the cool air.

I trail kisses along the words, which are woven through his other tattoos, and Killian's hand grips the back of my head, his fingers threading roughly through my hair.

I continue peppering wet kisses across his chest and down the center of his torso. His hand stays in my hair, but he doesn't move a muscle. My eyes meet his as I bend down and undo his towel, and when he realizes what I'm about to do, his pupils dilate.

Even at only half-mast, his dick is beautiful. My fingers attempt to wrap around his shaft. It's thick and soft like velvet. I stroke it a few times and it thickens under my touch. Bringing my lips to the tip, I give it an open-mouthed kiss. He smells clean, a mixture of soap and Killian.

I suck on the tip and a bit of precum drips out. It's salty on my tongue and has me thirsty for more.

Killian's grip on my hair tightens, and my gaze goes up, finding his eyes, which scream hunger and want, are locked on me.

Lifting his shaft up slightly, I run my tongue along the thick vein on the underside, my eyes never leaving his. When my tongue returns to the swollen head, more cum has leaked out, so I lick it clean.

"Jesus, fuck," Killian groans as I take him completely into my mouth, not stopping until he hits the back of my throat, causing him to growl out as he tries to stop himself from thrusting deeper into my mouth.

I pull back slightly and then take him all the way into my mouth again. With every bob of my head, his dick grows thicker, more cum dripping out. His grunts and groans are getting louder, and in return, I feel myself dripping wet.

I know he's getting close when I feel his dick swell, and I prepare myself to swallow him. But before that happens, my hair is pulled, and my mouth pops off his dick.

"I need to be inside you," he grunts as he lifts me from the ground and throws me onto the couch.

He tears my clothes from my body, then spreads my legs and pushes into me. Because I'm drenched, he slides right in, bottoming out. My back arches in pleasure, my butt lifts off the cushion, and I'm moved several inches up.

"Holy shit," I gasp. "That feels so good."

One of his hands takes both of mine and pins them above my head, the other gripping my throat to hold me in place.

"Of course it does," he says. "It's me and you."

And then he begins to fuck me.

I've never seen him like this. So overcome with emotion.

With every thrust, my climax rises closer to the surface. My ankles lock around his bare ass, and his thrusts get deeper, harder, rougher.

His eyes never leave mine as my orgasm reaches the edge and spills over.

"That's it, baby," Killian murmurs, his grip on my throat tightening. "Come all over my cock."

And with his words, I come harder than I've ever come in my life.

Killian's thrusts turn savage, unrestrained, and then he's growling out his orgasm.

His fingers leave my throat and I take in a deep breath, air quickly filling my lungs.

His lips land on mine and he kisses me with such love, my heart feels like it's going to explode.

"I'm the luckiest fucking guy alive," he whispers against my mouth when the kiss ends. "I get to keep you and kiss you and make love to you for the rest of our lives." He kisses me again and then pulls out.

"You paid off all my debt and deposited a shit ton of money into my account," I tell him now that my head isn't fogged up.

His eyes go wide. "You're my wife."

That's the only explanation he gives, because to him, me being his wife means he has the right to do what he did. I knew this would happen. It's who he is.

"Next time, you talk to me first."

I give him a stern look that has the corners of his lips twitching to break into a smile.

"Yes, ma'am," he agrees, clearly happy I didn't give him more shit. I wanted to. Believe me, I did. But I know what he did came from a good place. He loves me and wants to be, as Olivia would say, my prince charming.

I've been doing this alone for so long, but I don't have to anymore. And knowing it's Killian by my side, I don't want to.

Chapter Twenty-Seven

KILLIAN

THE ENTIRE DRIVE TO THE CONDO, GISELLE HAS been quiet and kind of...fidgety. She keeps checking her phone, but when I ask her if everything is okay, she tells me everything is fine.

The driver pulls into the parking garage and jumps out to help us with our bags while I grab our suitcases, which are significantly heavier than they were when we left, since we had to purchase beach attire when we arrived in Cozumel, and then Giselle insisted on buying several mementos from the touristy shops to remember our trip.

When we get to the door, she steps in front of it. "I need to go in first. Wait here."

She plucks my key from my fingers, which is strange since she should have her own. A few minutes later, she calls out my name and I take that as my cue to enter.

The condo has been completely redone. The walls, which were once a plain off-white are now a deeper shade of cream, with the back wall a dark coffee color. New art fills the walls. The furniture is the same, but a new leather recliner has been added to the mix. New pillows are in the corners of the couches. There's a new rug. And this is only the living room.

Giselle stands to the side as I walk through the condo. In the hallway, pictures of my friends and family line the walls in thick wooden frames. It's still masculine, yet it no longer feels cold. She's added warmth. My bedroom, office, the bathrooms, the kitchen. Every room has been transformed. And it hits me, she did all of this while in a different state and country.

"What do you think?" she asks shyly when I walk back out to the living room.

"I think you need to start your own interior design firm."

She laughs and it sounds like a sweet melody.

"I wouldn't go that far, but I'm glad you like it. I wanted your place to feel more like a home for you."

"You mean for us," I say, gripping her hips and pulling her into me. She comes willing, her arms encircling my neck. "We're married, which means you're moving in here. Now." Needing to feel her, I give her a soft kiss and she melts into my arms.

"Okay," she says, but then her body stiffens as if she's just remembered something. "What about my mom? She's getting out soon and I can't move her into here. There are only two rooms." She frowns. "And I can't kick you out of your own office."

"We'll figure it out," I tell her. "We still have a few weeks."

IT'S BEEN ALMOST A WEEK SINCE GISELLE AND I became husband and wife. Nick and Olivia officially put their places on the market and moved into their new home, which is just outside the city. Giselle is living with me in the condo and has spent every day after work organizing our stuff. What she doesn't know is we won't be living here for long. I have a plan.

We're on our way to my brother's place for my niece's birthday party. Giselle asked me to stop at the bookstore, so she can run in and grab her a gift. I told her I bought her a gift card, but she just gave me a look and told me that's not from her.

"Got it!" she squeals as she jumps back into the vehicle. She holds up a wrapped square.

"A book?"

"Not just a book. *The* book. *Alice's Adventures in Wonderland*." I should've known. "I also got her the movie since you told me she loves watching movies with you." She holds up a matching wrapped gift, only smaller in size.

We arrive at the party, and it's already in full swing. Kids are running around everywhere. There's a bounce house, several games, a creepy-looking clown painting the kids' faces, a cotton candy machine going, and tables of food and drinks. It looks like a damn carnival came to town in my brother's backyard.

"Killian!" Christina waves us over when she spots us standing there, taking it all in. She waddles her now very-pregnant self over to us and throws her arms around Giselle. "Welcome to the family!" she gushes.

"Thank you," Giselle whispers, and my eyes dart over to her. Why does she sound like she's ready to cry? "You look great." She nods toward Christina's belly.

"Thank you! Only a few more weeks." She grins happily, unaware my wife looks like she's a second away from losing it.

"We're going to get some food, and then we'll find the birthday girl," I tell Christina.

Taking Giselle's hand in mine, I walk us over to the corner where the food is. "You okay?" I ask her.

"Yeah, I've just never seen anything like this before." Her eyes glance around the backyard. "Were your birthdays like this?"

"No." I laugh. "I mean, sure, they were fun. Sometimes at the skating rink or a park, but nothing like this." Giselle nods absently.

"What about you?" I ask, wanting to know what's going through her head. She almost looks frightened by the extravagance of the party.

"Addy and I never had a birthday party. At least not one I can remember. My dad didn't want to overwhelm my mom. Sometimes we would go to dinner or he would bring home a cake, but that's it. I thought Olivia went all out for

Reed's first birthday, but this party makes it look like hers was reserved." She laughs.

"Uncle Killian!" Julia squeals. I turn around and she flies into my arms. "You're here!"

"I am. Happy Birthday! How old are you now? Eighteen?"

"No!" She giggles. "You always say that! I'm five!"

I set her on her feet. "Well, you certainly look older than five." I shoot her a wink, and she giggles some more.

"Come play with me in the bounce house." She tugs on my hand, and I look back at Giselle, whose face is completely devoid of all emotion.

"In a few minutes," I begin to say, but Giselle cuts me off.

"Go play with your niece," she insists. "I'll get us some food."

"You sure?"

"Yeah." She nods and smiles, but it's forced.

I want to ask her what's going on, but in front of everyone at a kid's birthday party isn't the right time or place, so instead I allow my niece to drag me to the bounce house.

I spend the next few hours playing games, getting my face painted, and—against my brother's warning that I'm going to pop it—jumping in Julia's bounce house with her.

Giselle and I eat lunch, and after singing Happy Birthday, have cake. We watch Julia open dozens of presents, and the entire time Giselle is here with me in body, but it's clear her head is somewhere else.

After wishing Julia Happy Birthday one last time and promising Christina and my brother we'll do dinner soon, we head home.

Giselle is quiet, lost in herself, and I try to think about what might've happened. Could all of this be simply because she's never had a birthday party? Her birthday just passed, so I make a mental note to throw her a party next year.

We get home and Giselle excuses herself to take a shower. When she gets out, she tells me she's going to head to bed. Normally, I would follow her, but something tells me she needs some time to sort out whatever is going on with her.

So, I tell her I'm going to watch some television. She gives me a chaste kiss goodnight and heads into our room.

A few hours later, I join her and she's fast asleep. I pull her into my arms, and she snuggles up against me, right where she belongs.

Chapter Twenty-Eight

GISELLE

IT'S MONDAY MORNING, AND I'M BEYOND exhausted—mentally and physically. Watching Killian with his niece yesterday was bittersweet. He says he's okay with us not having kids, but as I watched him, so clearly in his element at the party, I couldn't help but think, who the hell am I to keep this man from becoming a father?

But then I would try to place us in Christina's and Dylan's shoes, and the picture wasn't the same. Because I'm my mother's daughter and there's a chance I could one day end up like her—bipolar, depressed, and as a result, emotionally and physically abusive.

After I went to bed last night, I called my sister and we talked for a while. I told her about Killian and me getting married, and she congratulated us.

We also talked about mom and our childhood. She told me she spoke to her girlfriend about it, and she refuses to allow our mother's condition to affect her life. She's determined to live life to the fullest. I wish I could adopt her outlook on the situation, but it's hard. Addy has no desire to have kids. She wants to travel and see the world. She's blissfully away at college, while I'm trying to figure out how to have my own life and take care of my mom when she gets out of Serenity.

I stretch my body out and find Killian's rolled over on his side and is watching me. I know he's concerned about my behavior yesterday and wants to ask me about it, but how do I tell the man I love, I'm scared he's going to miss out on life's greatest blessings like having children because of me? And I'm petrified he'll one day resent me because of it.

Grabbing my cell phone, I check the time and realize I'm late.

"Shit!" I hiss, jumping out of bed and running into the bathroom. "I'm late!" I yell to Killian. "How long were you staring at me while the clock was ticking away?"

I run the brush quickly through my hair, and when he laughs a throaty laugh, I hurl the brush at him. Of course, he catches it and laughs harder.

"I have a ten o'clock appointment!"

"I'll drive you," he says, joining me in the bathroom.

We go about getting ready, brushing our teeth and washing our faces. We've only been living together for less than a week, yet it feels so much longer than that.

I always thought when I moved in with a guy it would take some getting used to. Who puts their toothbrush where?

Which side of the bed do we each sleep on? Do I cook and clean? Does he does the dishes?

My parents were hardly role models for how married living should go. But with Killian, it all just fell into place so naturally. I'm not sure what it will be like once his football season starts, but at least we have some time before he's traveling again.

We rush out the door, and on the way, he insists we go through a drive-thru for breakfast and coffee.

When we arrive, he shuts the car off, and we head to my office. Once we're alone in the elevator, Killian cuts across the small area and cages me into the corner, his body flush against mine. He kisses me with such force and passion, my entire body shivers in pleasure.

"I'm here when you're ready to talk," he murmurs against my lips, and my throat clogs with emotion.

How did I, Giselle Winters, the woman who spent the last year selling her body for money, get so lucky to end up with a man like Killian Blake? I don't deserve him.

"Thank you," I whisper.

The elevator dings and we enter Fresh Designs. I take my messages from the receptionist and head back to my office.

I unlock the door and have a seat behind my desk.

Setting my coffee and breakfast down, I pull my laptop out of my bag. I open it up and press the power button to turn it on as Killian falls into the seat across from me, and it's then I realize he's followed me in.

I can't help but laugh. This isn't the first time he's done this. Although, the last time he did it, it was because he had an appointment.

Oh, Jesus.

The screen comes to life, and I click on my schedule.

Sure enough, my ten o'clock appointment is with Killian Blake.

I glare, and he laughs.

"What the hell are you doing?" I demand, humor seeping out of my words. "Your condo is done."

"*Our* condo is done," he corrects me, and I roll my eyes.

And then it hits me...

"Killian, we didn't sign a prenuptial agreement."

He gives me an odd look.

"You know...a document that protects the rich people from being screwed over by the poor people they married when shit goes south."

It's kind of a joke, but it's still true. Killian doesn't take it that way, though.

"That's not funny, Giselle. I'm not having you sign a document that specifies what you get or don't get in case we divorce. We aren't divorcing, ever."

I open my mouth to argue, but he gives me a look that says he's not playing around. "Now, I'm here to hire your services."

"Okay." I laugh. "What would you like me to decorate now, Killian? Your locker room?"

"No, smart ass. Our house."

"Killian, I seriously have a lot of shit to do today. As much as I love having you in my office, I need to get to work."

"And that includes decorating our place."

He pulls a sheet of paper out of his pocket and pushes it across the desk.

I take it and read over it. It's a house listing. The address looks familiar. Where have I seen it? It's a five-bedroom, four-bathroom house with a three-car garage. An indoor/outdoor pool and a huge backyard, according to the images. When I see the name, I remember where I've seen this street name.

"This is Olivia and Nick's house?" I ask, confused.

"No, it's ours. It's two doors down from Nick and Olivia."

My eyes volley between the paper and Killian. "You purchased a house on the same street as Olivia?"

Oh my god! This man!

"We did. I had you sign the papers in Cozumel. You just didn't realize it. Everything is ours. And the house has a mother-in-law suite in the back. Your mom will have her own place. Bedroom, bathroom, kitchen, and living room. She'll even have her own sidewalk, so she doesn't have to walk through our house if she doesn't want to."

My jaw drops as I flip through the pages, reading all the details confirming what Killian said.

He bought us a house...two houses down from my best friend. I spring from my seat and fly into Killian's lap. He laughs as I straddle him and pepper kisses along his jaw, over his cheeks, his forehead, and lastly to his lips.

"Thank you," I murmur. "We don't need a house that big but thank you. For the mother-in-law suite and moving me near Olivia. Thank you."

Killian kisses me tenderly. "You're welcome. I would've moved us directly next door, but the old lady living there refused to sell." He mock-glares, and I laugh. "Once you're done decorating it, we'll move in. Think you can have it done before your mom gets out?"

"Yes!" I wrap my arms around his neck and kiss him.

His phone starts ringing, and I remember we're in my office, so I climb off him, while he pulls his phone out of his pocket and answers it.

"Hey bro, what's up?" He pauses then grins. "No shit? Yeah, we'll be right there. Do Christina's parents have Julia?" He listens to his brother. "All right, see you soon." He hangs up.

"Everything okay?" I ask him.

"Yeah, Christina went into labor this morning. They had to deliver the baby early, but he's perfect. Why don't we go visit them at the hospital and then we can head over to the house so you can check it out?" He stands, ready to go.

"Umm...well..." I try to think of a reason I can't go, but the truth is, I have no reason. My appointment this morning is with Killian, and he knows it.

He gives me a concerned look. "What's wrong?"

"Nothing. Sure, we can go by there on the way to the house. I just have an appointment this afternoon, so we can't stay too long."

"Okay." He smiles and takes my hand. "Grab your coffee and breakfast. You can eat on the way."

We arrive at the hospital, and after showing our identification, the receptionist gives us visitor passes and sends us up to the maternity ward. The door is open, so Killian knocks once and then we enter.

Dylan is sitting in the chair next to Christina's bed. She's holding their baby and they're both speaking to him. They look up, and Dylan stands and walks over to us. He gives me a hug and then Killian.

"Congratulations, bro," Killian says before walking over to Christina. He leans over the bed and gives her a kiss on her forehead. "He's beautiful," he tells her. "Looks just like his handsome uncle." He shoots me a playful wink, and my stomach plummets.

I stand frozen in place as I watch everything like an outsider. Killian sanitizes his hands, and Christina hands him the baby. He holds him in his arms like a pro as he walks over to show me him.

"His name is Kyle," his brother tells him.

"Hey there, Kyle," Killian coos. "How much does he weigh? Ten pounds?" he jokes.

Christina laughs. "Funny! Seven pounds, four ounces."

"Nice! Kid is going to be a linebacker." Killian grins, and Dylan laughs.

"Well, don't hog him, Kill," Christina chides. "Let Giselle hold him."

Killian looks up, and before I can get my facial expression under control, he sees the truth in my features.

He flinches, suddenly realizing why I struggled to come here, and then spends the next few seconds trying to make up an excuse as to why I can't hold the baby, his gaze filled with apology.

I look around and see Christina and Dylan watching us. Not wanting to seem rude or have to explain why I don't want to hold their baby, I walk over to the sink and wash my hands.

Killian whispers, "Are you sure?" and I nod.

He places the baby into my arms, and he's so tiny. I lift him up to my nose to see if he smells like Reed did when he was born, and he does. He smells like a tiny little miracle.

My throat begins to close, and it becomes difficult to breathe, as tears blur my vision.

Killian notices and steps forward, ready to take Kyle from me. And suddenly, I feel sick to my stomach. I hand him back the baby and dart to the bathroom, just making it to the toilet in time.

I throw up everything in my stomach as Killian holds my hair back for me. When there's finally nothing left to throw up, I stand and wash my mouth out in the sink then wash my hands and face. I glance in the mirror and see Killian watching me. Concerned. He's always concerned.

"I'm sorry."

He shakes his head. "No, I am. First the comment about being a stay-at-home dad, then taking you to Julia's birthday party, and now bringing you to see a baby. I know I've never been in a relationship before, but damn, I'm sucking at this." He chuckles humorlessly.

"Kill..."

"No, I couldn't figure out what was wrong yesterday at the party. I'm such an idiot."

"No, you're not. This is my problem, not yours. This is your family. Julia is your niece. Kyle is your nephew. Olivia and Nick have Reed and soon will have another baby. It's something I'm going to have to get used to, but you don't have to." I close my eyes and shake my head, until I feel Killian's hands on my hips. Then I open them back up. "Do you think maybe we rushed into things?" I ask, my eyes filled to the brim with tears.

"Baby, don't do this," Killian pleads.

"It's just..." I can't even get the words out.

I don't want to say what I'm thinking—that I'm being selfish by being with Killian. He deserves more. To be with a woman who isn't as broken as I am. To become a father. I'm bringing nothing to this marriage, while he's bringing everything.

"Giselle, please," he begs. "Let's go take a look at the house, okay?"

I nod my agreement, not wanting to disappoint him.

He has me wait for him outside the room while he tells his brother and Christina I'm not feeling well and then we head out.

The ride to the house is quiet, both of us lost in our own thoughts. When we arrive, the home is beautiful, but I can't find it in me to get excited. I go through each room, taking measurements and making notes while Killian and I discuss what each room could be: a gym, office, reading room, guest room.

But the entire time I keep thinking that if he were with someone else, the rooms would be labeled completely different: nursery, playroom, library, game room.

When we're done, he drops me back off at the office, and for the first time since we've been together, when we say goodbye, we don't kiss.

And as I walk to the elevator, I wonder if maybe it's a sign of what's to come.

Chapter Twenty-Nine

GISELLE

EVERYONE IS STANDING IN THE CHURCH, watching Reed get baptized. Nick and Olivia are all smiles as they watch their son squirm while the pastor says his speech. He dips his fingers into the holy water, then rubs it along Reed's forehead.

Reed giggles and everyone laughs.

Everyone is watching but Killian. Because the entire time I can feel his eyes on me. He's worried I'm going to lose it. When I agreed to be Reed's Godmother, it was before I learned my mother's condition could be hereditary. I considered telling Olivia I couldn't be who she needed me to be, but when I tried to make the words come out, I couldn't do it. I couldn't disappoint her. What are the chances something happens to them anyway? The Godparents only come into play if both parents die, right?

Killian and I step forward and repeat after the pastor, promising to guide Reed in his spiritual journey. Then the pastor sets him down and Reed toddles over to me, lifting his arms up for me to take him. So, I do.

"Gi Gi!" he squeals, and everyone laughs.

His tiny hands land on my cheeks and he squishes my face, placing a big wet kiss on my lips.

My eyes, of their own accord, meet Killian's, and his facial expression is caught between smiling and frowning.

Jesus, I'm so fucked up, and now I'm fucking up my husband too.

Like the toddler Reed is, he squirms to get down, and I set him on his feet. He runs over to his dad, and Nick picks him up, blowing raspberries against his little belly and making his squeal in delight.

The ceremony ends, and Olivia announces that everyone will be meeting at the restaurant down the street for lunch.

Needing a moment, I excuse myself to use the restroom. I'm washing my hands when the door creaks open and in walks Killian. He locks the door behind him and stalks toward me.

I don't even get a word out before he's lifting me onto the sink and spreading my legs. His fingers enter me as our lips crash against each other.

It's been almost a week since I've felt this connection with Killian. A week of sleeping together yet feeling like we're a million miles apart. Every night I can tell he wants to say something, but he's waiting for me. And I have no clue what to say.

He adds another finger and then another, pumping them in and out of me until I'm soaking wet.

He pulls my top down, and his lips wrap around my nipple, licking and sucking on it. And then he's pulling my panties off my body and lifting me into the air.

My back hits the hard wall, and he thrusts inside me. My arms wrap around his neck as my husband fucks me like a goddamn madman—punishing thrust after punishing thrust, not once slowing down or relenting. I find my release within minutes, and Killian's follows shortly after.

We're both breathing heavily, but he doesn't set me down. Instead, with his semi-hard cock still inside of me, his mouth smashes against mine with such force, I'm almost certain every emotion he feels is being projected into that one kiss.

"This has to stop," he demands.

"What?"

I try to get down, but he won't release me. I feel his cum dripping out of me.

"Pushing me away. Thinking you know what's best for me. I want you, Giselle. Baby, no baby. I don't give a fuck. It's you and me. So, whatever you're thinking, get it the hell out of your head. Got it?"

I nod in understanding.

Killian walks us back over to the sink and sets me down, spreading my thighs and using a wet paper towel to clean me up. I watch as he takes care of me. He always takes care of me.

"I want to take care of you," I blurt out, and he gives me a quizzical look. "You always take care of me. I hate us being so uneven. You give me so much, and I give you nothing."

Killian shakes his head and sighs. "If I have to spend the rest of our life explaining to you just how much you give me, I will. You give me so much." He lifts my necklace. "Your heart." He kisses my temple. "Your mind." A playful smirk splays across his lips. "Your body." He grabs my panties from the corner of the counter and puts them back on me. "Our life together has only just begun," he says. "Neither of us are experts at this, so how about we just learn as we go, okay?"

"Okay," I agree.

Killian helps me off the sink and it's then I remember where we are. "Oh my god! We just had sex in a church!"

Killian throws his head back with a laugh. "It's a good thing we're married."

"Giselle! Sweetie, you look so good."

I'm standing in the facility, staring at my mother, only it doesn't feel like it's my mother. She's glowing. She's dressed in a pair of jeans and a fluffy sweater. Her hair is straightened. And she looks beautiful.

"I look good? Mom, you look amazing!" I try to keep the shock out of my voice but even I can hear it. My mom laughs. *Laughs!* And it's not that crazy laugh she used to give us. It's melodic and genuine.

Killian and I are here to pick her up. The house is ready to move into and it will be our first time spending the night there. I was terrified of how it would go. That she wouldn't be ready. But she looks so healthy. Is it possible? Is she fixed?

"Where's Addy?" Mom asks.

"She's meeting us at the house," I tell her. "She's bringing her girlfriend, Kassie, with her for everyone to meet. But if you think it might be too much..."

"No." She smiles. "I'm so glad you both have someone." Tears prick her eyes, and I freak out.

"Mom, don't cry." My eyes dart around the room for the doctor, my heart picking up its pace. Damn it! She's going to lose it. "Excuse me, Dr. Burns!" I yell when I spot my mom's doctor.

He gives me a concerned look and comes over.

"She's crying," I point out, and my mom laughs through her tears.

"Sarah, you're leaving today." Dr. Burns gives her a hug, ignoring the fact that my mom is crying.

"She's crying," I say again.

"Giselle." Killian wraps his arms around me. "Your mom is crying because she's happy, baby," he whispers.

"But she's..."

"It's okay," my mom says, "Killian is right. I'm crying because I'm happy, but after everything I've put you through, I don't blame you for freaking out. I think it's going to take some time for everyone."

Dr. Burns nods in agreement. "We've found a therapist for your mother to see three times a week near you guys. Maybe you will consider going with her one day a week to talk things out."

"That would be great," my mom says with a smile. "Now, let's go home. My son-in-law told me all about this beautiful mother-in-law suite. I can't wait to see it."

The drive home is spent with all of us talking about everything that has been going on. Olivia being pregnant, Killian and my wedding and mini-honeymoon, my job and the possibility of getting a promotion soon. And then she brings up my dad.

"How is your father?"

Killian and I both go silent. She just got out. I can't tell her about my dad's other family.

"Giselle," she pushes, "I know."

My head whips around to her. "You know what?"

"About his other family. His other children."

"Should we maybe go back to the facility to discuss this?"

Mom laughs. "No, I've known for years. I'm sorry I never told you. He came to see me and told me you knew. I know you're angry with him, but I need you to know that I forgive him. What I put him through..." She shakes her head. "My being sick isn't what he signed up for."

Killian clears his throat. "While I think it's great you forgive him, I beg to differ. He married you. When he said those vows, he signed up for better or worse. Those times were the worse."

Mom grins, then leans forward and whispers, "He's a keeper."

I get choked up, trying to keep the tears from falling, but they spill over anyway. "Yeah, he is."

"You're right, Killian, we did make vows," Mom says, "and we did say for better or worse. But we fell out of love many years ago, and instead of letting him go, I held onto him. I was sick and depressed and scared. He deserves to be happy. And I'm ready to move forward. So please don't be too hard on him. He tried. *We* tried. But we didn't make it."

We arrive at the house and show her around, and she loves the mother-in-law suite I decorated.

Shortly after, Addy arrives with Kassie, and then Nick, Olivia, and Reed come over with dinner.

At some point in the meal, my eyes find Addy's and she gives me a soft smile. Words don't need to be spoken. This meal, this moment with our mother, was exactly what we prayed for, for so many years.

And it's because of Killian it was even made possible.

Chapter Thirty

GISELLE

"So, when are you due?" Celeste asks.

"Excuse me?" I glare at her.

We're standing in the bathroom of Assets. Celeste is reapplying her lipstick, and I'm washing my mouth from having just thrown up.

When Olivia found out I briefly worked at a high-end strip club, she insisted we all go and check it out.

She's never been to one, and apparently four months pregnant is the right time to experience half-naked women dancing on poles for the first time. Nick and Killian laughed, thinking she was joking. Olivia pouted. Nick, of course, gave in. So here we are.

"I don't know what you're talking about." I grab a paper towel and dry my face.

"Do you have the flu?" she questions.

"No!" I snap. "I think it's just nerves. It's my first time leaving my mom home alone. I've been working remotely from home since she got out."

My mom has told me several times that she's fine and I need to go about my everyday life, but I'm scared. The last time I came home, she was on the floor of the bathroom, a few minutes away from her death. And every time I attempt to leave, I imagine coming home and finding her too late. It's been over a month since she moved in and I'm still not ready to leave her yet.

"Yeah, okay." Celeste rakes her eyes down my body. "So, is it the nerves that are making you put on weight?"

"Not all of us pay a trainer to keep us in perfect model shape." I glare, and she shrugs.

"Whatever you say. Looks like I'll be throwing two baby showers instead of one." She winks and walks out of the bathroom just as Olivia walks in.

"You okay?" she asks.

"Yeah, Celeste is just being her usual bitch-self."

My side cramps up and I rub it with my fingers. It's been doing this the last few hours. Maybe I am getting sick. I've heard the flu is going around...

"What did she say?" Olivia asks with a laugh.

"That I'm getting fat." The pain in my side strengthens, and I place my hands against the sink to steady myself.

Olivia now looks at me concerned. "You're hardly fat."

"What do you mean hardly?" I turn the water on again to splash my face, and my eyes meet hers in the mirror.

"Well..." She flinches. "I mean..."

I turn toward the full-length mirror and assess my body. I look the same. Although, my pants were a tad harder to put on. I just chalked it up to Killian drying them by mistake.

"When are you due?"

Celeste's words send me running back to the toilet. There's nothing left to throw up, though, so instead, I spend the next five minutes dry-heaving. Olivia doesn't say a word, but when I rinse out my mouth again, I catch her face in the mirror, and she looks concerned.

"What?" I hiss as my stomach contracts—the pain radiating down my side.

"Is it possible?" Her gaze goes to my stomach.

"No, I'm on the pill."

Olivia scoffs. "Have you missed any? I only missed a few and POOF—" her hands shoot open at the same time her eyes go wide "—came Reed, and now this baby." She covers her adorable protruding belly.

"No..." I shake my head. "No, no, no. That shit happens to you, not me. I take them every goddamned day..." Except a few nights I ended up sleeping at Killian's place but left my pills at mine...and then when we went to North Carolina and then Cozumel. Holy fucking shit! I am just as irresponsible as Olivia.

"Giselle," Olivia says, "are you okay?"

"Yeah, I'm just going to go pee. I'll be right out."

"Is it possible that you're pregnant?"

"I don't know," I lie. "Please, just go tell Killian I'll be right out."

Olivia agrees and heads out of the bathroom.

I wait a few seconds and then go out the back door.

This seriously can't be happening. I'm so stupid. I thought I was invincible, like if the pills were there, I wouldn't get pregnant.

There's a reason doctors tell you to take them at the same time every day and not to miss any.

I flag down a cab and give him my address. I need time to think. This is my fault. I should've been more careful. I've been throwing up on and off for weeks, and I knew deep down there was a good chance I was pregnant. I just didn't want to deal with it.

I saw how Melanie having an abortion affected Killian. Could I do that? Could I abort a tiny baby that we created? No, I couldn't. Which is why I chose to live in denial.

I feel that sharp pain on my side once again, and my hand goes to my belly.

"Sir, I'm going to throw up. Can you please stop?"

He pulls over, and I barely make it out of the cab when I start throwing up nothing but acid. My knees hit the cement, and I try to release whatever is making me feel sick and nauseous.

My stomach cramps are now so unbearable, I can barely stand, so instead, I remain on all fours.

"Ma'am, should I call you an ambulance?" the driver asks, but I'm in so much pain, I can barely speak.

It's like the wind has been knocked out of me. I'm dizzy and queasy. Maybe I have food poisoning. This can't be how morning sickness is. Something is wrong.

"Yes, please," I choke out.

I stay doubled over as I wait for the ambulance to arrive. The pain is now so horrendous it's hard to see straight, hard to think. This isn't like any flu or food poisoning I've ever had. I'm losing my baby. I know it. I was afraid to admit I was pregnant. I considered, even if only briefly, not having this baby, and now I'm about to lose it.

When the pain gets so intense, my arms cave in and I fall to the ground. Worried about my baby, I cushion my belly, and my shoulder hits the cement hard. I pull myself into the fetal position, praying the ambulance gets here soon.

My eyes close.

It hurts so much.

I can hear the sirens.

I try to open my eyes, but I can't.

I hear the driver speaking to the medics.

"I-I'm pregnant," I try to tell them. "I'm pregnant."

"Okay, miss. We're taking you to New York General. We're just going to find your identification in your purse."

I think I nod, but I'm not sure.

They lift me onto a gurney and push me into the ambulance. My eyes are squeezed shut as I try to block out the excruciating pain as they let me know what they're doing every step of the way.

They place an oxygen mask over my face. I'm not sure when it's finally too much for me to handle, but at some point, I feel myself begin to black out.

My last thought: a plea to God to not take my baby. The baby I was in denial of, the baby I want more than anything in this world but was too afraid to admit, until the idea of losing him became all too real. Isn't that how the saying goes? You don't realize how much you love someone until he's gone...

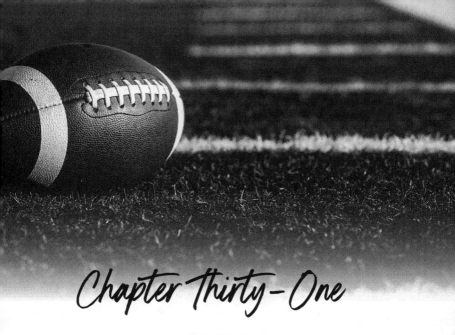

Chapter Thirty-One

KILLIAN

"SHE'S NOT IN THE BATHROOM!" I SHOUT. "I'VE checked every fucking stall. She's not there! Where is she?"

Celeste and Olivia are both wearing nervous looks on their faces. Not scared like they're afraid something happened to my wife, but nervous like they know something I don't.

"Olivia, you have to give me something here. Did she leave? Did something happen?"

Giselle has been off the last few days. She told me she was just stressed and tired, but it felt like something more.

Olivia glances between Nick and me. Then her eyes go to Celeste. "I-I don't know..."

"She's pregnant," Celeste blurts out. "She was throwing up and I pointed out that she's pregnant. She probably got spooked or something and left."

"Celeste," Olivia hisses.

"What? I'm sorry but the guy is assuming the worst here. She wasn't kidnapped or anything. She's just pregnant."

Pregnant.

Giselle is pregnant.

And she ran.

That may not be the worst-case scenario to Celeste, but that's only because she doesn't know Giselle doesn't want to have kids.

She's terrified at just the thought of becoming a mother.

And then it hits me—She ran. Like Melanie ran. I pull my phone out and dial her number, and it rings and rings and rings and then goes to voicemail.

"We have to find her," I say. "She..."

I can't say the words out loud. That there's a real possibility that another woman, who's pregnant with my baby, is about to...fuck! I can't even think the words. This can't be happening. Could I forgive Giselle if she does what I think she's about to do? Could we get past it?

Olivia's phone rings and she pulls it out of her back pocket. "Is it Giselle?" I ask.

"No, I don't recognize the number." She answers the call. "Hello?" Her eyes dart over to me. "Yes, I am." Her hand that's not holding the phone goes to her mouth in shock. "Okay...Okay, thank you."

She hangs up and tears pool in her eyes, and million scenarios run through my head of what could've happened, but there's only one thing in this moment I know for sure: I can forgive Giselle for anything as long as she's okay.

I knew she didn't want to have kids. We didn't use protection. Yes, it's on both of us, but she's not over what happened with her mom. She's been afraid to leave her for weeks since we brought her home. She's alone and not in her right mind. Fuck! This can't be happening...not again.

"She's at New York General," Olivia says, snapping me out of my thoughts. "They couldn't tell me anything over the phone, but I'm her emergency contact. All the nurse could say is she's in surgery and should be out within the next hour and will need someone to bring her home once she's released."

My heart plummets. Giselle had surgery. There's no way she ran straight to the hospital to have an abortion. Something else has to be wrong.

Without waiting for anyone else to follow, I start to run toward the entrance. We came in a cab tonight in case we both drank...which Giselle didn't.

I hail a cab and Olivia, Nick, and Celeste jump in as well. After I tell the cab driver where to go, the ride there is silent with worry.

We get to the hospital, and I go straight to the front desk. "My name is Killian Blake. I'm Giselle Blake's husband."

"Killian," Olivia says, "when the nurse called, she said Giselle Winters."

Shit! We hadn't gotten around to getting her driver's license changed yet. We're still waiting on the documents to go through.

"Giselle Winters," I say. "I'm her husband."

"And you are?" the nurse asks Olivia.

"Olivia Harper."

"I have permission to speak to you. She's just coming out of surgery. She'll be moved into recovery, and once the doctor has checked on her, she'll be able to have visitors."

"Why is she in surgery?" I ask.

"She was brought in for appendicitis."

I let out a sigh of relief. She didn't run...maybe the throwing up wasn't that she was pregnant, but that her appendix was about to burst.

"Do you know if she's pregnant?" I ask.

The nurse's expression gives nothing away. "I don't have that kind of information. I'm sorry."

Everyone sits down to wait, but I head over to billing to make sure whatever my wife needs, she gets. I know she doesn't have insurance, and we haven't added her to my policy yet, but I'm going to make damn sure they understand she gets the best treatment.

After requesting a private room for her recovery and giving the woman my credit card to charge everything to, I sit down to wait with the others.

Then I remember Giselle's mom is at home and would want to know about her daughter, so I give her a call to let her know what I know. When she tells me she's on her way, I offer to go and get her, but she scoffs. "I've been hailing cabs since before you were born," she says before we hang up.

For the next couple hours, we wait to hear something from the doctor. Sarah shows up and lets me know she called Adrianna, who is on her way, despite her mom suggesting she should wait until we hear from the doctor.

"Family of Giselle Winters," a nurse finally calls out, and we all stand. "I can only bring one of you back at a time until she's brought to her private room."

"Go ahead," I tell Sarah. As much as I want to see my wife, I know she's been waiting a long time to be able to be there for her daughter.

"Thank you," she says, pulling me into a hug. "Thank you for loving my daughter."

Chapter Thirty-Two

GISELLE

I'M STARING AT THE UGLY, DREARY-LOOKING pictures on the wall as I wait for Killian to walk through the door.

I don't know what I'm going to say...what he's going to say. I don't know what he knows or doesn't know.

I left without telling him and ended up having emergency surgery to remove my appendix. Instead of telling him something felt wrong, I chose to hide it and run.

I put myself and our baby at risk.

I can only imagine how mad he must be with me.

Mentally, I'm preparing myself for the shit he's going to give me. And I deserve it. So, I'm shocked when, instead of Killian, in walks my mother.

"Oh, Giselle," she coos.

She frames my face with her hands and gives me a kiss on my forehead. "I'm so glad you're okay."

The tears that were pricking my eyelids, spill over. My entire life all I wanted was for my mom to be a mom, and here she is doing just that.

My side is in pain, the drugs are barely helping because my options are limited due to being pregnant, but none of that matters, because right here in this moment, my mom is holding me.

"I-I'm pregnant," I blurt out.

My mom smiles. "Did you finally figure it out on your own or did the doctor tell you?"

I gasp. "You knew?"

"Well, I have been pregnant a couple of times." She winks.

"Did everyone know but me?" I laugh, but then remember Killian doesn't know...or maybe he does but didn't mention it.

"I think you always knew," Mom says, grabbing a chair and sitting next to my bed.

She's right.

In the back of my mind, I knew something was off, but didn't want to have to face it.

"I think I did too," I admit.

"Is the baby okay?" Mom asks.

"The doctor said so far everything is good. They did an appendectomy. Luckily, I'm only ten weeks, so they were able to go in and do the surgery easily. They've ordered an ultrasound for the morning to check everything over, and I'll be here for the next few days."

Mom grabs my hand and squeezes it. "I know you were brought in here because of your appendix, but it seemed like maybe your husband didn't know where you were until Olivia got the call from the hospital. Were you running?"

I let out a sigh. "I was...I told Killian before we even got married, I didn't want to have kids."

I hate having to admit this to my mom, that because of what she put us through, I didn't want to have my own children.

Realization dawns on my mom, causing her to frown. "Oh, sweetie." She pulls me in for a gentle hug, and I melt into her arms. I've missed my mom so much. Why couldn't the doctors have figured out what was wrong with her years ago? "Please don't do this to yourself or to your husband."

"You said it yourself. Dad couldn't handle you being sick. What if I become Bipolar? What will it do to Killian and our children?"

"That won't happen because we know what to look for. We will recognize the signs and get you the help you need. I wasted so many years unable to be the mom you girls deserved. The wife your father wanted. We won't allow that to happen to you."

"What if I get sick and Killian cheats on me like Dad did to you? He says he'll handle it, but what if he can't? What if he leaves me?"

But even as I say the words, I know in my heart Killian would never do such a thing.

"You can't live with what ifs, sweetie," Mom says. "That man loves you so much."

"She's right, I do." I startle at the sound of Killian's voice as he walks into the room. "We were told only one person at a time, so I let your mom go first, but I couldn't wait any longer." He shrugs unapologetically. "So, where were you attempting to run to?"

"I'll leave you two to talk," my mom says, standing. She bends at the waist and kisses my forehead. "You've spent enough time being affected by my illness. It's time you start living, sweetie. It's time we all do." Then she whispers into my ear, so only I can hear, "I'll be back in the morning to check on you and my grand baby."

Once she leaves, Killian sits in her place. He takes my hand in his and gives the inside of my wrist a soft kiss.

"I was so worried," he murmurs. He kisses the center of my palm. "I was so mad when I found out you ran, but when Olivia got the call from the hospital..." He kisses the top of each of my knuckles. "Every worst-case scenario ran through my head, and my only thought was that you had to be okay." He looks me in the eyes. "I just found you. I can't lose you."

"I'm pregnant."

He grins but quickly schools it, unsure how I feel. I hate that he can't just simply be happy.

"I forgot my pills a few times, and I haven't gotten my period in the last two months..." That was my first red flag I might be pregnant, but I chose to ignore it.

"I'm ten weeks along. The doctor said as of right now the baby is okay, but they've scheduled an ultrasound for tomorrow."

"And how are you?" Killian asks.

"I'm okay. The doctor said I'll be here for a few days and then I need to take it easy for a few weeks once I'm discharged."

"And how do you want to handle the pregnancy?" he asks softly.

"What do you mean?"

"You have choices, Giselle. Abortion, adoption, or keeping the baby. I'm your husband, and I'll stand by your side no matter what you choose to do."

I stare at this beautiful, selfless man who loves me so much. There was never a choice. I always wanted a baby with him. I was just too scared to admit it. Scared I would end up like my mom, and Killian would end up like my dad. But we aren't them. We're us. And it's time I start throwing that damn ball so he has something to catch.

"I want to create a family with you, but I'm scared," I tell him honestly. My hand palms his cheek, and he moves closer.

"Then I'll be brave for the both of us," he vows right before he gives me a passionate kiss that I feel all the way down to my bones.

"ARE YOU READY FOR YOUR ULTRASOUND?" THE ultrasound tech asks, kicking the brakes out from under the bed and pushing it toward the door. I give Killian a look, and he smiles warmly at me. I know with him by my side, I'll be ready for anything that comes my way.

"Yes," I tell her, my eyes never leaving my husband who's holding the door open for the tech so she can push me to wherever they do the ultrasounds.

When we arrive, the room is pitch black, with only a single light coming from a computer monitor. The tech rolls me next to the monitor and presses down on the brakes.

"You can sit in that chair," she tells Killian.

He thanks her and drags the chair next to me, taking my hand in his and giving the inside of my wrist a kiss.

While she types away on the computer, Killian moves a few wayward hairs out of my face and leans in to kiss my forehead.

"I'm nervous," I admit to him.

He smiles softly. "I love you. Whatever happens, we'll handle it together."

"I'm going to put this paper across your lower half, so I can lift your gown," the tech says.

Once she does so, she squeezes some warm blue goo onto my belly and begins to search for the baby.

The room is quiet, and my heart begins to pick up speed. I wasn't awake when the doctor did the ultrasound after my surgery, so I've yet to hear my baby's heartbeat, and now there's a chance I might not ever.

Just as I finish my thought, a whooshing sound fills the silence, and the tech smiles. "That's the baby's heartbeat. One hundred and seventy. Good, strong heartbeat."

She explains that with me only being ten weeks along, there's not much to see. According to her, our baby is the size of a strawberry. I laugh absently at what she says, but the only thing I can really focus on is the continuous whooshing sound.

Our baby has a heartbeat. He, or she, is alive in there.

I look over at Killian, and he has tears streaming down his face.

Lifting my hand to his cheek, I wipe one of the tears. "When I used to read fairytales, I fancied that kind of thing never happened, and now here I am in the middle of one."

Killian's shoulders shake with laughter as his tears fall faster. "*Alice's Adventures in Wonderland.* Chapter four: The Rabbit Sends in a Little Bill."

"You really did read the book," I say back through my own laughter and tears.

Epilogue

KILLIAN
TWO MONTHS LATER

"W E C O U L D H A V E T H I S I F Y O U W A N T," I T E L L Giselle as we sway to the music on the dance floor.

We're at Olivia and Nick's wedding reception, and Giselle has sighed and gushed over every detail.

Apparently, a pregnant Giselle is an emotional Giselle. She seems to shed tears—happy and sad—over everything, from what to eat, to seeing a baby playing at the park, and it's absolutely adorable.

She's been reading every book imaginable about what to expect when she has the baby, and she's even been seeing a therapist to discuss how she's feeling.

She's facing her fears head on, and I'm so damn proud of her for that. She's eighteen weeks pregnant, and we found out a couple days ago we're having a girl. Olivia and Nick are having one as well, and the women are now hell-bent on them becoming best friends.

"I loved our wedding," Giselle murmurs. "I don't want what other people have. I want what we have."

She kisses me softly then rests her head on my chest. It's well past midnight and almost everyone has retreated back to their rooms.

Olivia and Nick are on their way to Florida for their honeymoon. Although, I'm not sure you can call it a honeymoon when they're bringing Reed and going to Disney.

I can tell Giselle is getting tired on her feet, but she insisted on one more dance before we head up to our room. We could've driven back to our house from the Hamptons, but I thought a weekend away would be nice. Plus, there's a surprise waiting for Giselle when we return in the morning.

"I need to use the restroom," she says. When she leans in, she whispers, "Meet me in the bathroom in three minutes."

My dick twitches at her words, and I can't help my grin.

My pregnant wife is always horny, which suits me just fine.

I watch, as she saunters toward the bathroom, and begin to count down the seconds until I'm inside of her.

While I'm waiting, my phone vibrates in my pocket, so I check to see who it is. It's from Sarah, and it's only one word:

GISELLE

I SCURRY ACROSS THE DANCE FLOOR TOWARD THE bathroom to make sure it's empty. I've been craving to have Killian inside me all night, and I can't wait another minute. I've already seen the Yacht Club's bathroom, and it's more extravagant than most homes.

When I open the bathroom door and step inside, there are three stalls. I need to make sure they're all empty.

I'm not even three steps in when I hear grunting and moaning. I stop in place, shocked.

Apparently, someone else had the same idea we did.

Just as I'm about to turn around and give them their privacy, I hear, "Fuck, Celeste."

My hand covers my mouth to silence my gasp.

Is Celeste having sex in here? And with who? It couldn't be...

The door swings open, and in walks Killian. He locks the door and stalks toward me like a man on a mission.

"Shh..." I put my finger up to my lips. "Someone is in here. We need to go."

His brows go up, and he takes my hand to guide us out of the bathroom.

But before the door opens, Celeste moans out, "Yes, right there!"

"Is that..." Killian whispers, and I stifle a giggle, nodding my head.

We exit the bathroom quietly, and then I answer him, "Yeah, Celeste is totally having bathroom sex!"

"Goddamn." Killian laughs. "I guess I'll just have to wait until I get you up to our room to get between your thighs."

He pulls me close and gives me a kiss.

KILLIAN

THE NEXT MORNING, AFTER STOPPING FOR breakfast, we head home. Once we arrive, Giselle heads straight back to her mom's suite. She always does.

The therapist they're seeing together says it'll take time before Giselle feels comfortable enough to not check on her mom.

When it's late at night, she just peeks in, but when it's earlier, she'll hang out and they'll have coffee or tea together. They're finally getting the relationship they've longed for.

About twenty minutes later, she returns, and when she doesn't find me in the room, she calls out my name, her feet padding down the hallway as she searches for me.

When she finally gets to the last door on the left, she turns the knob and enters. "Killian!"

Her hands come up to her mouth as she takes in the nursery.

"When did you do this?"

She steps farther into the room and takes in all the Alice in Wonderland décor.

When I got ahold of her Pinterest page, I hired her boss, Lydia, to decorate it.

Giselle has been busy since she got her promotion, and I wanted her to enjoy the fruits of the labor instead of her having to do the labor herself.

"It's beautiful," she breathes.

Her hand glides over the mahogany wood crib and stops to feel the bedding. She eyes the walls which have been transformed into scenes from the book with floor-to-ceiling trees and animals having tea parties.

"It's exactly how I imagined it would look," she says, coming over to me when she's done checking it all out. "Thank you."

She stands on her tippy-toes and gives me a kiss.

"I'd like to take the credit, but Lydia did all the hard work."

I take her hand in mine and guide her to our room. Pulling my shirt off, I throw it onto the dresser.

Giselle comes up behind me and wraps her arms around my waist, and I look down at her hands before I pull her around to face me.

"Not just for the room, Kill," she says. "Thank you for loving me...broken and all."

I unzip then lift the yellow sundress Giselle is wearing over her head. Then take a moment to appreciate all of her new curves that pregnancy has brought with it.

I can't help it. Every time I get her naked, I have to stop and see if she's grown any more. I love watching our baby grow inside her.

As I trail kisses along her neck and down her collarbone, I pick her up and move her to the center of our bed.

Hovering over her, I begin to worship my wife's body as I make my way down to her wet cunt.

I give it a kiss before I make my way back up to her lips, giving her a hard kiss before I back up slightly, needing to look into her beautiful blue eyes.

"I already told you, Giselle. I'm in deep. There's nobody I'd rather be broken with than you."

About the Author

Reading is like breathing in, writing is like breathing out.
– Pam Allyn

Nikki Ash resides in South Florida where she is an English teacher by day and a writer by night. When she's not writing, you can find her with a book in her hand. From the Boxcar Children, to Wuthering Heights, to the latest single parent romance, she has lived and breathed every type of book. While reading and writing are her passions, her two children are her entire world. You can probably find them at a Disney park before you would find them at home on the weekends!

Made in the USA
Middletown, DE
21 July 2024

57786131R00205